A Death in the Venetian Quarter

Also by Alan Gordon

Jester Leaps In
Thirteenth Night

A DEATH IN THE VENETIAN QUARTER

A MEDIEVAL MYSTERY

ALAN GORDON

ST. MARTIN'S MINOTAUR ❧ NEW YORK

www.minotaurbooks.com

Library of Congress Cataloging-in-Publication Data

Gordon, Alan (Alan R.)
    A death in the Venetian quarter : a medieval mystery / Alan Gordon.—1st ed.
    p. cm.
    ISBN 0-312-24267-0
    1. Istanbul (Turkey)—History—Siege, 1203-1204—Fiction. 2. Crusades—Fourth, 1202-1204—Fiction. 3. Fools and jesters—Fiction.

PS3557.O649 D43 2002
813'.54—dc21

                                                            2001048750

First Edition: March 2002

10 9 8 7 6 5 4 3 2 1

To my son, Robert Louis Gordon,
with love from his collaborator,
coconspirator, and occasional coach

ACKNOWLEDGMENTS

In addition to those mentioned in the historical note, the author gratefully acknowledges the work of Pierre Gilles, the Reverend H. J. Chaytor, Horatio Brown, Sigfús Blondal, Michael Maclagan, Rodolph Guilland, Bryan Tsangadas, Benjamin Hendrickx, Grinna Matzukis, Adele La Barre Starensier, Anna Muthesius, and the many contributors to *Eyewitness Travel Guides: Istanbul* (1998), especially whoever did that amazing illustration on pages 20–21.

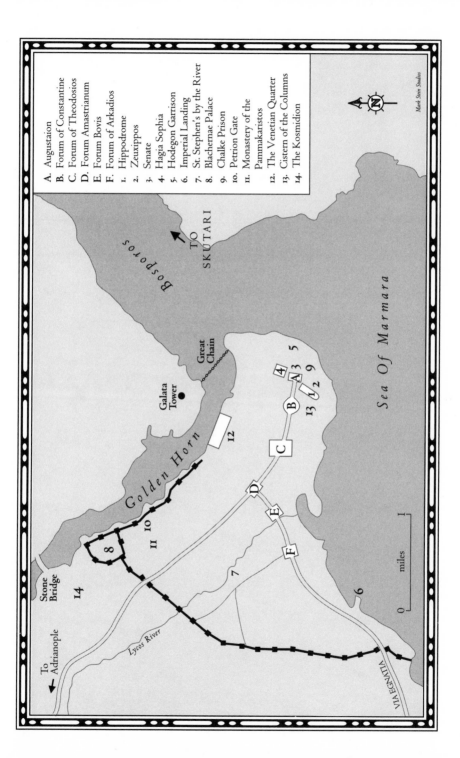

A. Augustaion
B. Forum of Constantine
C. Forum of Theodosios
D. Forum Amastrianum
E. Forum Bovis
F. Forum of Arkadios
1. Hippodrome
2. Zeuxippos
3. Senate
4. Hagia Sophia
5. Hodegon Garrison
6. Imperial Landing
7. St. Stephen's by the River
8. Blachernae Palace
9. Chalke Prison
10. Petrion Gate
11. Monastery of the Pammakaristos
12. The Venetian Quarter
13. Cistern of the Columns
14. The Kosmidion

Mark Stein Studios

N

Bosporos

TO
SKUTARI

Great
Chain

Galata
Tower

Golden Horn

Sea Of Marmara

Stone
Bridge

To
Adrianople

Lycos River

VIA EGNATIA

0   miles   1

A deed has been disclosed which no rhetoric can explain; a crime has been discovered which no mime can represent, nor jester play, nor comedian describe.

—St. Jerome, "To Sabinanius," Letter CXLVII

A Death in the Venetian Quarter

ONE

Good madonna, give me leave to prove you a fool.
—WILLIAM SHAKESPEARE, *TWELFTH NIGHT*,
ACT I, SCENE V

I blame the Pope.

It was in the power of Innocent III to stop the whole thing. They said after it was over that he tried, he sent a letter, but it was sent too late, or it arrived too late, or the leaders of the Crusade ignored it or suppressed it. A letter. As if that would stop anything. A papal envoy, that's what was needed, someone who would show his might and miter to the rank and file, let them know that they were looking directly at excommunication and Hellfire. But all the Pope did was send a letter, and send it late at that.

And I blame that bishop, that French madman, what was his name? Foulkes? Fulk? There was a truce in the Holy Land, something that had survived even after both Saladin and the Lionhearted had come face to face with the Ultimate Undoer of Plans. Yet this preaching simpleton couldn't leave well enough alone, had to pick at old scabs, urging so many to become unholy innocents to attack the infidels once again. And then he died before things even got going, the coward. Which just spurred the Crusaders on even more.

Then there was the boy, Alexios. I still don't understand why he wanted to be emperor after seeing what happened to his father. You would think seeing one family member deposed and blinded by another would have a discouraging effect on ambition. The son managed to flee that fate, only to return as the puppet of an invading army. He was to get his wish, of course. Become Alexios the Fourth. How long would he sit on the throne, six months? Something like that, then Mourtzouphlos would garrot him with a bowstring. The boy should have studied his history. Those who do not are condemned, period. But I'm getting ahead of my story.

And I truly blame the Doge. There's some dispute as to how the Crusaders ended up as Venice's private expeditionaries, but I put old Dandolo at the heart of it. The legend was that he was blinded in Constantinople and still carried a grudge, but I don't believe that. It was greed, pure and simple, if ever greed could be pure and simple. He hoped to eliminate Venice's greatest trading rival in one bold swoop, after which the entire Mediterranean would be his playground.

And I blame the Count most of all. Boniface of Montferrat, the leader of the Fourth Crusade. A lesser man might have let his honor get in the way of his ambition. Not Montferrat. A smarter general would not have let a blind nonagenarian doge outmaneuver him before he even set foot on a boat. Not Montferrat. Throw in a measure of avarice equal to that possessed by any of the great families of Venice, and you produce doom for thousands and destruction of an entire empire.

Well, no matter who was responsible, it didn't change my situation. I was trapped inside the high walls and towers of Constantinople. Outside the seawalls were two hundred Venetian ships, carrying the armies of the Fourth Crusade, the first to strike at Christians rather than infidels. Inside the walls, four hundred thousand people wondered what was going on, whether this was an attack, a siege, or just a Crusade passing through and an opportunity to sell inferior supplies at inflated prices. The Greeks paid lip service to God and put their real faith in their walls. The Varangians and the other mercenaries sharpened their axes and prepared to die defending the current emperor, something they neglected to do for the last one when he was being deposed and blinded by this one. The merchants buried their gold, and everyone started hoarding supplies, just in case. Except the Jews, of course. No walls protected them. They lived across the Golden Horn, under the shadow of the Galata Tower. Nowhere to hide. They just waited and hoped that the oncoming storm would pass over them. Sometimes that worked for them, sometimes it didn't.

And I? I did what any self-respecting fool would do while the world collapsed around him.

I threw a party.

It was a select gathering of five, all the members of the Fools' Guild who were in Constantinople. There was Rico, the dwarf, who could juggle insults and invective as well as I could juggle clubs and knives. He was the current favorite of the current emperor, Alexios the Third. There was Plossus, a recent graduate of the Guildhall who would more likely be found walking on stilts or on his hands than on his feet; Alfonso, the Bolognan troubadour who now traveled the circuit from Thessaloniki to Constantinople, relaying news and instructions from the Guild to us and our reports back to them; myself, locally known as Feste, Guild name of Theophilos, original name . . . well, modesty intrudes; and my heart, my life, my beloved, my wife, locally known as Aglaia, originally Viola, quondam Duchess of Orsino and possessor of a few other titles.

The occasion was the ascension of Aglaia from Apprentice Fool to the rank of Jester, an accomplishment quite remarkable given that she started her training at the late age of thirty-three and that she completed it within a year and a half. The elevation was a tribute to both her talent and the superb training she received. Did I mention that I was her teacher? I didn't? There's that modesty again.

My wife and I lived in a set of rooms south of the Blachernae complex, where the Emperor kept his palace. More sumptuous quarters than I've generally had in my career, but Aglaia was the Empress's Fool and I did quite well with my own performing, so we could afford to live in some style.

When the others arrived, I led her to a stool in the center of the room and bade her stand upon it. Then the four of us stood around her, each holding two cups.

"Fellow members of the Fools' Guild, welcome," I said. "We are gathered to honor our newest member, who shall henceforth have the Guild name of Claudia and shall be entitled to all the honors and dignities accorded to any of us."

"Are there any honors and dignities accorded to any of you?" asked Aglaia.

"None whatsoever," I said. "Now, Claudia, there are traditionally two toasts given in praise of new members. The first is with water, the second with wine."

"Why water?" she asked suspiciously.

"To Claudia!" we shouted in unison, and splashed her from four directions.

"Oh, hell," she spluttered, her makeup running down her neck in white rivulets.

I handed her a cloth and a cup of wine.

"To the Guild!" we cried, and drank.

"To the Guild!" she agreed as she wiped her face, and she downed her cup.

Rico, who was an excellent cook when given the opportunity, had braised a joint in red wine and garlic. We attacked it with vigor, finishing with almond tortes that Plossus had brought from a baker near the Forum of Arkadios.

"Jester in full in what, eighteen months?" moaned Plossus when he had eaten his fill and then some. "I spent three years in training at the Guildhall to get there. It's not fair."

"It's because she trained under me," I said. "And had some interesting experiences before that. Bow to her talent, youth."

The wine and jokes flowed freely, although Aglaia did not partake unduly of the former.

"Are you unwell, milady?" commented Rico, noticing her sobriety. "Or do you scorn our wine?"

"Well, since you ask, I have an announcement of my own," she said. "I told my husband this afternoon. We are expecting a baby."

"How did this happen?" exclaimed Plossus with an innocent look on his face.

"Like Feste said, she trained under him," said Rico, and she nudged him with her elbow.

"Congratulations," said Alfonso. "When will its ugly face appear to frighten the world?"

"In about six months, if my others were anything to go by," said Aglaia.

"So, you will be drinking less wine and cutting back on your acrobatics," I said, more for my information than anything else.

"Yes," she replied. "I should still be able to juggle up to the end. Fortunately, the Empress is more interested in my company and conversation than my tumbling."

"Unlike myself," I said. "Well, as Chief Fool of Constantinople, I suggest that we talk a little business while we're still sober enough."

"Who says we are?" said Rico.

"The Venetian fleet anchored by the Abbey of Saint Stephen today," I continued.

"We heard," said Plossus.

"Which leads me to wonder why we received no advance notice about them from the Guild," I continued, looking at Alfonso.

"When I left Thessaloniki, the fleet was on its way to Negroponte," he said, shifting uncomfortably. "It's difficult for us to follow a fleet by land, and the Guildmembers with the Crusaders can't exactly swim to shore with their reports clenched in their teeth. You expected them to show up here sooner or later."

"Who is with the Crusaders?" asked Rico.

"Just a few troubadours. You can't expect an army to travel with fools for entertainment. They need men who can rally the troops with heroic song, not make them laugh. There's Giraut, Gaucelm Faidit, Raimbaut's with Montferrat, and Tantalo's more or less in charge of the lot of them."

"Tantalo's a good choice," I said. "I haven't trusted Raimbaut since Montferrat knighted him. He let it go to his head. Now, he wants lands to go with the title."

"Good singer, though," said Alfonso. "Not bad with a sword, either."

"I thought the troubadours were going to try and persuade the armies to go straight to Beyond-the-Sea," said Plossus.

"They failed," said Aglaia.

"The leaders showed the men Alexios, had him cry his tale," said Alfonso. "The army now thinks that Constantinople eagerly awaits the return of the true emperor, and will overthrow the current one the moment he appears."

"They're in for a rude awakening," I said. "The Greeks don't know this boy from Adam. The last thing they want is a Venetian proxy on the throne. So, we stick with the Guild plan. We find some way of persuading the two sides to work this out peacefully. Maybe get the

Greeks to provision the Crusaders enough to send them happily off to Jerusalem."

"A generous financial contribution to the Venetians would help assuage their affronted honor," added Aglaia.

"I don't know," said Alfonso doubtfully. "They swore all sorts of oaths to come here. They're very big on oath-taking. The Venetians may be here for the gold, but the Crusaders are here out of religious fervor."

"They have succumbed to the fever of the fervor," commented Plossus.

"And the boy Alexios now has the favor of the fever of the fervor," added Rico.

"I'm a believer in the favor of the fever of the fervor," finished Aglaia.

"All right," I said hastily, forestalling the continuation of the game. "In the morning, we'll start collecting information. Rico and Aglaia to the Emperor and Empress. Plossus, head down to the Akropolis and watch the fleet's movements. Try and get a good count of the ships."

"What about me?" asked Alfonso.

"Go back to Thessaloniki," I said.

His face fell. "But I'm needed here," he protested. "You'll need every one of us."

"I need you to get word to the Guild that it's finally happening," I said. "Speak to Fat Basil in Thessaloniki, then come back. But don't come into the city. If there's a full-scale war going on, you won't be able to do us any good. Stay in Rhaidestos. There may be a flood of refugees coming through. Find out from them what happened. If you don't hear from us within two weeks of your arrival, report back to Fat Basil."

Alfonso took a jug of wine and refilled all our cups, excepting Aglaia's.

"Good luck to all of you," he said quietly.

We drank in silence.

"This is no kind of party," said Aglaia suddenly. "I have just become a fool, I have a brand-new lute, and I want to sing."

She pulled out the lute I had given her and started strumming. The rest of us grabbed what instruments lay at hand and joined in, the coarse squeakings of the dwarf blending with the beautiful baritone of the troubadour. We sang into the night, and not a serious note was sounded until our three visitors had passed out on the cushions and my wife and I staggered into our bedchamber.

I embraced her, patting her belly gently.

"Boy or girl?" I asked her.

She considered the question carefully.

"Girl, I think," she said. "I don't know why, it just seems like one."

"Then let her resemble her mother in every way," I said. "Perfection should be duplicated. I've never been a parent before. You'll have to tell me how it's done."

"In my previous experiences, with hordes of servants," she laughed. "But I learned one or two things over the years. It's time for me to be the master and you the pupil."

I yawned and lay back.

"When there's time," I said. "First things first, unfortunately."

I woke at cock's crow with my normal hangover. Aglaia slept on, lovely despite the caked ruins of her whiteface clinging to her cheeks. I carried a bucket out to the well in the courtyard and hauled in some fresh water. Rico was up when I returned, doing his stretches.

"I'm going for bread," I said.

"I'll go with you," he replied.

We walked down the street to a small square near the foot of the

Fifth Hill. We purchased bread, cheese, and fruit for the day. Even now, the market was buzzing with the news of the fleet. As we walked back, we had to flatten ourselves against the wall to let a squadron of Imperial Guards trot by, followed by several wagonloads of large stones and lumber.

"Breakfast for the catapults," I said.

"Ever been through one of these?" asked Rico, subdued.

"One of what?"

"War," he said. "Bloody slaughter, rape, pillage, that sort of thing."

"Yes," I said. "Have you?"

"When I was a boy, before the Guild recruited me, my village was raided several times by bandits. The militia came and engaged them. It wasn't a pretty sight. But that was nothing compared to this."

"Hopefully, this will be nothing," I said.

"And if not?"

"Then keep your head down."

"Too late, it's already there," groaned the dwarf. "Look, why don't you come along with me to Blachernae today? You can sound out your friend, the eunuch."

"He's not exactly a friend," I said. "But that's not a bad idea. After we break our fast."

The others were up and about. Plossus was doing a full split on the floor, touching his toes, while Aglaia was scrubbing her face thoroughly with a rough cloth.

"Water and whiteface make paste," she muttered. "My complexion may never recover from this."

I peered into her unadorned face and sighed with admiration. She smiled up at me, then started applying the new day's makeup.

Alfonso finished packing his gear, picked up his lute and waved.

"Here," I said, handing him some rolls and apples for the road. "Safe journey. Don't dally overmuch in the courts of love."

"If I don't, people will be suspicious," he objected. "I have to uphold my reputation. Indeed, that of all troubadours. Milady, I bid you fare-well."

He kissed her hand gallantly, and she curtsied as if she were still a duchess.

"Regards to Fat Basil," said Rico.

"I'll await word in Rhaidestos," promised Alfonso, and he left. We soon heard him singing as his horse clopped away, but both sounds faded quickly.

"And now we are four," said Plossus.

"Don't forget our brethren in the ships," I said. "We'll meet back here nightly. Be careful."

Plossus stepped through the window onto his stilts, which were leaning against the building. "Stand aside, world!" he cried. "Plossus the Colossus walks among you." He strode away to the laughter of the children playing in the courtyard.

We picked up our bags and walked to the inner Blachernae gate. The complex had an interior wall separating it from the city, just in case the population decided to rebel. Once inside, we passed by the domes of the Church of Saint Savior in Chora and the Church of the Theotokos, passed the older palace and marched up to the marbled and frescoed ornateness of the new palace.

We used the side entrance, of course. Aglaia gave me a quick kiss and hurried off to the Empress's quarters, while Rico and I passed through a series of rooms until we reached the Imperial Throne Room.

Emperor Alexios Angelos was up before noon, an indication that he was taking the arrival of the Venetian fleet seriously. He was in his sixties, a hale man with hearty appetites and bad legs who dyed his thick, black beard daily to maintain its virile appearance. He was on his throne with his feet propped up on a cushioned stool, the Imperial legs being massaged by his favorite mistress, a sultry Egyptian who played the flute quite badly.

He had his ministers and generals with him, all looking worried and confused. He saw us enter and smiled wanly.

"The fools are here, everyone," he said. "Finally, some worthwhile advice."

We bowed, and set up quietly near the foot of the throne. A soldier came in, panting and sweaty, and saluted.

"Out with it," said the Emperor.

"They've raised anchor and set sail toward the city," he gasped.

"Did they come ashore at all while they were anchored?" inquired Theodore Laskaris, one of the Emperor's sons-in-law and one of his more competent generals.

"No, milord," said the soldier.

"They didn't even stop to forage," said Laskaris. "That's bad. They're determined to come straight for us, that's what I think."

"How much of a navy do we have left?" asked the Emperor.

Michael Stryphnos, the Lord Admiral, looked glum. He had acquired his post by way of being the Empress's brother-in-law and had spent his time embezzling the funds allocated to restoring the navy. Perhaps he never expected that he would actually have to take to the sea while admiral. "We can put maybe twenty ships in the water against them," he said.

"And how many are in their fleet?" the Emperor asked the soldier.

"We counted about two hundred," he replied.

"Well, that would be more, wouldn't it?" commented the Emperor. "Didn't we used to have a bigger navy?"

"Not really," said Stryphnos quickly.

"Oh, yes," said the Emperor. "I remember having more. You've let it go, haven't you, Admiral? Diverted a little ship-building money to your own needs?"

[11]

His brother-in-law said nothing.

"I think he's an excellent admiral," chirped Rico.

"Your reason, my foolish little one?" inquired the Emperor.

"For he has single-handedly destroyed a mighty fleet," said the dwarf. "Too bad it was his own."

"Hmph," said Alexios, not particularly cheered. "Maybe we could borrow someone else's fleet. Isn't that what we've been doing? What navy do we usually use when we need one?"

"Venice's, Your Majesty," said Laskaris.

Alexios slumped back in his throne, sighing.

"I suppose that won't do this time," he said.

"No, Your Excellency."

"All right, see how much they want to go away," commanded the Emperor. "And, my Lord Admiral, since you don't have a navy, I want you to follow the fleet from the shore. Take five hundred knights with you."

"Yes, sire."

"We do still have some horses left, don't we?" thundered the Emperor.

"Yes, sire," said Stryphnos, and he bowed and left.

"And we'll be eating them inside a fortnight," Rico muttered to me.

"Dear me, I had better warn Zeus," I said. "All that money I've spent keeping him stabled here would go to waste."

"Better keep him handy," said Rico. "You never know when you might have to leave in a hurry around here. Look, your ball-less friend is trying to catch your eye."

I looked up to see Philoxenites, the Imperial Treasurer, jerking his head toward a corridor, then vanishing down it. I played on a bit to give him time, then stood and stretched and strolled out of the room as if I was heading for the nearest chamberpot.

TWO

The concession to the Venetians of a Quarter in Constantinople, with shops in the district of the Ferry, between the gate called the Jews' Gate and the gate called the Watch Gate, with all occupied and unoccupied lands, and comprising the three wharfs or landing stages on the shore of the Golden Horn.
——FROM THE ALEXIAN CHRYSOBULL (1082 A.D.)

Philoxenites kept his offices at the northeast corner of the palace, with a view overlooking the Golden Horn. He was a large, bald man, a source of much ridicule among the masses, but he was a wily, manipulative, ambitious schemer. That in itself did not distinguish him from the average member of the upper echelon. What did was his knack for thriving no matter who was on the throne or in favor of the Emperor. He had his fingers in every pie in Byzantium, which made him a useful source of information as long as you kept your back to the wall.

He was a eunuch, something favored by those who knew him. Such creatures should not be allowed to reproduce.

He waved off our usual preliminary banter, though observing the social amenities. I always made sure he drank first, just in case.

"To Byzantium," he said, smirking as he lifted his cup to his lips. "I might as well get right to it," he began as I cautiously tasted my wine. "There's been a death in the Venetian quarter. I thought you might want to look into it."

"Who died?" I asked.

"Fellow by the name of Bastiani," he said. "Camilio Bastiani. A silk merchant."

"And why should the death of a merchant interest me?"

"I thought all humanity interested you."

"I don't have time for every single one of them. There's probably a sparrow falling somewhere that I've missed as well. What's so important about Bastiani?"

"He's a Venetian."

"So? Venetians die. There're thousands of them sailing toward martyrdom as we speak."

"Which makes the timing of Bastiani's death all the more interesting."

"Why? What makes this particular Venetian significant to you?"

He walked to the door, opened it briefly, and glanced in both directions. Satisfied that no one was listening, he closed the door and pulled a chair close to mine. His appearance did not improve with proximity.

"He was my principal informant inside the Venetian quarter," he said softly. "And a possible conduit to the fleet if we needed to open negotiations quietly. He is a major loss."

"To you or to Byzantium?"

"Everything I do is for Byzantium," he said with a straight face. "I think you must know this by now."

"With a healthy dose of personal gain," I observed.

"One's wealth should be commensurate with one's value, don't you think?" he said.

I let that go by. I've lived most of my fool's life in poverty, at least as far as gold was concerned. If I had wanted to be ambitious, I would have stayed home.

"All right, the timing is suspect," I said. "Why do you need me? Why not use Will and Phil like you usually do?"

William and Philip were Englishmen who had joined the Varangian Guard. Philoxenites had close ties to the Varangians, and these two in particular did his dirty work with efficiency and no small amount of personal pleasure.

"Will and Phil are otherwise engaged," he said. "They are soldiers first, and there is a bit of a war brewing, as you have probably observed. I can't draw on them now. But even if I could, I would prefer using you."

"Why?"

He looked out his window at the seawall. A squad of Varangians was getting a catapult in position at the top of a tower.

"The jurisdiction over the area makes this a delicate situation," he explained. "There have been various chrysobulls between Venice and ourselves over the years that have made the quarter virtually independent, although the Logothete is nominally in charge. The Venetians have their own officers, courts, and judges. We can't just barge in and stomp around looking for a murderer, even if the victim is one of their own."

"And the murderer may not be from the quarter at all."

"Exactly!" he said, beaming at me as if I were a student in his class.

"Tell me more, and I'll see if it interests me enough to pursue it further," I said.

"These are strange times when the Imperial Treasurer must entertain the fool," he said. "Bastiani lived in a three-story building inside the Porta Viglae. The landlord is a man named Vitale. Poor housing, but the merchant was a stingy man by all accounts. He has no family here. There is rumor of a wife in Venice, but that's not certain. His ships came into the wharf on the other side of the gate, and his offices were in the smaller embolum used by the silk merchants."

"I know the place," I said. "I've passed by it when I've entertained at the hospital there."

"Your charitable work does you credit, I'm sure. Last night, Bastiani took his evening meal at a communal table in the embolum with his fellow merchants, then went home alone. His landlord saw him go to his room on the top floor. Bastiani bade him a good evening, then shut and barred the door. That was the last time anyone saw him alive."

"What happened to him?"

"When he didn't appear for the morning meal, the landlord went up and knocked on his door. There was no answer, and it was still barred. When they broke down the door, they found Bastiani lying on his bed in his nightclothes. The room was otherwise undisturbed. His eyes were closed, and he failed to respond to the ruckus raised by the door being smashed in. He was dead."

"How was he killed?" I asked.

"That is a puzzle," admitted the eunuch. "There was no mark on him, no evidence of violence. The only unusual thing was that his face was bright pink."

"Poison of some kind."

"That would be my conclusion, but how was it done? There were no indications that he had eaten or drunk anything in his room. The last meal he had was a communal one, and nobody else at the table suffered any ill effects. The boarding house was a short walk from the embolum, and there are no taverns to lure the pedestrian between the two buildings. So, there you have it."

"I do have other matters to attend to, you know," I said.

"Not any more," he said. "Please believe me when I tell you that we are working toward the same goal."

"What do you know of a fool's goals?" I asked.

"Last year, you trusted me enough to alert me to a plot against the life of the Emperor's deposed brother," he said. "You and your talented wife mentioned the advantages of keeping Isaakios alive in the event that his son came knocking at the gates with an army behind him to claim the throne. Your advice has proved all too prescient. Because of all these factors, I've allowed your activities to proceed unhampered."

"Most of the time," I said.

"Most of the time," he conceded. "As the only official who bothers watching the doings of fools, I've developed some idea of your goals. Would I be correct in saying that you seek peace?"

"Who doesn't want peace?" I said.

"Two hundred ships full of soldiers for a start," he said. "The pursuit of peace can be quite dangerous. My goal is the preservation of Byzantium. Peaceful preservation would, of course, be the most desirable. But if peace can only be bought through subjugation, then there will be war."

"I understand entirely," I said. "You say you wish the preservation of Byzantium. You said nothing about preserving the current emperor."

He leaned back in his chair, his hands making a tent before his chest, his eyes narrowed to slits.

"I know what I said, and I know what I didn't say," he said finally. "Right now, I need to know who killed my informant, and why. If there is to be a siege from Venice, then we have the matter of ten thousand Venetians already in the city. If they struck at my informant as the first step toward insurrection, then I want to know about it. Find out for me."

"And then?"

"And then I'll decide what to do with the information."

"What if I refuse?" I said.

"Then I have you arrested as a foreign spy," he said. "Along with your lovely wife, your stilt-walking friend, and the Emperor's dwarf."

"Can't have that happen," I said. "All right. But on one condition."

"Yes?"

"I'm only gathering information. If you want anyone killed, seek elsewhere."

His eyebrows crawled up his forehead.

[17]

"My friend, I would never ask you to do anything that vile," he protested.

I nodded and headed to the door.

"I have plenty of men available for that sort of thing," he added.

I hesitated, then turned back toward him.

"Who do you have to contact the Crusaders now that Bastiani's gone?" I asked.

"That's none of your business," he said.

"Maybe not," I said. "I am not interested in getting anyone in trouble. Far from it. But if Bastiani was killed because someone wanted to destroy your means of communicating with the Venetians, then anyone else you might consider using could be in danger right now."

"A good point, Feste," he said. "I will warn them. If necessary, would you undertake the task? I'm guessing you have some friends in the enemy ranks."

"I'll think about it," I replied, and then I left.

The Venetian quarter was once the Jewish quarter before the Jews were kicked out of the city. All that was left to show they had been there was a small burial ground and the Porta Ebraica, the Jews' Gate. This now marked the easternmost point of the quarter. Not quite four hundred paces west was the Porta Viglae, which marked the other end. In the middle was the Porta Drungarii. The gates were in the seawall, a thick monster soaring some forty feet into the air, dotted with towers. Opposite each gate was a wharf.

The whole district nestled between the base of the Third Hill and the Golden Horn, with the seawall more or less bisecting it. Ten thousand Venetians were jammed into every available bit of space, along with their churches, their stores, and their warehouses. Land was at such a premium that many locations combined different functions. The Church of Saint Akindyni, the chief church of the quarter, also did a very nice business as a bakery. I heard that the communion wafers were excellent.

To the west was the Moslem quarter. To the east, the Amalfitani, the Pisans, the Genoese, competitors of the Venetians in trade, rivals in everything else, always with one hand on a ledger and the other reaching under the table for a dagger. There were walls between the districts, and for good reason.

On top of the hill, the Vigla kept watch over everything. I doubt that any of them saw Bastiani die.

I had no trouble finding Vitale's boarding house. It was at the end of an alley by the hospital, a basic brick cube pressed against the northern wall. I glanced to my right and marked the embolum. The eunuch was right—there were no taverns in this area, no obvious brothels beckoning to the passerby with too much time and money on his hands. That's not to say Bastiani couldn't have stopped by someone's room and shared a private bottle or two, but I wasn't looking to go door to door asking his neighbors if any of them had murdered him recently.

Vitale himself was sweeping out the door when I came up. He was a portly man with a florid face, and the slight exertion he placed on the broom caused him to sweat profusely without having a noticeable effect on the dirt. He had ample time to see me approaching, but the appearance of my whiteface caused him to gape a bit. I bowed, and he nodded his head back at me.

"Feste the Fool, at your service," I said. "Are you the one called Vitale?"

"That is what they call me," he said. "I've seen you about. You're a funny fellow."

"Thank you, good sir," I said. "Then it won't surprise you to know that I am here on funny business."

I looked up and down to see if anyone was listening, then leaned

[19]

toward him until the bells on my cap were practically dangling in his eyes. "They say there's been a murder here," I whispered. "Is it so?"

"Well, don't know that I'd be calling it a murder so quick," he said hurriedly. "One of my tenants passed away during the night."

"But under mysterious circumstances, yes? Tell me everything."

He looked at me suspiciously. "Why should I?"

I took his arm and pulled him inside the doorway, glancing behind me.

"I collect gossip," I said. "A bit of scandal is worth several dinners to me. And it may be worth something to you as well."

"Really?" he said, more interested now.

"I have a patron, a wealthy man," I explained. "He has, shall we say, unusual tastes, even for this debauched city."

"Go on."

"He has a particular interest in macabre settings. Places of sudden death, whether suicide, murder, or just the unexplained. He has been known to take impressionable young ladies into these rooms, close the door and . . . well, I'm sure you can imagine the rest."

"Shameless!" exclaimed Vitale, his lips glistening. "To think that such shocking behavior goes on in this city. And he would be willing to pay?"

"For one night's entertainment, it could be as much as a year's lease is worth to you," I said. "But it must be the right kind of atmosphere. That is why I'm here, as sort of an advance scout. May I see where it happened?"

"Certainly, certainly," he said, dropping his broom with glee. "It's on the third floor."

He started up the first flight with a bustle but slowed considerably on the second and was wheezing heavily by the time he reached the top.

"Begging your pardon, good Fool," he gasped. "The excitement and all."

"Take your time, good fellow," I said. "Which room was his?"

"The middle one in the back," he said as his breath caught up with him. "We have six rooms on each floor, three in front, three in back. He preferred his privacy, so he chose the one with no view."

"What was he so private about, do you think?"

Vitale shrugged. "It was no business of mine, as long as he paid the rent regular, which he did. Last night, he came home as usual, said good night as he passed me, and turned in. I serve a morning meal here. When he didn't come down, I went up to get him. I knocked, no answer, knocked louder, still no answer. I thought maybe he went out during the night, but when I tried to push the door open, I found it was still barred from the inside."

"Which concerned you."

"Of course. I dashed down to the first floor, got a couple of the other tenants, and we ran back up and broke the door in."

He pushed it open to reveal a small room, sparsely furnished. A bed was in one corner, the bedclothes scattered. A cedar trunk was in the opposite corner, and a chamberpot was upended nearby. No bottles, plates, cups, any indication of food or drink. There were no windows, and the room stank.

"I'll clean the pot up and throw some rushes in before your patron uses it," Vitale assured me hastily.

"I should think so," I huffed. I scanned the room, looking for anything that might be of use. "Where did you find him?"

"He was in bed, lying on his back, his eyes closed. I wasn't the first one in the room, one of the others was, but I could see him through the door. I nearly dropped dead myself, had one of my coughing fits with all the excitement and galloping up and down the stairs so many times. I would have said it was a natural death, except when I looked at his face, I saw the pink in it. Never seen anything like it."

"Do you think it was murder?" I asked.

"I think it was witchcraft, to tell you the God's truth," he said, his eyes wide.

I gave the room one more glance, then stepped out. He closed the door behind him, and a thought struck me.

"You said you broke the door in," I remarked.

"Yes, sir. The boys knocked it right off its hinges."

I pointed to the hinges, which were whole.

"What say you to that? And where are the broken pieces of the wooden bar?"

He looked at me oddly. "Well, sir, since one of my tenants is a carpenter, I had him fix it up as quickly as possible. I want to let the room out by week's end. And as for the broken pieces, they went into the fire already."

"A pity," I said. "The scene may be too disturbed now for my patron to derive the true sense of mayhem that he requires. Let me ask you this: Did Bastiani receive any visitors here?"

His eyes narrowed. "I don't know what you mean, Fool," he said. "I run a respectable establishment here."

"To be sure," I said. "Perhaps you could direct me to some of the others who saw him? And let me pay you for your pains." I tossed him a couple of bronze coins which he pocketed quickly.

"Let's see, the only one who would be here right now is John Aprenos," he said. "He rooms with the carpenter on the second floor. He was one of the ones who helped me break the door in."

I suspected that Vitale's shoulder never touched wood during that incident, but I was content to let him make himself part of the story.

Aprenos was lounging on a pallet, one of two in the middle room facing the front of the building, with a window over the front door.

He was drinking and blinked a bit uncertainly when he saw me. Mounted on the wall by him were three spears and a shield.

"What's this creature?" he growled.

"Feste the Fool," I said.

"Well, I'm John, the Huntsman," he replied. "I've no need for fooling."

"He wants to hear about Bastiani," Vitale informed him.

"What for? He's dead," said Aprenos, rising unsteadily to his feet. He was a lanky fellow with powerful arms.

"I'll leave you with him," whispered Vitale. "More cleaning to do. Let me know what arrangements need to be made for your patron."

"Thank you," I said. He lumbered down the steps.

"What's this to you?" asked Aprenos.

"Curiosity," I said. "I search out curious incidents, then recount them to others."

"It's a curious way to make a living," he said.

"Precisely," I replied. "What can you tell me about your late neighbor?"

"Not much," he said, scratching his neck. "Kept to himself, didn't say much, died alone."

"Did he ever have any visitors here?"

"Well," he said, chuckling. "There was some woman who came by. He would sneak her in, but Tullio and me saw her a few times. That's the fellow who sleeps in the other pallet. He's a carpenter. He's at work."

"Why aren't you?"

"The gates are closed," he said. "They're not letting people out until they know what's happening with that fleet. So much for my living. I'll have to find some day work until things settle down."

"About this woman—would you recognize her if you saw her?"

"Maybe," he said doubtfully. "Just some drab from the street as far

[23]

as I know, never paid her much attention. Haven't seen her in a while."

"Any idea how he died?"

"We all thought poison, from the face," he said. "That color pink's not a usual color for a man. But neither is white, and here you are."

"Here I am," I agreed. "Any idea who might want him dead?"

"I didn't know him that well. I only saw him when we came home at night. You'd be better off asking the other silk merchants."

"Fair enough. Would you know where I could find your friend Tullio?"

"Sure," he said. "Down at the embolum, finishing up the coffin. Funeral's tomorrow."

"Thank you, friend John. I hope that you hunt again shortly."

He waved and returned to his bottle.

As I came out of the house, I saw a woman, cloaked and veiled, standing at the far end of the alleyway. She started when I came out, and then she vanished off to the right. I ran to the main street and looked for her, but she was gone.

Probably worth checking out, I thought. A man will tell his mistress many things, even when he's awake. And if she was a common prostitute, all the better. I know quite a few men who will pay such a woman just to pretend to listen while he talks about himself. But first I would have to find her. I had a few ideas on how to tackle that particular problem.

In the meantime, there was the embolum. It was a large rectangular building just inside the Porta Viglae, with several silk and leather shops clustered inside the columns of the loggia running along the outside. Inside were storerooms and a large central trading area. On the upper floor were dormitories for visiting sailors and traders.

Bastiani was laid out in a corner of the central trading area. Business continued as usual in the rest of the room as bolts of silk were passed under the eyes of the traders for inspection, then assigned to different storerooms. The traders were making neat little entries in large leatherbound ledgers, so that the room was filled with tiny scratching noises.

The coffin was resting atop a pair of sawhorses, and the body was in full view, not so much for the viewing but because the coffin lid had not been prepared yet. Tacked to the wall behind him was a banner depicting the Lion of Saint Mark, made of silk, of course. Next to the coffin, a young, fair-haired man was busy cooking something in a small pot suspended from a tripod over a small brazier. He dipped into the pot a wooden spoon, held it up, and watched a yellowish concoction drip from it. He shook his head irritably and picked up a handful of stale cheese from a nearby table. He sniffed it, grimaced, and tossed it into the pot, stirring rapidly.

"Is it ready to eat yet?" I inquired.

He glanced at me, noted my makeup.

"A proper question from a fool," he replied. "It will never be ready to eat. I'm making glue. Nothing like cheese for glue, you know."

"I have had cheese that tasted like glue, so I'm not surprised," I said. "Are you Tullio?"

"I am he," replied the carpenter, turning to a group of pine boards on the ground. "Looking for some juggling clubs? I could turn out as many as you like once I'm done making the lid."

"Actually, I was looking for this fellow in the box."

"There he is. Friend of yours?"

"Not really. I was wondering if there was going to be a wake. Perhaps I could provide a little entertainment."

"Ah. The fool makes money off the dead."

"As does the carpenter," I replied. "I heard you even fixed a door as part of the deal."

"You've been to Vitale's?" he exclaimed. "Whatever for?"

"Curiosity," I said. "Bastiani was a neighbor of yours. Did you know

[25]

him well? I'm looking for some personal information I can work into my tribute."

"Not well," replied Tullio. "He lived upstairs. We said hello in the morning. Sometimes we would walk this way together."

He picked up a few boards and laid them lengthwise on the coffin, lining them up until the body was covered. He notched the wood at the point where it hung over the end, then picked up a saw.

"What do you think killed him?" I asked as he trimmed the edges.

"No idea," he said. "There's murmuring about murder, but I think that's mostly to save face. If he's a suicide, he can't be buried in consecrated ground."

"Why would anyone want to kill him?"

"He's a merchant," said Tullio. "If a merchant is murdered, it's probably over money. If he kills himself, it's probably for the same reason."

"Logical thinking for logical times. But these are strange days at the moment."

"True enough," he agreed, trimming a second board.

"I heard he had a woman," I said.

"Who told you that?"

"Your roommate."

He laughed. "Was he sober?"

"Not very."

"Poor John. He needs to be galloping through the forest, impaling the poor woodland creatures. He hates being cooped up like this. I'll have to bring him along with me, get him some work."

"Is he any good?"

"When he drinks only water, he can knock a squirrel off a branch from fifty paces. He's been called by the Emperor himself, at least when his legs were still good enough to hunt regularly."

"Was he right about the woman?"

"Yes," said Tullio. "The only one ever to go into Bastiani's room that I know of. Don't know her name, but I think she plies her trade by the Forum of Theodosios. Looking for a little female company, Fool?"

"One can never have enough, friend Carpenter. Now, if you will point me toward the man in charge of the funeral, I will leave you to your labors. I'll come by about the clubs some happier time."

"It may be a while for that to come about," he said. "The man you want is Andrea Ruzzini. He's the older man standing by that oaken table."

I thanked him and sought out Ruzzini. He was a hale fellow in his fifties, with a good deal of brown left in his beard and hair and with arms and chest powerful enough to suggest he still pitched in with the loading of the bales on occasion. At the moment, he was counting a stack of silver.

"Begging your pardon, noble sir," I said when he had finished and made an entry in his ledger.

"Yes?" he said in a gruff voice.

"I have come to offer my condolences over the death of your colleague, and my services as well."

He looked at me sourly. "We have no need of jesting at a funeral, Fool."

"But I am a singer, too. If there is a wake, then I could provide you with the appropriate music for the occasion. I know your city, your language, and your songs quite well."

"Our city is here," he said. "Most of us were born here and grew up speaking Greek before we spoke Venetian."

"As you can hear, I speak that language, too. Sir, a proper wake needs music to send the departed to Heaven in the spirit of joy."

He looked across the room at the coffin.

"All right, we might as well," he said. "He had little joy in his life. Let him at least have some now. Come back later tonight. We'll be maintaining the vigil here."

"And the funeral?"

He grimaced. "We're negotiating terms with our protectors. Our cemetery is outside the city walls. They won't let us bury him unless they have an armed escort to keep us from joining our compatriots on the ships. I think we'll be able to bury him tomorrow."

"Very good, sir. I—"

But I was interrupted by a boy rushing in yelling, "Come quickly! They're tearing everything down!"

People rushed from the room. I followed, curious to see what was happening. The commotion was coming from the other side of the gate.

A Vigla squadron was pulling down a house by the seawall. The former occupants were standing by piles of furniture and other belongings, watching the activity with forlorn expressions. A captain was standing in front of them, reading from a scroll.

"All buildings against the outside of the seawall in this quarter are to be torn down," he proclaimed. "You have one hour to remove all your possessions. After that, we take no responsibility. This is by order of the Emperor Alexios Angelos."

The house came crashing down with a splintering of timbers and an eruption of dust. The guards stood back, some of them coughing, then started loading the wreckage onto wagons to cart away.

Ruzzini stormed up to the captain, his face ruddy. Two of the Vigla drew their swords as a precaution.

"Captain, this is an outrage!" shouted the merchant. "We are your friends and neighbors. Have we no rights at all?"

"You shouldn't have been allowed to build against the walls, anyway," said the captain. "We have to clear them to defend the city."

"But Captain—"

"Look, Ruzzini, you have no say in this!" shouted the captain. "If you have a problem, take it up with them!"

He pointed with his sword and the crowd turned and then collectively gasped.

A ship, a merchantman larger than any floating against the three wharves, had come around the tip of the seawall. Dozens of shields, with all manner of coats of arms painted on them, hung over the sides. The sails were furled, but from the topmast flew the flag of Saint Mark and the emblem of Montferrat, and three banks of oars projected from the hull. As the ship cleared the seawall, another appeared behind it, and another behind that.

The fleet was surging up the Bosporos.

THREE

[They] call themselves Venetikoi; nourished by the sea, they are vagabonds like the Phoenicians and cunning of mind.
—NIKETAS CHONIATES, *O CITY OF BYZANTIUM*

The great iron chain that stretched from the Galata Tower on the far shore of the Golden Horn to the Eugenios Gate by the Akropolis was slowly raised until it blocked the entrance to the harbor. The Venetians watched it desolately, knowing that their ships and cargoes were trapped inside for the duration of the siege, and their fortunes with them.

The fleet did not attempt the chain, nor the shore by the tower. It seemed to be heading toward the opposite shore of the Bosporos. As invasion wasn't imminent, I decided to continue my investigation. I'm not much good at stopping fleets, anyway.

I first went for religious counsel. This might surprise anyone familiar with my general distrust of established churches, but the particular cleric I sought had his own peculiar expertise. In this city, the Patriarch of the Church was appointed by the emperor. The more corrupt the emperor, the more corrupt the Patriarch, and the more corrupt the Patriarch, the more corrupt the Church. And of the two hundred churches scattered across this city, from the grandeur of the Hagia Sophia down to the little two-benches-and-a-cross emporia, the most corrupt was Saint Stephen's by the River. It was from this husk of a church that Father Esaias spun his webs.

Few had seen his face. I was one of the few, and I didn't care to repeat the experience. He hid it beneath a simple cowl and lived in a luxurious apartment concealed within the crypts beneath the church. A small cadre of padres surrounded him, each more deadly than the next. The depredations of the rich and powerful occupy a rarefied world of their own, but the commonplace crime that afflicted the rest of us was Esaias's bailiwick. He had a piece of almost every act of extortion, theft, prostitution, fraud, and smuggling in the city. And that was his good side. He had no enemies that anyone knew about. At least, not for long.

When Aglaia and I had first arrived in the city, we had struck an alliance with him—one of necessity more than desire, but it had proved mutually advantageous on more than one occasion, so it continued. Fortunately, the goals of the Fools' Guild did not generally butt into the business of the underworld, so there was no need for us to challenge each other. Not that we thought there never would be such an occasion, but so far, so good.

The house of worship was on the west bank of the Lycos river, which entered the city from the northwest and was more or less sucked dry before it could reach the sea. It was a medium-sized brick church, with no distinguishing features except the sense of menace it projected over an already menacing neighborhood.

Father Theodore was standing inside the entrance, watching me approach. A burly man with no discernible expression on his face, he was a fearsome swordsman. He wore one sword openly outside his cassock today. I expected that he had some smaller weapons concealed inside, but I had never put that theory to the test and never wanted to.

"Good afternoon, Father," I said. "How's business?"

"A bit busy at the moment, Feste," he replied. "You wish to see Father Esaias?"

"If he could spare a moment, I would be most grateful."

[31]

"You know the way," he said, and he stood aside to let me pass.

I descended the stone steps to the crypts and approached an altar. I stood before a screen on which Saint Stephen looked benignly at me. I tapped lightly on it. Saint Stephen looked at me with one painted eye and one real one. I crossed myself piously. The real one winked, and the screen slid aside.

Father Melchior was on the other side. He greeted me warmly and motioned me over to a cushioned chair.

"Good to see you, Feste," he said. "Father Esaias will be here shortly. He's hearing confessions."

I heard a slap and a muffled yelp from another room. Melchior glanced in its direction.

"That fellow should be confessing soon," he observed.

"I hope his sins were not too grievous," I said.

"His penance should be purely monetary. Wine while you're waiting?"

"Yes, thank you."

Father Esaias came in and plunged his bony hands into a basin.

"He is forgiven, Father Melchior," he said, scrubbing hard until there was no trace of blood. "Get him cleaned up and send him on his way."

"Yes, Father," said Melchior, and he left the room.

"My apologies, Fool," said Father Esaias as he dried his hands on a towel. "There is panic in the air today. I have to administer reassurances." He sat in a chair opposite mine and poured himself some wine. "Business or social?" he asked.

"Business, I'm afraid," I replied. "I'm looking for a prostitute."

"I can refer you to several. What did you have in mind?"

"It's not for me, it's for a friend."

He snorted.

"Perhaps you'll tell me what you really want," he said.

"A silk merchant by the name of Bastiani was poisoned last night

[32]

in the Venetian quarter. He had been known to receive visits from a young lady who normally works the Forum of Theodosios. I'd like to talk to her."

"As would I," he said sharply. "The ladies of that forum aren't allowed to make private calls. Either she's one of ours and she's working on the side, or she's a competitor. And I dislike competitors. What does she look like?"

"I got a glimpse of her, I think, but she was cloaked and veiled."

"That doesn't sound like one of ours," he said. "Their wares are usually on display at all times."

"Maybe at the forum, but not for private visits?"

"Perhaps," he conceded. "But you've given me little to go by. I'll drop a word and see what turns up. Forgive me if it isn't my main concern at the moment."

"I understand completely, and I thank you for any help. And please let me talk to her before you begin disciplining her."

"Why does this merchant concern you?"

"Anything Venetian concerns me. What do you think of the present state of the world?"

He shrugged. "We will act according to how the situation develops. What goes on in Blachernae? You were there this morning, weren't you?"

"Confusion and blame. No coherent course of conduct, yet. Normally, no sane army would attempt these walls, but given the disarray of the Empire, the Crusaders might have a chance."

"Are you still friendly with that Varangian captain?"

"Henry? Yes."

He put his goblet down with a thud.

"In our own way, we are as patriotic as any faction in this city," he said. "Tell him that we can't help him outside the walls. We're no good on open plains where stealth is not a strength. But if the walls are

[33]

breached and the foreigners brave the alleys, they will find them as deadly as any terrain they have ever encountered. We will guarantee that."

"I'll pass it along," I said. "Whence comes this loyalty?"

"If the Crusaders win, they take the traditional three days of looting," he said. "That won't affect our holdings—we've already moved our wealth away for safety. But if they steal from the rest of the city, that cuts into our future prospects."

"And, as you said, you dislike competitors."

"Precisely. Go in peace, my son." He raised his hands in blessing. As it was meant sincerely, I thanked him and departed.

And yet, I did not feel especially blessed.

I hurried home to rejoin my fellow fools. Aglaia was already there, preparing the meal. Rico arrived soon after, and Plossus last of all, somersaulting through the window.

"Food," he cried. "I have had a hard day of counting. It has made me hungry."

"Counting ships makes you hungry?" wondered Aglaia as she placed a bowl of stew in front of him. "That's strange. Counting sheep makes me sleepy."

"I have been counting ships that are shipping counts," said Plossus. "Along with earls, knights, and all the rabble they've brought along to do the real dying."

"We heard there were two hundred in the fleet," said Rico.

"A gross exaggeration," said Plossus. "There are a hundred and ninety-seven. Forty of the big transports, a hundred horse transports, and the rest galleys. It took most of the day for them to pass by the city. What a glorious sight they made! The knights on the ships hung their shields over the sides just to flash their colors at the Greeks.

People were bringing blankets and baskets of food to the Akropolis to spend the day watching them."

"What were the people saying about it?" I asked.

"Lot of disbelief, nervousness. No one seemed to have heard the fleet was coming until they saw it, so they are wondering about how prepared the Emperor is to face it. Everyone is confident that the walls will hold, but they are a little distressed that there was no local navy opposing the invasion."

"Did the boy Alexios's name come up?"

"Not once. I guess Blachernae's done a thorough job of suppressing that bit of information from the rest of the city. Other than that, there was little hostility, little uproar. A couple of archers in the Varangian Guard loosed a couple of arrows from the seawall, but it looked more like they were betting on the distance than actually trying to hit anything. The fleet's too far away."

"Any sign from our people?"

"I heard some singing from the *Eagle*, but couldn't make out what it was. Probably Tantalo—it was the first ship up the straits, a real monster, and it was flying mostly Venetian colors."

"Yes, I saw it when it passed the Golden Horn," I said. "Good work, lad. What's happening with the Emperor?"

"Agitation, in a word," said Rico. "He wanted no distraction from me. He wouldn't even make time for that Egyptian minx, which is unheard of. She sat by the throne and pouted prettily, but he's called for his horse and armor and sent for the Ikon of the Virgin from the Church of the Theotokos."

"He means to ride?" exclaimed Aglaia. "He can barely walk on those legs."

"He's afraid," said Rico. "He mutters about God's revenge upon him for what he did to his brother. He's lashing out at all of his generals and advisors. It's not exactly inspiring."

"He should let the battle come here," said Plossus. "If the army goes after the Crusaders, they'll be spread too thin."

"Strategic, but not popular," I said. "If the people don't see some active pursuit soon, they'll turn against him."

"That's what the Emperor says," said Rico. "He's talking about sending a delegation to the Crusaders, but he's waiting to see where they land first."

"Something we need to know as well. And the Empress?"

"Consulting astrologers, as usual," said Aglaia. "She's taking the invasion as a personal affront after all the hard work she's done quashing unfavorable omens."

"She shouldn't take it so hard," protested Rico. "She did her best. There's hardly a statue left unmutilated in the entire city, thanks to her."

"Nevertheless, she's upset. Most of all, because she fears the Empire will fall before she's finished remarrying off her daughters."

"Not to mention the fact that two of them could end up widows," I commented. "Palaiologos and Laskaris are going to be right in the thick of battle if it gets that far. You marry your daughters to generals, you take your chances."

"There's that," agreed Aglaia. "But at least the first two daughters are married right now. And Palaiologos is claiming his old leg injury is acting up, which may prevent him from going to war."

"Convenient," laughed Rico.

"And there's a bit of a scandal brewing with the third daughter," Aglaia continued.

"What's little Evdokia done to disgrace the family now?" asked Plossus.

"There is no one capable of disgracing that family," said Rico.

"She's fallen for a married man," said Aglaia.

"Not for the first time," said Rico.

[36]

"No, but this one's in prison."

"Ouch," I said. "That doesn't sound promising. Criminal or political?"

"Political, I think. Alexios threw him in a few years ago for the usual suspicions of conspiracy. Evdokia met him while making the charitable rounds, and now her charity has narrowed considerably in its scope. All of which has nothing to do with the Crusade, but it's what occupies Euphrosyne's attention while her world is being destroyed."

"All right," I said. "For the moment, we watch and wait. Rico, you should drop hints to Alexios about paying the Crusaders off whenever you deem it appropriate. Aglaia, do the same with Euphy. I don't know how much contact she'll be having with her husband, but you never can tell when she'll pop into the throne room and start haranguing him. Plossus, keep sounding out the factions, see if the wind starts changing. If the people get up in arms about the current Emperor, I want to know about it immediately."

"And while we do all this, you will be doing what?" asked Aglaia.

"I've been roped into a little investigation for Philoxenites," I said. "Plossus, you know the Venetian quarter better than I do. Ever hear of Camilio Bastiani?"

"Silk merchant," he replied immediately. "Nothing unusual about him. Kind of a quiet fellow."

"He just got a lot quieter," I said. "Someone poisoned him."

"Really? When was this?"

"Last night. Philoxenites said he was his informant on the quarter and his link to the fleet."

"Always the quiet ones, isn't it?" mused Plossus. "Well, that's news to me, but no surprise, I suppose. The eunuch has informants everywhere, they say. He thinks someone from the quarter did it?"

I filled them in briefly on what I had learned.

"And why, pray tell, does this concern us?" asked Rico.

"When I find out, I'll let you know," I said. "In the meantime, I'm going to the wake tonight, and then I'm going to get rid of the outfit and makeup and show up at the funeral."

"Disguised as a common human," sighed Aglaia. "Oh, well, go ahead. Abandon your wife and child-to-be. I knew this marriage would have days like these."

"Want me to go with you?" asked Plossus.

"Not just yet. Too many fools might alert the murderer."

"Too few fools could get you killed," pointed out Rico.

"I've worked alone before, and I haven't been killed yet," I said, picking up my lute.

"You never manage to succeed in reassuring me, you know?" said Aglaia, smiling brightly. She came over and kissed me.

"Until tomorrow night, everyone," I said, and went back into the night.

The night patrols were out enforcing curfew, but I had all manner of documents from various imperial sources allowing me safe passage. We all did, justified by so many late nights entertaining others. The gates to the Venetian quarter were heavily guarded tonight. More to keep the Venetians in than to keep anyone else out, I supposed. The captain himself came out to verify my legitimacy, but we knew each other, so it was no ordeal.

"Someone having a party in the middle of all this?" he asked. "Some cheek if you ask me."

"A wake, as it happens," I said. "I'm making mournful music for a murdered merchant."

"A wake, is it?" he said, looking uneasily through the gate. "There will be many more of those in the next few days. You'll be a busy fool, Feste."

"Any idea who killed him?"

"Don't know anything about it. Our jurisdiction stops right here."

He opened the gate for me and I went through.

"Have a nice wake!" he called after me, and the gate clanged shut behind me.

Though night had fallen, the Venetians were out, gathering in small clumps at the street corners, drinking in the taverns and casting baleful glances at the seawalls. There was a constant muttering in the air, a resentful flurry of words that swirled through the alleys and thudded into the piles of furniture brought in from the houses that had been torn down earlier that day.

I caught my share of stares, wandering the streets in my whiteface. Some actually shuddered as they turned and caught sight of me, making a ghost of me in their minds before realizing it was only Feste, that drunken madcap. I unslung my lute, tuned it, and started strumming as I walked along, warning the unwary so that they need not fear my approach. And in this manner I reached the embolum.

There were several men inside, ranging from some in their teens to a pair of graybeards who chatted quietly with Ruzzini. Tullio was not there, but his handiwork remained with the remains, the finished lid resting against the wall by the coffin. There were a dozen candles surrounding the late merchant, the light flickering across his face, glinting off the coins someone had placed over his eyes. Christian or not, some old traditions carried on.

I nodded at Ruzzini, who pointed to a small bench in the corner. I sat down unsteadily, nearly falling, then took a swig from a small wineskin. I saluted the ensemble, then began to play quietly.

Venetian tunes were largely about traveling the seas, sailing to distant lands to seek your fortune, sometimes never to return. They provided an apt metaphor for death, the last voyage. I selected the more sentimental ones, hoping the combination of the tunes and the occasion would steer the mourners toward the melancholy and the maudlin. And that seemed to work. Some of the older fellows became wistful, even weepy, as they sipped their wine and gazed at the Venetian flag hanging on the wall behind the coffin. I was hoping that someone might say something revealing when a blond young man with barely enough fuzz to call a beard stormed up to confront me.

"Enough, Fool!" he commanded angrily. "That music meant nothing to Bastiani. Do not sully the honor of Venice by playing it in his presence."

"I beg your pardon, kind sir," I said, slurring my words a little. "I meant no offense. What shall I play?"

"Play something Greek," he spat. "He cared more for Byzantium than he did for us."

"Hold your tongue, Signor Viadro," said Ruzzini sharply. "You dishonor the dead."

"He had no honor in life," retorted Viadro. "Why should he have it now?"

"Peace, Domenico," said another man, a dark-haired fellow of about thirty with a quiet authority to his mien. "He wasn't flawless in life, but who is? You go too far. Bastiani was one of us, and we will treat him according to our traditions."

"Traditions, Ranieri?" said Viadro, mockingly. "Our Venetian way of life? I was born and raised here. I've been to Venice once in my existence, and I honor it more than any of you true Venetians who travel back and forth and know its every bridge and canal by heart. All you do is for the sake of expediency. Placate the Greeks while they tear down our homes and lock us within these walls within walls. That's what Bastiani did, and what did it get him? Murdered in his bed."

"He was murdered?" I gasped, looking stupidly at the youth.

"Quiet, Fool, I wasn't speaking to you," snapped Viadro.

"What are you saying, Domenico?" asked Ranieri softly. "That the Greeks killed him? Those are dangerous thoughts right now."

"All thinking is dangerous to you," retorted Viadro. "The times are dangerous, and the time for thinking is past. Venice knocks at our gates. Shall we tell Venice we're at home, or hide behind the gates and hope they give up and go away?"

"They are across the water, and we are here," said Ranieri. "The Greeks have their mercenaries and outnumber us forty to one. And silk makes poor armor as far as I'm concerned."

"It isn't the quality of the armor, it's the strength of the arm that makes the army," declared Viadro, holding his arm up and flexing it. He was powerfully built. I would have lost to him in a second if strength were what mattered.

"You're too headstrong, boy," pronounced Ruzzini. "You speak as if you could take on anything outside this quarter. You're too young to remember how it used to be here. We are completely at their mercy while we live within these walls. You weren't here in '71. Those of us who were could tell you how quickly the Greeks could turn on us. The entire quarter imprisoned on the whim of an emperor. All our goods confiscated. They didn't have enough prisons to hold us, so they put us anywhere, in rootcellars, warehouses, church crypts. Many of our people died in those crypts. Thirty years ago, and the Greeks still haven't finished making reparations. Do you want to bring all of that back down upon us again?"

He mopped his brow after making this speech. Viadro fumed, but remained silent. One of the graybeards came over to take his arm, but he shrugged it off and retreated to the safety of a bottle.

I played on, late into the night. The graybeards were asleep first. Then Viadro went, having expended his energy in speech and then dousing it with wine. Others followed as the candles around the coffin burned down to nothing.

Eventually, my hands slipped off the lute, my eyes closed, my body sagged against the wall, and I began to snore lightly. The routine has fooled people on more than one occasion, and this proved to be no exception.

"What on earth possessed you to bring a fool here?" muttered Ranieri.

"He showed up this afternoon looking for work," said Ruzzini. "He was most impressive selling his wares. As a merchant, how could I not respect that?"

"Odd, him popping up like that. Like a vulture after the kill."

"Fools and Death go together," observed Ruzzini. "We've had fools singing at wakes before. I thought he sang rather well."

"He knows our music," conceded Ranieri. "Which makes me wonder how someone who knows Venetian music should turn up in Constantinople."

"He's been here a while," said Ruzzini. "Over a year, I think. And that younger fool, what's his name?"

"Plossus."

"Yes, Plossus. I've seen him perform here many a time, and he speaks our tongue fluently."

"Better than our patriotic Viadro," said Ranieri, laughing quietly.

There was a pause. I suspected that they were watching me. I kept the snoring regular.

"They all look so peaceful," said Ranieri.

"Except for Bastiani," said Ruzzini. "Strange. The dead usually appear at rest, but Camilio seems as tormented in death as he did in life. I fear his soul will walk among us yet."

"Nonsense," said Ranieri. "He couldn't do anything to anyone when he was alive. Why worry about his shade?"

"If he was so harmless," started Ruzzini, then he paused. "I don't want any more deaths," he said finally.

"Why are you telling me this?" asked Ranieri, sounding almost amused.

"You heard me."

"People who don't keep their heads sometimes lose them," said Ranieri. "Everything will work out fine if you just stay calm and collected. With all that's happening right now, Bastiani's death will soon be forgotten."

"I want no more murders."

"It had nothing to do with us," insisted Ranieri. "Why do you keep saying this?"

A rooster crowed in the distance. Then another.

"We're at a wake," said Ruzzini. "Let's call it a prayer. There's been little enough of that as it is."

He came over to my bench and nudged me. I sat bolt upright and started strumming wildly, blinking as the first rays of the sun came into the room.

"Enough, good Fool," said Ruzzini, handing me some coins. "I've paid you for your singing, only. You sleep on your own time."

"Sir, show me a vocation where they pay you for sleeping, and I will gladly prentice to it," I said, standing and bowing.

"There is one," he replied. "It's called emperor."

I laughed. "Very good, sir. May I have your permission to use that in the future?"

"Be my guest. Just don't tell anyone that it came from me."

"Of course, sir. In the meantime, could you tell me where the Mass is to be held? I might like to attend."

"You would?" said Ruzzini in surprise. "You didn't even know poor Bastiani."

"Sir, I have spent the night sleeping by him," I said. "What greater intimacy can there be? Truly, sir, it is my custom, having performed at the wake, to pay my last respects as well."

"Very well, then. It will be at the Church of San Marco, on the other side of the Porta Ebraica."

"Thank you, sir," I said, and started to walk out.

"Fool!" he called.

I turned. He came up to me, suddenly looking his years, and took my hand in his.

"Thank you," he said. "It was good hearing the old songs."

"It was an honor to sing them," I said. He loosed his grasp, and I left the embolum.

ƒOUR

Mors ultima ratio (Death is the final accounting).
—LATIN SAYING

Feigning sleep for the night had left me exhausted, but I saw no opportunity to rest. I threw a cloak around my motley, then took off my cap and bells and wrapped them securely so that they would not jingle. I stuffed them inside my bag and pulled out a broad-brimmed hat which I pulled on so that my foolish aspect was somewhat concealed. Then I ducked into a nearby alley and dipped a cloth into a rainbarrel. I scrubbed hard until the makeup was off, a process that left my skin feeling raw but at least woke me up a bit. I made sure no one was looking, then changed under the cover of the cloak into normal clothing. Normal for anyone but a fool, that is. Having approximated a civilian, I then went to church, hoping that my non-Venetian garb would be shielded by the cloak.

I arrived just as Bastiani's coffin was being carried in, the church bell tolling for the Office of the Dead. The church itself was a small one, constructed mostly of wood. That was unusual for this city, but as the Venetians were the principal importers of lumber, they took care to set aside enough for their own religious needs. I had heard that the foundation was actually from an old Jewish temple that was on the site before the Jews were shunted across the Golden Horn. There was enough to that story to cause the Venetians to maintain their cemetery outside the city walls, lest they risk sharing eternity side by side with the Jews. Even the dead bicker, I suppose.

The coffin was placed on a pair of trestles in the narthex, with Bastiani's feet toward the altar. Feet to the East, ready to journey on to Jerusalem, according to the tradition. Of course, if it ever actually happened, he'd be bound to run into more Jews once he got there. Maybe if they could all figure out a way to get along better in life, they wouldn't have to worry so much about getting along in death. But I didn't expect to see that happen in my lifetime.

I spotted Tullio standing by his tripod, the coffin lid leaning against the wall. The glue pot was bubbling, sending its slightly rancid odor wafting into the sanctuary where the scent battled with the smoke from candles and incense. I kept my head bowed on the off chance that anyone might recognize me despite my plain face. I knelt and crossed myself just like I was a good churchgoer, took a candle, lit it, and added it to the collection surrounding the deceased. Then I took a seat in the rear corner so that I could observe the proceedings unobtrusively.

The silk merchants had their own burial society and sat in the front on this occasion. Viadro staggered in a bit after the others, looking somewhat the worse for wear. Ruzzini looked haggard after so little sleep, but Ranieri was awake and alert, scanning the congregation as intently as I was. I kept my face down and my hands clasped in prayer as his gaze swept over me.

The priest, a fellow of my own age but with gray streaking his tonsure and a pronounced tremor in his hands, began the service. The psalms were sung, but since this Mass was for the dead, they ended with the *Requiem aeternam* rather than the *Gloria Patri*. *Eternal rest give unto them, O Lord, and let perpetual light shine upon them.* The candles around the coffin were not cooperating with this plea, burning down a little too quickly, spitting a bit as they did so. The uneven light allowed me to glimpse a woman sitting in the back row on the opposite side, dressed in mourning, a black veil covering her face. Her hands, which were all I could really see of her, were young and pale. She held a purple silk kerchief in one of them. She was squeezing it so tightly that I thought she might compress it into stone.

I did not see anyone else watching her. There were other women present, but none seemed as affected by the service.

"Deliver me, O Lord," cried the priest in a quavery voice, "from eternal death in that awful day when the heavens and earth shall be shaken, and Thou shalt come to judge the world by fire."

"Quaking and dread take hold upon me, when I look for the coming of the trial and the wrath to come," responded the congregants.

"When the heavens and the earth shall be shaken," continued the priest.

"That day is a day of wrath, of wasteness and desolation, a great day and exceeding bitter."

"When Thou shalt come to judge the world by fire."

"O Lord, grant them eternal rest, and let everlasting light shine upon them."

"Deliver me, O Lord, from eternal death in that awful day, when the heavens and the earth shall be shaken and Thou shalt come to judge the world by fire," finished the priest.

I thought that he would go directly to the absolution, but he stood at the front of the congregation, fixing them with his gaze.

"The heavens and the earth are being shaken," he said softly. "We are being judged. 'Thou art Peter, and upon this rock I will build my church; and the gates of hell shall not prevail against it. And I will give unto thee the keys of the kingdom of heaven.' Matthew, chapter sixteen, verses eighteen and nineteen. That rock, that unshakeable rock, was Peter, who went to Rome and was martyred. That Church, that unshakeable Church, was Rome, and the keys of the kingdom of heaven are there, nowhere else. They are not here, not in this city founded by man. This city, which immures itself within these walls. This city, which is so often shaken by the trembling of the earth itself rising in revolt against it. This city, which one may only enter through gates—are these not the very gates of hell? Christ was never here. Peter was never here. And this trembling city shall not prevail against the unshakeable rock that is Peter's Church, that is Christ's Church, that is Rome."

I saw Viadro nodding furiously in agreement. Ruzzini looked apprehensive, Ranieri thoughtful. I wondered how many here knew that Rome no more wanted the Crusaders in Byzantium than Byzantium did.

The priest walked up the aisle to the coffin and walked around the deceased, sprinkling him with Holy Water. Then he took a thurible from a deacon and waved it around so that the smoke from the incense whirled past the body.

The prayers for absolution were spoken. The congregants filed passed the coffin. I joined in the line, noting as I paid my respects that a crumpled purple silk kerchief had been tucked into one of Bastiani's hands. Then Tullio came up, dabbed the edges of the coffin with glue, and placed the lid carefully on top.

There was a cart waiting outside with a solitary mule before it. A detachment of Varangians stood a respectful distance away, their axes held at the ready in this enemy territory. My friend Henry was in charge. I didn't know if he could recognize me without my whiteface, but I kept my hat pulled low just in case.

The coffin was placed on the cart, and the procession headed toward the gates to the city proper. It was my intention to follow the veiled woman, either to the burial or wherever she was going from here. But to my surprise, I saw Ranieri hang back, then slip away toward the embolum.

I hesitated, wondering at my course. It was strange that he wouldn't go to the burial, and Lord knows I wanted to find out more about him after last night, but I didn't know if I would have the opportunity to locate her again.

"Here's a pretty puzzle," said a voice softly in my ear. "How may a fool walk in two directions at once?"

I turned to see a young man watching the funeral procession. He was dressed in Venetian garb but seemed more of a dockhand than a merchant.

"What are you doing here?" I muttered.

"Thought I'd pay my last respects," replied Plossus. "It's morning. No point in gossiping with the Greeks before noon. Is that the lady you seek?"

"Possibly," I said. "And I'm becoming interested in friend Ranieri."

"I'll take the lady," said Plossus. "I told your wife I'd keep you out of trouble. A married man following a beautiful young woman is always in trouble."

"All right," I said. "Meet me at the Bull and Lion later."

The clergy and the congregation began to chant the *In paradisum*. Plossus ambled down the steps of the church and joined the rear of the procession, singing along lustily. I glanced toward where Ranieri was walking. He turned suddenly, looking back at the church, but I was already behind a pillar. He satisfied himself that no one was following him and continued on his way. I stayed about a hundred feet behind him until he came to the embolum.

He looked around again before entering but did not spot me standing just around the corner of a nearby building. I waited until he was well in, then walked quickly to the protection of the colonnade. Checking for anyone watching me, I sidled over to the entryway and peeked inside.

I saw Ranieri's back as he vanished into one of the storerooms at the rear of the building. I marked its location, then strolled around the building, just in case there might be a window on the other side. Of course, there wasn't one, curse the luck. I returned to the front of the building and waited.

He emerged after a long interval, pushing an enormous crate on a dolly. He shut the door behind him and paused for a moment, catching his breath. Then he went at the crate again, bracing his shoulders securely against it, his legs straining mightily with the effort. He came to the door of another storeroom, opened it, and pushed the crate inside. He emerged a few minutes later with an unladen dolly, and repeated the process. I counted five crates moved before he finished.

When he emerged from the embolum, I was across the street, buying some rolls from a stall. He walked toward the gate to the wharf. I followed at a discreet distance, but he didn't even bother looking behind him this time. He passed the gate to the outer part of the quarter and continued until he reached the end of the wharf. He looked across the Golden Horn for a long time, then nodded and turned around. He made his way to a tavern just off the wharf and sat down to a midday meal.

I looked where he had looked but saw nothing. Maybe nothing was what he wanted to see. Maybe all I had seen was a routine inventory transaction, so important to him that he would skip the funeral of a colleague to perform it. And maybe it was something else. I resolved to find a time to break into that storeroom.

But at the moment, I was watching a man eat and getting hungry myself. I spotted some of the other merchants returning from the funeral, going back to business. I saw no point in remaining, so I left the quarter, transformed myself back into a fool, and headed south.

The Bull and Lion was a tavern situated south of the Great Palace, not far from the Boukoleon Harbor from which it took its name. It was particularly known for an outstanding mussel stew, and it was a bowl of this that I found in front of Plossus, who had also returned to motley.

"How did you get here so quickly?" I said. "The cemetery is out on the Adrianople road. You had twice the distance to cover."

He pointed to his stilts, which were resting on the floor behind him.

"Picked these up on the way back," he said. "I can double my walking speed, as long as I don't fall down."

"And do you ever fall down?"

"Only if it will get a laugh. Have some stew."

I joined him with a will, and we passed the time in silent appreciation of the fruits of the sea.

"Anyhow," he continued, "I wasn't that far away. Your mysterious lady did not attend the burial."

"Really?"

He tore off a piece of bread and started soaking up the sauce.

"Tell me, O Elder Fool, for I am but a tender youth, why women become prostitutes."

"Out of desperation and poverty."

"Hmm," he said. "She seemed neither desperate nor poor."

"Sometimes they are gentlewomen who have fallen on hard times."

"Well, if that's what hard times are like, let me fall as well."

"What do you mean?"

"She lives in a nicely appointed mansion on the Fifth Hill. Nothing ostentatious, but nothing you'd be able to purchase from what you make off the streets."

"A courtesan, perhaps. One who entertains a select and affluent clientele."

"Maybe," he said doubtfully. "But it did not seem like that kind of house. Of course, I couldn't see inside. It was set back from the street with a fearsome iron gate and a stone wall protecting it."

[51]

"Any servants?"

"I saw none, but there must be someone. At the very least, a house-keeper. And here's another odd thing—none of her neighbors know her name. She only emerges cloaked and veiled, usually at dusk. The people I gossiped with are a bit spooked by her. They think she may be a witch."

I guffawed. "You've solved it, lad. He was killed by witchcraft, and she was the witch with the craft. Case closed."

He looked pained. "It could be an explanation," he protested.

"Then why was she so distraught at the funeral?"

"A spell or potion gone wrong?" he said hopefully. "She was trying to make him fall in love with her, and killed him by mistake." He paused. "I don't always sound this stupid, do I?"

"No, not most of the time," I assured him. "But one thing I know about witches. The ones who are not outright frauds are women without magic but with a vast knowledge of herblore. Which would include poisons. We'll have to find out more about her. If nothing else, I want to know what she knows about Bastiani."

"We'll add it to the list of things we have no time for," grumbled Plossus.

"You'd be surprised how much spare time one has during a siege," I said. "Lord knows no one will be wanting us for entertainment. I hope you've been saving your money."

"I paid my landlady for another month," he replied. "She was surprised that I was planning to stick around that long. A lot of people are already fleeing the city."

"The more fool they," I said. "It's safer here."

That's the sort of completely misguided assertion that I come up with every now and then. Events were to prove me wrong. Sometimes, I really hate events.

We went our separate ways after lunch. Plossus was off to the neighborhood by the Hippodrome to sound out the factions. I decided, since I was in the neighborhood, to drop by the Senate and see if I could get a word with my friend, Niketas Choniates.

Choniates was a senator as well as being Logothete, which made him one of the highest functionaries in the bureaucracy. The Senate, of course, was a completely spurious institution, consisting of a self-important body of wealthy men with no real power. Every time there was an uprising against an emperor, the Senate would back the man in charge until the emperor had him executed, at which point they would hail the emperor and thank God for his miraculous escape and beneficent leadership. The real power and money in this city stayed with the denizens of Blachernae, their relatives and their favorites. But the Senate maintained the trappings of government.

Choniates was an exception to the rule, however. A smart man, he took his duties seriously. I figured that as Logothete, he would take more than a passing interest in these events, especially given his nominal responsibility for the Venetian quarter. And, most of all, he was one of the finest gossips I had ever known. Gossiping is a skill, truly an art, and to have an ear to events in the largest city the Christian world had ever known was a gift indeed. During my time here, we had become sharers of information, both for its usefulness and for the sheer indulgence of it.

I passed by the Hippodrome and cut through the Augustaion, the great square by the Hagia Sophia. The Senate House was at the east side of the square, an enormous structure with huge marble columns, a magnificent arch over the entrance, friezes running rampant along the top, the whole thing some 150 feet wide. They say the current building dated to the time of the Emperor Justinian, who rebuilt it on the same site as the one originally put there by Constantine himself. Amazing how a useless institution can endure for so long. It gives me hope for the survival of the Fools' Guild.

The senators were all scurrying back after their own noon meals, or their noon assignations with their mistresses. I mingled with the crowd, imitating the gaits of some of them to the quiet amusement of their servants, until I saw Choniates.

"Nik!" I shouted.

He turned and marked me.

"Feste," he exclaimed in surprise. "I thought we were having lunch next week."

"I want to talk to you. Something's come up."

"I did notice the invasion," he said dryly.

"Something local. When are you free?"

He frowned. "Not right now. We're debating whether we should urge the Emperor to fight the invaders or to reconcile with them. We have to decide if our advice will drive him to do the exact opposite and what it is we really want. What about lunch tomorrow?"

"Fine. I'll meet you by the Pillar of the Blind."

He waved and hurried off.

The Great Horologion in the square indicated that it was one o'clock, which meant that I had gone close to thirty hours without sleep. I decided that was long enough and headed home for a nap.

I woke in time for dinner, staggering in to the derisive applause of my companions.

"We were debating whether or not to rouse you," said Rico. "Much depended on the quality of the food and if we wanted to share it with you. Fortunately, Plossus did the cooking tonight, so there's plenty to go around."

"It's heartbreaking when one's sincere efforts are rejected so cruelly," sighed Plossus. "They did not teach us cooking at the Guild."

"That is sadly apparent," said Aglaia. "You'll have to get Rico to give you some lessons. Good morning, my love. Have something."

[54]

"Thanks," I said. "What's the word from Blachernae?"

"The fleet is harbored at Chalcedon, across the Bosporos," said Rico. "They've occupied the Emperor's palace there and are raiding the area for provisions. The Greeks are following them from the opposite shore but, lacking fins and gills, are confined to standing at the edge of the straits and yelling rude things across the waters. Had I known that was all it took to be a soldier, I could have been a general myself."

"The Emperor?"

"Still here, but he rides tomorrow."

"Well, unless his horse can swim, I doubt that we'll see any battle then," I said.

"We will if Euphy finds out Alexios is planning to ride himself," said Aglaia. "She still needs him alive right now."

"Isn't marriage wonderful?" mused Plossus.

"Enough of the wars," she said. "What's going on with your investigation?"

I filled them in on what Plossus and I had seen and learned. The other two listened with interest.

"You say that this Ranieri had to exert himself to push these crates?" asked Aglaia. "Even using a dolly?"

"So that every sinew was taut and defined," I said. "You would have enjoyed watching him, my dear."

"That aside, it occurs to me that silk, even in bales, is still light."

"That occurred to me as well," I said. "Something else was in those crates."

"Do you know whose storeroom they came from?" asked Rico.

"Not yet," I said. "But I'll find out. Would you all be up for some burglary, perhaps tomorrow night?"

"All of us?" said Aglaia delightedly. "What fun!"

"Two for performing to distract the crowd, and two to break in. I was thinking Rico and myself for the criminal part of the affair. I spotted some serious padlocks on the doors, and he's the best lock-picker of all of us."

"Then, milady, I shall have the honor of escorting you tomorrow," said Plossus with a deep bow. She returned it, smiling.

"There's still the matter of the woman," I said. "Anybody know anything from the description?"

"No," said Aglaia. "But I'll gossip with the ladies tomorrow and see what I can find out. You know, you still haven't said how you thought Bastiani was killed."

"Poison, I assume," I said.

"But if it was poison, when was it given to him?" she asked.

"I don't know yet," I said. "There was no sign that he had eaten or drunk anything in his room, so I figure that he had been given it before he came home."

"I don't agree with that," she said.

"Why not?"

"A poison that takes that long to take effect? Yet it caused no other symptoms? No vomiting, no headaches apparent to others? Name me one that does that."

"I can't right now," I confessed.

"Me, neither," said Rico. "And I'm pretty good with them."

"You must teach me more about that subject," said Plossus.

"No need," said Rico. "You want to poison anyone, just cook them dinner."

"So, he must have been poisoned in his room," she persisted. "Which means that the poisoner must have been in there, and cleared up the evidence afterward."

"But no one saw anyone go in with him, or come out later," I said.

"You only spoke with three people so far," she said.

"True enough. But you'd think they would have noticed our mystery woman."

"Maybe she just vanished into smoke," suggested Plossus. "She's a witch, isn't she?"

"Witchcraft?" she scoffed. "A woman acts oddly and everyone immediately leaps to the conclusion that she's a witch. They could say the same about me."

"And we do," said Rico. Then he ducked as an apple sailed over his head. Even dwarves have to duck sometimes.

"And you're assuming something else that may not be correct," she said.

"Which is?"

"That the woman at the funeral and the woman visitor are one and the same. Maybe the mistress of the mansion is merely a loved one and the prostitute from the forum is a separate visitor."

"That could be," I said. "I think that Plossus and I are going to have to insinuate ourselves into the community a little more. I fear that Philoxenites is right in worrying about an insurrection coming out of that quarter. The sermon this morning was almost a call to take the cross."

"It would be suicide, don't you think?" said Plossus. "They wouldn't even have to wait for the Varangians to knock them off. All the Venetians need to do is give someone an excuse to wipe them out, and the Pisans and the Genoese will be over the walls in a heartbeat."

"I didn't think the Pisans and the Genoese got along that well," said Aglaia.

"When it comes to stomping Venetians, they are in complete agreement," I said. "They're the best allies the Greeks have right now. All right, we'll meet back here for dinner tomorrow and plan the evening's burglary. Good night, gentlemen."

"But you've only just gotten up," protested Plossus.

"Lad, let me explain to you once again about married people and their peculiar behavior," said Rico, tugging at his sleeve.

They left. We cleared the table and went to bed.

Later, as we held each other, she brought up the poisoning again.

"Always the romantic," I said. "That's what I love about you."

"I just think that if we could figure out the how, it would help us figure out the who," she said. "You say that he turned pink?"

"Yes. Perhaps it was done with cosmetics."

"You're not taking me seriously," she muttered.

"I'm a jester," I reminded her.

"When we're alone, you're my husband," she reminded me. "You can stop performing. At least, in that manner."

I propped my chin up on my hands and looked into her eyes.

"When we're alone, I shall perform however you wish me to," I said. "And I was wrong about one other thing."

"What was that?" she said, smiling as I gathered her to me.

"I know one woman who is truly magical."

And now, my fellow fools, I shall turn this narrative over to my good wife.

ƒIVE

Most adept at prognosticating the future, she knew how to manage the present according to her own will and pleasure, and in everything else she was a monstrous evil.

—NIKETAS CHONIATES, ON THE EMPRESS EUPHROSYNE

And about time, too. Dear God, it's hard enough trying to get a word in edgewise with this man when he's speaking, but just try wresting a pen away from him!

But even Feste cannot be everywhere at once. Yes, fellow fools, I call him Feste here, even though I should be using his Guild name. I cannot bring myself to do that. He was Feste when I first met him, and Feste when we fell in love, and even though he's Theophilos to the Guild, Feste is what springs to my lips, whether in passion or in scolding, and there's been plenty of both. I know his true name, too. He gave it when we took our wedding vows, possibly the first time in thirty-odd years that he had uttered it. There have been other names as well, both for him and for me, but for the telling of this tale, it shall be Feste and Aglaia.

I'm used to courts. I grew up in one, married into another, raised my first two children there, to the extent that I was allowed. My fortunes took an interesting turn when I married my second husband. Most women marry a fool for love first, then get practical on the next husband, but I did it the other way around. With a disposition like that, it is small wonder that I became a fool myself.

And, oddly enough, becoming a fool gained me access to the greatest court in the world, something that being a mere local duchess never would have done. But, as the Empress's Fool, I came and went in Blachernae unchallenged, while mere kings and generals were made to wait at the front gate, staring as I strolled by in my motley and white-face.

At the time of the Venetian invasion (I will *not* call it a Crusade! The noble names that men attach to their murdering!), Euphy, as we called her in private, was around sixty, although she would claim forty, and that only when her grown daughters were in the room to refute anything less. She had set a fashion years ago by appearing unveiled in public. Now, when a veil might have had a more than favorable effect on her appearance, she wore makeup to create the illusion of beauty. So much makeup that you could peel it off in one piece and use it as a mold of her face.

She had been much abused in life, had Euphy, victimized by circumstances, the machinations of the court, the jealousies (rightful ones, I might add) of her husband, and, worst of all, the absence at this stage of her existence of jealousies of her husband. But where others so buffeted will accept their fates philosophically, Euphy fought back. She fought back from exile, from forcible tonsuring, from the beheading of her lover, she fought back. Where others would have gone mad, she . . . well, she went mad, there's no denying that, but with the madness came a fierce cunning. She mastered the grand Byzantine traditions of spying, manipulation and murder, and practiced them with ruthless joy.

And did it as a woman would, not as some pale imitation of a man. While other women would say, Oh, he's treated her very badly, what can we do? with Euphy, it would be, Oh, he's treated her very badly, should I have him killed?

Women, in those rare occasions when we gain control over the world, can easily surpass men in the exercise of cruelty. I think this may be why men are afraid to let us have control over the world.

[60]

I realize, in writing this, that I am betraying a certain admiration for the woman, mad and murderous as she was. Yet do I not, as a fool, wear an excessive amount of makeup? Have I not, as a fool, killed my share of men? I have lived too much with the mockery of others to place my conduct above theirs, no matter how piously the Guild paints its stated goals. We use many of the same tactics that have given the Byzantine Empire its reputation, justifying the means by the ends. But in the end, I sometimes think that we are no better than anyone else.

On the morning after the merchant's funeral, I entered the Empress's chambers to find it in more of an uproar than usual. Her three daughters were there, engaged in a bout of competitive wailing, each on a different pitch, each on a different topic, while Euphy looked down from her throne with an exasperated expression.

"They can't make him fight," cried Irene. "He's not well. He can't help it if his injury flares up. He can't even get out of bed."

"He can't because he won't," screamed Anna. "Which means my husband has to fling himself into the middle of battle just to keep the family honor intact, all because your husband's a coward!"

"At least you have husbands," sniffed Evdokia. "I'll never find one in the midst of all this. It isn't fair!"

I am giving you the gist of their plaints. The actual oratory went on and on until Euphrosyne stood up. The motion was so sudden that everyone in the room stopped to watch her, except for the three daughters, who were building to a shrieking shrewfight and not paying attention.

One should always pay attention to one's mother, especially when she is powerful and insane. Fortunately, all she did this time was walk up to them and slap each in turn, Evdokia hard enough to send her sprawling.

"Why do you always hit me the hardest?" sniveled Evdokia from the floor.

"Because you need the most sense knocked into you," I answered before Euphy could say anything.

The Empress turned and stared at me, and I wondered for a moment if I had overstepped my bounds, but then she broke into a broad smile.

"The fool speaks wisely, daughter," she said to Evdokia. "As usual. Good morning, Aglaia. How are you today?"

"Well, Your Grace, and thank you for asking," I replied, then I gave that statement the lie by rushing out of the chamber to spill the contents of my stomach into a rather ancient urn.

I returned as soon as I was able to find Euphy back on the throne.

"Come here, woman," she ordered, and I walked up the three steps a bit unsteadily to stand on the platform next to her.

She took my head between her hands and peered closely into my eyes.

"You're with child!" she exclaimed.

I nodded.

"My apologies, Your Grace," I said. "The morning sickness caught me unawares."

"Perfectly acceptable," she said. "Is this your first?"

"Yes," I said, lying again. There was no need for her to know my background. There were two children from my first marriage, but they were being raised by a regent since the death of my first husband.

"Well, you must come to me for advice," she pronounced proudly. "I know everything there is about raising children."

There were looks of disbelief on three of the faces in the room, but they prudently refused to challenge this assertion.

"As for Your Petty Lownesses," she continued, addressing her daughters, "I want you to start putting some iron in your spines. We show a united front to the people, no matter what the truth is. One of you will be Empress after me, but only if you deserve it. Most likely Anna, I think. She's the only one who married a real man."

"I married a fine man," protested Irene.

"He was fine enough when you married him," said Euphy. "That's why I picked him for you. Marry your daughters to generals, keep the stock strong, that was my thinking. Too bad he had the accident. Even worse that he survived it, if you ask me. If he had died right away, we could have found you someone better by now."

"You didn't find me any great prize," muttered Evdokia, her cheek still reddened from the blow it received.

"That was your father's doing, not mine," said the Empress. "What did you expect? You're the youngest, your only value was for the alliance, and a fat lot of good you did for us there."

"He was a brute," protested Evdokia.

"And you cheated on him," said the Empress. "You have always had the morals of a cat in heat. He threw you out, you came slinking back here, and you've turned down several perfectly acceptable matches I've arranged for you. Why should I listen to you complain now?"

Anna's maid came in and whispered something to her mistress. Her face fell, and she stood and bowed to her mother.

"I must go bid my husband farewell," she said.

"God be with him," said the Empress. "And remind him."

"Of what, mother?"

"If he loses, he doesn't get to be Emperor. I will see you at lunch, dear."

"Yes, mother."

Anna left, and Euphy turned her attention back to her other daughters.

"Go attend your invalid," she commanded Irene, and the woman slunk away, her shoulders bowed.

"Father would never treat me like this," she muttered, but the Empress pretended she did not hear her.

Evdokia remained, chewing her thumb nervously. The Empress pointed at her.

"You stay here," she said. "You will attend me today. We'll have some mother-daughter chats." She bared her teeth in a gruesome approximation of a smile. "It will be fun."

"Yes, mother," whispered Evdokia.

A tinkling of tiny bells approached us rapidly, and a moment later the Emperor's flutist burst into the room to kneel before Euphy. She was breathing hard, something I suspected she did to draw attention to her overexposed bosom. The bells adorned her wrists, ankles, and earlobes, and clattered away throughout her conversation.

"What is it, girl?" asked the Empress in Arabic.

The flutist had been hand-picked by Euphy to be the Emperor's mistress. The Empress had known that his attentions were turning away from her as she got older, but she was determined to hold sway over his passions. So, she did it by proxy, tolerating his being besotted with this Egyptian wench while using her to spy on him, control him, and divert him from any other amorous distractions.

The two of them always conversed in Arabic, believing that none of the servants or ladies-in-waiting spoke it. They never suspected me, of course. Growing up in Sicily, I had a very fine Arabic tutor from Bugia, who taught me mathematics and the Greek philosophers as well as his language. I no longer have need of mathematics or philosophy, but the language has served me well on many occasions in this city of many tongues.

"He means to ride today," said the flutist.

"He what?" shouted Euphy. "How could he? I told you to take care of him, to wear him out last night."

"He wouldn't have me," she said tearfully. "He's never refused me before, but now he's determined to go."

Euphy treated her like a daughter, which is to say she stepped down from her throne and slapped the girl, snapping her head back and rattling her bells.

"You're a worm," said Euphy contemptuously. "You should have known how to wrap him around your little finger by now. By God, girl, if I was twenty years younger and had your figure, I would be ruling all of Europe. Well, it seems that I must speak with my husband before he gets himself into any greater trouble. Fetch my crown!"

Her servants scattered about the room retrieving the accoutrements of her royalty. A gorgeous purple silk cape was draped around her heavily brocaded gown, with enough jewels stitched into the fabric to finance an army if she were willing to part with them. The crown was gold, of course, studded with more jewels.

"How do I look?" she asked, preening slightly.

"Magnificent, Your Highness!" chorused the room.

"Captain, attend me," she said to her bodyguard. "Evy, you come along. Watch and learn. Let my ladies carry my train."

Her entourage assembled, servants fore and aft. On the captain's signal, they launched the Empress down the halls of Blachernae.

She did not tell me to follow her. But neither did she direct me to stay. So, I followed her.

Her captain, a well-muscled fellow who swung a sword as long as he was tall, led the way, shoving aside the odd servant or courtier unfortunate to find himself in the Empress's path. Each set of double doors was opened with a crash, shivering hinges and sending tremors through the palace. Finally, we reached the Imperial Chamber.

Alexios was sitting on a padded sawhorse while his servants bustled about him buckling on his armor. His sword and spear leaned against the throne. I spied Rico sprawled across the throne itself, tootling away on a whistle, paying no attention to us. Alexios looked up at our entrance, a puzzled expression on his face that cleared only slightly when he spotted his wife at the center of the maelstrom.

"Oh," he said. "Hello, my dear. And is that Evy with you? My, how you've grown."

"Just where do you think you're going?" demanded Euphrosyne. And, just like that, he looked like any common henpecked husband rather than the Emperor of Byzantium.

"Well, um, I was going out," he began.

"Out? Out where? You're not thinking of going to battle at your age."

"Actually, I was. They expect me to."

"Who does?" she demanded.

"Well, the citizens. The people. You know, the ones I rule."

"The ones you rule. Yet you are off to battle because they expect you to. Sounds like they rule you."

"Now, my dear, this happens to be the sort of thing an Emperor is expected to do every now and again." He motioned to his servants who carefully lifted him off the sawhorse and stood him on the floor. He grimaced as his legs took the weight of the armor.

"You can't even stand up without help," she said scornfully.

"That's why we have horses, my dear," he replied. "Wonderful creatures. Carry you straight into battle, and not a word of complaint from them. I truly like horses."

Rico stood on the throne, seized the Emperor's spear, and used it to vault across the room.

"Here, Your Bigness," he said, handing it to him. "Spit a few Frenchmen with it."

"Thank you, little friend," said the Emperor, taking it. "Would you be so kind as to bring my sword?"

The dwarf somersaulted across the floor, grabbed the sword, and dragged it slowly back. He raised it slowly over his head, then collapsed under the weight.

"It would take a mighty arm to wield this blade," he said. He proffered it to the Emperor, who seized it and waved it clumsily about.

"How do I look?" he asked.

"Like a fragment of a man," Euphy said. "What will happen to me if you get yourself killed?"

"Oh, I expect you'll manage," he replied easily. "Get Laskaris to run the place—he's the best of the bunch."

She burst into tears. He looked at her impassively.

"That won't work any more," he said. "Go back to your plotting, Euphrosyne. If God sees fit to extend my life a little longer, then I will see you when I return."

The tears stopped immediately. She turned and marched out of the room, Evdokia running to keep up. The Emperor watched them leave.

"And if He doesn't, then I will see you in Hell," he muttered. "By God, it would almost be worth dying in battle to get away from her."

He turned and caught sight of me. "Go," he said, frowning. "Go and attend your mistress."

Rico chased me out of the room, squawking, "Go! Go!" like he was some deranged crow. I ran down the corridor, then slowed as I turned the corner and waited for him to catch up to me.

"Isn't marriage wonderful?" he sighed.

"Easy for you to mock," I said. "You've never been married."

"I've been saving myself," he informed me proudly.

"Really?"

"I figure that if he takes a spear in battle, I might have a chance with the flutist."

I giggled. I couldn't help it.

"She's beneath you," I said.

[67]

"Not yet," he said. "But that would be the general idea. Did Euphy really think she could talk him out of going?"

"She forgets that he occasionally takes being Emperor seriously. Will he really ride to battle?"

"Just enough to give the city a good show," he said. "He'll wave his sword, shake his spear, flash the ikon, then send the Guard on ahead of him. His fighting days are long past."

"How about the bribery?"

"I've brought it up. He said, 'Is there enough gold in the world to make them go away, I wonder?' It's a good question. How did she like the idea?"

"I haven't had a chance to mention it. The day has been filled with dramatics, and the quality of the acting has been poor."

"Well, watch your back. When this family starts feuding, the words don't last long. Sooner or later, the knives will come out. I'll see you tonight."

We thumbed our noses at each other and left for opposite sides of the palace.

I returned to the Empress's chambers in time to see the captain dragging Evdokia down the hallway as she shrieked, "But I don't want to go to my room!" A door was slammed and bolted, and the shrieking faded.

The Empress was nowhere to be seen but had left a trail of battered ladies-in-waiting in her wake. I helped one of them get to her feet. Her name was Isadora, and she was from a wealthy family in the city who thought placing her with the Empress would further her prospects. So far, it had only taught her how to take a punch and keep smiling. Not the worst thing to learn, but still.

"Thank you, Fool," she whispered to me, as I dabbed a kerchief at the blood on her lip. "It is fortunate that I am not expected to leave the palace anytime soon. I'd hate to be seen in public like this."

"Wear it with pride," I said. "The men are always boasting of their scars. Why shouldn't we?"

She smiled wanly.

"May I ask you a question?" I whispered.

She glanced around, then nodded.

"I've become curious about a woman who lives on the Fifth Hill. She dresses in mourning and lives alone in a mansion set back from a high wall. The rumor is that she's a witch. Do you know . . ."

Then I stopped, for she had turned quite white.

"Please, Aglaia," she whispered fearfully. "Never mention her in this room."

"But—"

She shook her head and walked away, leaving me holding a bloodied kerchief.

What was that all about? I wondered. Perhaps it was just simple superstition. Lord knows it ran rampant in this palace, with the tone set by the Empress. But when Euphy encountered a witch, she was more apt to trade recipes than to run away. What was special about this one?

It was too hard a knot for me to untie for now. I decided to let Time untangle it for me.

A servant came running from Euphy's bedchamber. To my surprise, she came directly to me.

"She wants you," she said. "Quickly!"

I looked at the female debris about me, gulped, took a deep breath, and headed in.

She was pacing the room, still in her imperial regalia, the crown askew. She stopped when she saw me, then strode toward me, her hands extended toward my face.

I did my best not to flinch. She seized my head in both hands and peered into my eyes.

"A daughter," she said. "That is my prophecy."

"I think so as well, Majesty," I replied.

She nodded, satisfied, and released me. I rubbed my jaw where her fingers had dug in.

"Daughters are difficult," she said.

"So I see."

"The problem is, we spoiled them. Treated them too gently. They have no idea what the world is like, then suddenly they're being married off and learning the hard way. My fault, but there's nothing I can do to change the past. All I can do is change the future, and I have devoted every minute of my existence to that end."

"Your untiring efforts in that regard are an inspiration, Highness."

"Stop it," she said sharply. "The one person I can count on to be honest in this entire city is you, Fool. Don't play up to me when I need you the most."

Well, compliments from an unexpected quarter. I never expected her to praise me for my honesty. It showed what a thorough job I had done in deceiving her.

"All right, Euphy," I said. "What do you want from me? I won't bother tuning my lute for this occasion."

"I can't keep Evy locked up forever, as much as I wish I could. We have to show the people how strong we are, and that's everyone in the family. She will be out making her charitable rounds as usual. You know she's fallen for this prisoner."

"Yes, I've heard."

She sighed.

"Romantic folly is the worst kind," she continued. "One must be clear-eyed about men. Marriage is a relationship where the two parties use each other for their own ends. If you don't want to be used, you can't let love get in the way. That's a lesson I've learned a little too late in life. I want to teach it to my daughters while they're still young."

"And Evy needs to learn it the most?"

"Exactly," she said, pleased. "I want you to become her companion. Go with her on these outings. Worm your way into her confidences, and report back to me. She has bodyguards, but they don't fully perceive what is happening with her. I need a woman in there, and you're the only one I trust right now."

I bowed.

"I will do this, of course," I said. "But don't you think she'll suspect me?"

"I've already thought about that," she said. She opened her door a crack, then beckoned to me. I peered through to see the ladies and servants working on their needlepoint and gossiping, all while keeping their ears pricked up in our direction.

"Traitor!" Euphy screamed suddenly, causing me to jump. I turned to look at her uncertainly. She was grinning maniacally. "You stupid, evil tramp! You think you have a license to mock to my face? Who knows what you do behind my back?"

"But, Your Majesty," I protested, realizing the scene we were playing. "I was only trying to help."

"I alone decide what is best for my daughters," she shouted. "How dare you take their part! Go tell your little jokes to them if that's the way you feel."

She flung open the door and shoved me through it.

"If it please you," I began, then stopped as I saw her pull back her arm. This is carrying verisimilitude a bit far, I thought just before her fist connected with my jaw. I pulled back at the last second to soften the blow, but she was remarkably strong for an old woman. I was knocked back onto the floor, skidding about ten feet on the smooth black marble. She slammed her door shut, and I sat up, surrounded by the stares of the other women. Some of them seemed frankly pleased at my discomfiture.

I inspected my lute for damage, but I had managed not to fall on it. I was glad, for I had only had it a few days, a gift from my husband. I then inspected my jaw, which I had had for much longer, a gift from my parents and of much less value. It was sore and tender. I suspected that a bruise would emerge. I pulled out my makeup kit from my bag.

"That's one advantage I have over all of you," I announced to the ladies as I powdered the flour-chalk mixture over my jaw, wincing a bit. "I can still show my face in public after that. Good day, gentle-women. I leave you to the whims of this considerably less gentle woman."

I walked out a bit unsteadily, but my head cleared by the time I reached the gate from the Blachernae complex. That was a blessing, at least. I needed a clear head tonight.

I was going out with my husband to commit a burglary.

$\mathcal{S}$IX

Let's vary piracee
With a little burglaree.
—W. S. GILBERT,
THE PIRATES OF
PENZANCE

I often marvel at the correspondence between religion and superstition in our world. One would expect the Church to push pagan beliefs and rituals out of the way, relegating them to the odd heathen sacrifice in a remote cave or a witches' sabbath deep in the woods. Yet somehow the opposite was true. The greater the influence the Church had over a given area, the greater the concomitant use of talismans, worship of relics, interpretations of the stars, and casting of fortunes.

Perhaps it was because of the Church's emphasis on saints and miracles rather than faith and morals, the rallying of armies to conquer Holy Lands rather than the rallying of minds and spirits to chasten sin and bring the gifts of goodness and charities on our own doorsteps.

All I truly know was that in this city of over two hundred churches, there was such widespread practice of arrant nonsensical magics that an ancient Greek or Roman—or even better, a Druid—dropped into the middle of the city would find himself right at home.

The Hagia Sophia was the largest church in the world, or at least that part of the world that was known to us. Perhaps some enterprising monk even as we speak was building some bigger monstrosity in India or Cathay, but no one around here had heard anything about it. So, this pile of marble, porphyry, gold, tiles, and gems rose to the heavens from this shaky patch of land, all for the greater glory of God. Truly, it was a palace of a church, and it would be churlish to note that Our Savior set foot in a palace only once in His life that I can recall, and he didn't particularly enjoy the experience.

The building was so infused with the trappings of holiness that it was no wonder that its congregants believed the very stones and tiles had powers. It had stood for so long that the powers had become specialized. Each of the 104 columns was invested with a particularized healing quality. One drew the lame; another supposedly cured maladies of the kidneys. Another, set in a gloomy gallery off to the side, reportedly helped those who had lost their sight. I had never heard of anyone actually being cured by this tall piece of rock, but the legend seized it and named it the Column of the Blind.

I watched the poor souls come into the gallery, stepping uncertainly. A pair of young deacons took each of the pilgrims by the elbow and led them to the column, which received their gifts and prayers with a face of stone. The deacons, I noticed, were not averse to accepting tips to further their holy work.

The bureaucrats of the Senate and the Great Palace complex frequented this gallery solely to amuse themselves by watching the blind stumble toward the column. They sat in the pews, twisted away from the altar, eating their lunches, laughing among themselves. I watched them with disgust.

"So many born blind, so many who have been blinded, so many who just refuse to see," murmured a voice behind me.

"Hello, Nik," I said without turning around. "Do you have time for a real lunch?"

"With you, always," he said. "Let's go to that place in the Genoese quarter."

We left separately, passing through the Augustaion. As I walked by the Column of Theodosios, I marked Ranieri going the other way. I had been in such a suspicious frame of mind lately that I was ready to follow anyone at a moment's notice, but lunch with Niketas was my priority now. Where was Plossus when I needed him?

Niketas found a table in the back and was ordering a marrow-bone custard for the two of us when I sat down. He was a middle-aged man like myself, though stouter. We jesters tend toward the slender due to our regimen of exercise and constant dashing about. I had never seen Nik do anything more strenuous than lift a spoon to his lips or wag his tongue.

We came here because the place catered mostly to the local Genoese. It was unlikely that we would find a Greek who would wonder about seeing us together and impossible that we would run into any Venetians. Given the topic of conversation, it was a good choice.

"Now, what was so urgent that you needed to move up our luncheon date?" he asked.

"For once, I've come to ask you something in your official capacity."

"As a senator?" he laughed. "You've never thought much of that position before."

"As Logothete," I said.

"And you generally think even less of that," he said. "When did my bureaucratic powers become interesting to you?"

"Since the death of Camilio Bastiani," I said.

He raised an eyebrow at that.

"Who wants that looked into?" he asked quietly.

"You know I can't tell you that," I said, while simultaneously nodding my head to the north.

"Ah," he replied, glancing in that direction. "Well, I can make my own guesses. Bastiani died in his sleep, I heard."

"I think he was murdered. So do his friends."

"I didn't know he had any," said Niketas.

"What do you know about him? The quarter falls under your jurisdiction. You probably know it better than anyone outside of the Venetians."

"He came to the city about fifteen years ago, I think," he said. "Went about his business efficiently, kept a low profile. Never gambled, either with ships or with dice. Kept a carefully steady margin of profit and otherwise drew little attention."

"What about family? I heard something about a wife, but nobody said anything at the funeral."

"There's a wife. Children, too."

"I haven't seen them about."

"That's because he left the whole family in Venice," said Niketas. "Arranged marriage, did his duty, continues to support them, goes back to visit when his business requires the voyage, but makes his fortune here."

"Not much of one," I said.

"Why do you say that?"

"He lived in a boarding house in a tiny, windowless room. Not the mark of a rich man."

"Then it may surprise you to know he was one," replied Niketas, grinning.

"Really?"

"As I said, he didn't gamble. The money went back to Venice. He lived simply because he had no desires. This was all that he did."

"He must have had some desires," I said. "Rumor had it there was a woman here."

"Then I am glad for it," said Niketas. "He always struck me as a lonely, crabbed individual, trapped in his life. If he had found some beggar's mite of happiness before he died, good for him."

"But you don't know who the woman is?"

"This is the first time I've heard anything about it."

"Hm. If a merchant is murdered, it's usually over money," I mused, remembering Tullio's words. "Who inherits?"

"The family back in Venice, I suppose."

"What about business competitors?"

"Every silk trader in the city would be one," said Niketas. "Even his fellow Venetians. The denizens of that embolum present an ever-shifting series of alliances. They invest in shipments together, secretly sell each other out for better independent deals, then they reform for the next one. The only thing they won't do is collude with any of the other quarters."

"Could Bastiani have been doing that? Entering into some kind of pact with the Genoese or Pisans?"

"I doubt it. As I said, he didn't like to gamble. The quarters police themselves, and any outside contact would be scented quickly and dealt with."

"Maybe it was dealt with," I said. I leaned forward to whisper. "There is some belief in Blachernae that a Venetian uprising is being organized. What do you know of it?"

"Just the same rumors," he said.

"Was he the type who would participate?"

"Not him," he said firmly. "He cared little about his fellows. I cannot see him taking up arms for Venice. It would cut into his profits. And now you have me wondering if he was killed because he knew too much about it."

"I am beginning to lean in that direction myself."

"I have to get back to the Senate," he said, rising. "We are bravely deciding upon a wait and see position. But I will keep my ears open. Come by anytime, Feste."

He paid for the lunch, and left.

I saw a pair of familiar faces when I came out of the tavern. Henry, a captain of the Varangian Guards, was standing in the street, his adjutant Cnut by his side. They were in full armor, as always, their enormous axes resting casually on their shoulders.

They were chatting amiably with a group of Genoese, who were listening intently and nodding a lot. The conversation ended with hand-shakes all around, and the two soldiers turned and caught sight of me.

"Hallo, Feste!" bellowed Henry. He was a good-natured Englishman who took soldiering seriously but little else. Even for a Varangian, he was powerfully built, with any number of scars that he would proudly display at the slightest hint of a request. Cnut was much younger, a stripling sent from his native Denmark to gain military experience, something lacking at home of late.

"Well met, good soldiers," I said.

"Hello, Feste," said Cnut. "What brings you here?"

"What brings me anywhere? Good food, good wine, and someone else paying for them. How about yourselves?"

"Just getting some of the city defenses organized," said Henry. "Time for people to decide what side they're on. Either you're a Greek or you're a Venetian, that's the choice."

"Said the Englishman and the Dane to the Genoese," I said. "And there are Frenchmen with the Venetians, too."

"That just means I get to combine pleasure with business," chortled Henry. "It's about time we had a proper war around here. Things were altogether too boring."

"So I hear," I said. "Someone told me you're now doing escort duty for funerals."

"Exactly my point," said Henry. "Escorts for the dead! A waste of our talents. If this keeps up, I'll end up using my axe to hew wood."

"I'll beat your sword into a plowshare if you like," I said. "I admire your bloodthirst, but what will you do if there is no war? They could still make peace, you know."

"Now, where's the fun in that, eh, Cnut?" scoffed Henry, slapping the younger fellow on the back, which resulted in a loud clanging noise.

"How about you, lad?" I asked Cnut when the reverberations had faded.

"Oh, I would like to see battle," he said. "Father sent me here for experience, and I haven't had much, except for marching."

"There's plenty of experiences you can have without getting yourself killed, you know."

"You can stay home in bed and grow old if you want," said Henry. "But the true test of a man is with steel."

"Steel cuts all men, the brave and the cowardly," I replied. "Well, may you get what you came for, my friends. And I wish you well. There is no shame in surviving battles, either. Remember that."

We made our farewells and parted.

I spent the afternoon roaming the Great Palace complex, juggling far and wide. I could find no sight of Ranieri. But as I came up to the lighthouse, I saw a crowd gathered, watching the fleet as it sailed north up the Bosporos. Needless to say, they were completely uninterested in my little performance.

In the evening, I watched from a discreet distance my wife fooling around with a younger man. I was not alone in watching them—they were surrounded by a crowd of Venetians. I was leaning against a corner of the embolum, my back to the alley leading to the side entrance.

To all outward appearances, I was a Venetian myself, abandoning the motley and makeup for dark clothes and a voluminous cloak. I had also added what I thought was a rather dashing mustache and beard, but all it did was produce peals of laughter from my beloved when I showed myself to her. She told me afterward that it helped her forget about the throbbing pain in her jaw, which was good. When I saw the size of the bruise under her whiteface, I had to be restrained from storming Blachernae and committing reginacide.

Aglaia's duties to the Empress generally kept her inside Blachernae, but she was a superb street performer when given the opportunity. It was the first time I had seen her work with another fool besides myself, apart from when all four of us performed together.

Plossus and she transformed into a variety of couples: mother scolding son, old lecher pursuing virtuous maiden, squabbling siblings. When he donned his stilts and began to juggle, she pulled out her lute and matched melodies to his movements.

There was an odd mood in the quarter tonight. A suppressed excitement combined with apprehension, a sense that the world could end soon. Children chased each other in and out of the flickering pools of light cast by the torches, while couples held each other close, wondering how much longer they had together.

Plossus was now standing on his hands on top of the stilts. Suddenly, he let one fall so that he was balanced on just his right hand, ten feet off the ground. As all eyes turned upward, I reached behind my back and tapped the cloak.

Rico, who had been clinging to a leather harness that wrapped around my chest, slipped to the ground behind me. I held out my arms for a moment, shielding the alley from view with my cloak, while he noiselessly fiddled with the padlock on the side entrance to the embolum. I heard a soft click and a satisfied grunt. Checking to make sure no one was watching me, I stepped backward until I found the door. Then I went in.

I had a small burglar's lantern that I held in front of the door where I had seen Ranieri move his crates. Rico examined the padlock, then selected an iron key from several on a ring at his waist. He slid it gently inside the padlock and turned it. The lock fell open.

"Cake and candy," said Rico. "Shall I do the others?"

"Not yet," I said. "Let's get these crates open."

I was wondering how we could pry them open without being heard from the outside. Just then, I heard the crowd start singing along with our two colleagues, a fervent, patriotic air.

"Perfect time for a sing-along," said Rico as he slipped a short crowbar under the lid of the first crate. I did the same on the other side, and the lid came away with a creak. Rico pulled himself up to the top of the crate, and we took a look at something blue and fluttery.

"Just a bale of silk," said the disappointed dwarf.

I took my crowbar and tapped the bale in a few spots. The third tap produced a muffled clank.

"Not just a bale of silk," said Rico. He slipped inside the crate and stuck his hand carefully into the bale. He grunted, then pulled out a sword that reflected the lantern brightly. He held it up.

"Does this make me the true king of England?" he asked.

"Better put it back," I said.

He replaced it, then squatted to see what else was there.

"I count over fifty blades," he said. "Good steel, no fancywork around the hilts. I wonder what kind of worms spun them."

"Come on out. We'll check the others."

The next crate held four dozen shields stacked under the barest of coverings. A third opened to reveal crossbows along with a slew of bolts. I shuddered upon seeing them.

"What gave you the shivers just then?" asked Rico, ever watchful.

"Ugly things, these," I said, holding a bolt up to the light. "Took one through my thigh a couple of years ago. Lucky I still have the leg."

"Well, just because you had one little unpleasantness with a crossbow doesn't mean they're all bad," he reasoned. "I find them useful once in a while. When you're my size, you think highly of anything that can even the odds."

"Want to take one as a souvenir?"

"No, thank you," he replied. "I already have one back at my place."

The remaining crates produced more of the same.

"Whose storeroom is this?" asked Rico.

I held my lantern up to the door. There was an engraved plate bolted onto it with the name of Bastiani in large letters.

"Interesting inventory for a dead man," said Rico.

"Or a good storage room for a live one," I said. "If the weapons are found, they could always blame the deceased."

"What should we do about all of this?" asked Rico. "Tell the eunuch?"

"I'm not sure," I said. "We need to know why the weapons are here. Are they supplies for an insurrection or just kept as a precaution in case their Pisan and Genoese neighbors decide to take advantage of the times and attack the quarter?"

"Or maybe someone's just smuggling arms," added Rico. "And your friend Bastiani got wind of it somehow and was killed before he could pass along the information."

"So, if we alert Philoxenites now, we don't discover who's behind Ranieri. We'll just frighten them into inactivity."

"Not the worst result," he said. "But you also want the murderer, don't you?"

"I don't like letting him run around loose," I said. "At the very least, I want to know who it is before we decide what to do about him. Maybe I can convince Philoxenites to hold off any action until we've learned the full story."

He gestured at the opened crates. "We didn't bring our glue pot with us. They'll know someone's been poking around."

"Let's put the lids back. If they're not checking inside every day, they might miss the damage."

We replaced the lids as snugly as we could, then closed the door and locked the padlock.

"Where next?" he whispered.

"Ranieri brought the crates out of that one," I said. I held the lantern up. The plate read "Ranieri."

The lock succumbed quickly to Rico's manipulations, and the door swung open. The room contained many more crates than had Bastiani's, many of them stacked to the ceiling.

"Where do we begin?" I wondered, looking around.

Rico peered around the corner of the pile.

"There're a few more in back," he said. "It looks like the front stack was placed to conceal them. Unless they're all put anywhere."

"Ranieri seems too careful a man to be messy," I said. "Let's try it."

We had just finished prying the lid off the first crate when Rico looked up in the direction of the street. The singing had died down.

"Someone's coming," he whispered.

"Hide," I said, handing him my crowbar. I crept to the door to the main room of the embolum. To my dismay, I heard the padlock on the front door being unlocked and voices in the alley by the side. There was no other way out. The best tack was to take the offense. I stepped out of the storeroom, closed the door, and set the padlock so that it appeared locked without actually being so. Then I blew out my lantern and placed it under a table.

Torchlight preceded the entrance of several young men who stopped when they saw me standing motionless in the darkness.

"Who are you?" one of them called in Greek.

"Who are you?" I replied in my best Venetian dialect.

"You're not supposed to be here," he said. "Lay down your weapons."

I held my cloak open to show that I wore no sword. I did have a knife and dagger secreted about my person, but I wasn't ready to give them up just yet.

"Which one of you is my contact?" I demanded.

They stared, then looked uncertainly at each other.

"Come, men of Venice, I have little time," I continued. "I've been waiting far too long. If I'm not back on my boat before daylight, we may all be dead men. Who is my contact?"

One of them stepped forward. "You are from the fleet?" he asked.

"Children," I said, shaking my head in amazement. "Useless. All right, I'm going. If anyone comes in here looking for me, tell him I will return tomorrow at this time. Now, get out of my way."

I strode toward them. For a moment, I thought I might pull it off, but the one who had just spoken to me blocked my path.

"We heard a noise like someone was breaking into this place," he said.

"That was me," I said. "This is where I was told to go."

"Maybe," he said. "Or maybe you're just a common burglar."

"Do you see me with any stolen goods?" I demanded. "Or tools to break down doors? Use your head, boy. Now, let me go. Our Doge awaits my word."

He put his hand on my chest.

"If it is so important that the fleet contact one of us, then you shall stay," he declared. "Tie him up."

The others, given something simple to do, grabbed me. In a minute, I was trussed to a chair.

"We'll be back with our elders," said the youth. "Then we'll figure out what is happening here."

They ran out, leaving me bound and in the dark.

But not alone. As soon as the last youth exited, a knife blade slid through the crack of the doorway to Ranieri's storeroom to dislodge the padlock. Moments later, Rico and I were running through the back alleys of the quarter.

We found my bag, which I had stowed for safekeeping before this venture. I was in full makeup and motley in under two minutes, the Venetian garb and fake facial hair tucked under my juggling clubs.

"Should be enough to conceal your identity," muttered Rico. "Good try with that story, by the way. You almost convinced me that you were a Venetian spy, and I know you."

"Seemed like a good idea at the time," I said, picking up my bag.

"Mind you, I was a little worried that you would walk right out, leaving me cowering in that crate. I could have been shipped anywhere."

"Cheap way to travel, though. Did you find anything interesting while you were in there?"

"Just some ornamental bush packed up to be sent to somebody's mother-in-law," he said. "No weapons concealed among the leaves. But I only was in the one crate. There were still about forty others, and I don't think we can get away with doing this again. Once they discover someone has been poking his nose in there, they'll get rid of the contraband and increase the security."

"Agreed," I said. "Let's go find the others."

We strolled back to the embolum, arriving as if we had just passed through the gate to the quarter, and joined our colleagues in time for some eight-handed juggling. We noticed my recent captors come in with Ruzzini, Ranieri, Viadro, and several other silk merchants. Moments later they emerged, looking around wildly, pointing in all directions before scattering.

We finished with Aglaia standing on Plossus's shoulders and Rico on mine, while the clubs went back and forth on two levels. Then Rico scooted around the perimeter of the crowd, collecting coins, while Aglaia and Plossus packed their gear.

Rico returned, his cap filled with silver.

"A most profitable night," he said. "At least, financially."

$\mathcal{S}$EVEN

"What's a drunken man like, fool?"
"Like a drowned man, a fool, and a mad-
man."
—WILLIAM SHAKESPEARE, *TWELFTH*
NIGHT, ACT I, SCENE V

"There's something wrong about dividing the proceeds four ways, don't you think?" commented Plossus as Rico sorted out our Venetian take the following morning. "It seems to me that those who did most of the performing also did most of the earning."

"What about those of us risking prison?" asked Rico. "It was a joint venture, share and share alike. If we had gotten caught, would you have volunteered to do a quarter of the sentence?"

"At least you made it back for the big finish," said Aglaia. "That was fun. We haven't done a four-fool routine in a while."

"You're gaining weight, by the way," said Plossus. "Next time, I'll take Rico and you can stand on your husband's shoulders. It's only fair—he's the one who got you in that condition."

"But you're stronger than I am," I said. "So, you get to carry her. Just make sure you don't drop her, or you'll have to answer to me."

"And if you are going to commit a burglary, couldn't you at least steal something?" continued Plossus. "All this breaking in just to get information. What's the profit in that?"

"In this case, precious little," I said. "We didn't even narrow down which of the merchants might be in contact with the fleet. They all showed up."

"I think they're all in on it," said Rico. "The embolum is the center of the insurrection. Bastiani wanted out, or they figured out he was reporting back to the eunuch, so they killed him."

"How?" asked Aglaia.

Rico shrugged.

"I keep getting back to how it was done," she said. "Figure out the how, and you'll figure out the who."

"I'm still stumped as to how go about doing that," I confessed.

"I'd like to see his room," she said. "Any way you could get me in there without drawing too much attention?"

"Actually, there is," I replied. "I told the landlord that he might receive a visit from a wealthy and debauched patron who liked to seduce young women in macabre settings. Care to play an impressionable maiden?"

"That would be a stretch," scoffed Rico.

"I vaguely remember what that was like," she said, glaring at him. "All right, we'll do that tomorrow night."

"I volunteer to play the debaucherer," cried Plossus.

"Nonsense," I replied. "Nobody seduces my wife unless they are me. Are you two off to the palace today?"

"My liege is afield," said Rico. "I'll wander the city and see what I can learn."

"And I must make the charitable rounds with my lady Evdokia," said Aglaia. "Chatting all the while in my foolish feminine way."

"I think Plossus and I had better insinuate ourselves into the community some more," I said.

"I'll fetch my stilts," said Plossus, and soon after, we were back in the Venetian quarter.

We hit the south end by the larger embolum. Too much performing near the silk merchants would arouse suspicion, and I didn't see any need for an immediate resolution of this matter. Besides, there were other commercial circles with their own pools of information. We set up outside the seawall near the Great Wharf and began.

The children gathered first, as was usual, but the halt in the shipping brought about by the raising of the great chain meant that a lot of dockworkers were idle. Soon we were surrounded by a rough, burly group who called out a number of rude suggestions as to our parentage. We reached into our bags of comebacks and soon had them laughing at each other as well as our own antics.

Working with a young fool always brought out the competitor in me, and Plossus was a particularly skilled colleague, not at all beneath some friendly scene-stealing. And, I must confess, I was feeling a bit jealous after seeing him work with my wife last night. No good reason for it, but I found myself digging for all the tricks that my advantage in years could give me.

It was a successful performance and soon spilled over into a nearby tavern favored by the dockworkers. The house ale was a lethal concoction with a foul aftertaste. My guess was it had been brewed with water from the Golden Horn itself. This nevertheless did not prevent any of our newfound friends from consuming vast quantities of it, but even with their tongues so amply loosened, we learned nothing to help us further in our search. The main complaint we heard was over the lack of work, but no one seemed eager to blame his situation on the fleet.

We shifted after lunch to the central wharf outside the Porta Drungarii. As we passed by an open shed, I spotted Tullio putting together a number of crates and stacking them against the wall.

"So, this is where you work," I called to him.

He waved and kept going.

"I have to get these done quickly," he said. "Who knows how much longer people will be able to pay me? And I have to pack my tools and move them out of the shop before the invasion comes. Everything on this side of the wall will be fair game."

"Do you really expect them to challenge the seawalls?" asked Plossus.

"They have to challenge them somewhere," he replied. "I'd rather not take any chances."

"How will your friend the huntsman take to having you working in his sleeping quarters?" I asked.

"As long as he's drinking like this, he'll sleep right through anything I do," said Tullio.

"Then may his snoring drown out your sawing," I said. "Godspeed."

He nodded pleasantly, and we set up by the wharf.

"It is a holy profession, carpentry," commented Plossus as he pulled his clubs out of his bag.

"Because Our Lord apprenticed to it?" I asked.

"No, because it is devoted to the making of holes," he said. "And I am often struck by the fact that Our Lord, who was raised by a carpenter, died on a carpenter's creation. I wonder if He appreciated the irony."

"Careful, lad," I cautioned him. "You may mock any church in my presence, but show respect for the First Fool, Our Savior."

Another crowd, another retreat into a tavern, this one on Drungary Street, just inside the gate. Venetians who still had active jobs poured in for dinner, and we strummed away and led them in increasingly raucous songs.

I spotted Viadro and nodded in his direction. Plossus followed my glance. The youth was seated on a a stool by the tapster, downing one cup after another.

I walked over to him and called to the tapster, "My good host, this fellow drinks with my coin. I will usurp your position and fill his cup from now on." I tossed some coins onto the bar and snatched a bottle and Viadro's cup. "This way, sirrah," I beckoned, and he followed me, puzzled.

"What are you doing?" he asked.

"Good master, I am attempting to make amends for my behavior the other night," I said, slurring my speech heavily. "I offended you with my choice of music, it seems."

"Odd," said Plossus. "Normally he offends just by the quality of his voice."

"Hush, boy. Sir, you must drink with me."

"Drink with a fool?" said Viadro, amused.

I stood up and slammed my bottle down.

"Sir!" I bellowed. "I spend my life figuring out ways to get others to buy me drinks. For a fool to buy a drink for somebody else is the highest possible compliment in our profession. I asked you to drink with me, now drink!"

"Humor him," Plossus muttered to Viadro as I poured another round. "He gets like this. He'll get angry, then weepy, then he'll pass out. It's all harmless. I'll take care of him."

"A toast!" I cried, holding my cup aloft. "To the memory of your late friend."

"He was no friend of mine," said Viadro.

"There, you see?" I said. "He offends so easily. I told you what happened the other night?".

"You tell me so many things, how am I supposed to know which one you're talking about at any given moment?" replied Plossus.

"I was hired to play for a dead Venetian at a Venetian wake," I explained. "So, what would you expect me to play?"

"Venetian music?"

"Exactly!" I shouted triumphantly, then I sat down and almost toppled off the bench. "And this gentleman gets angry with me."

"Why did he do that?" asked Plossus.

"I do not know," I said. "Says the dead man, what was his name again?"

"Bastiani," muttered Viadro, staring into his cup.

"Right, Bastardiano," I continued, prompting a quick laugh from Viadro. "Says he's a traitor, or something. Now, how was I supposed to have known that?"

"I don't see how you could have known," said Plossus.

"So, you see, signore," I said to Viadro, "the offense was mine, for which I humbly beg your forgiveness, but it was an offense of ignorance, as is usually the case with me, for I am but an ignorant fool."

"You are forgiven," said Viadro, trying to rise, but I grabbed his wrist and poured him another drink.

"To Venice!" I shouted, and he was forced to join that one. I spluttered and coughed as I sipped, which allowed me to spill most of it onto the floor. Viadro didn't waste a drop of his.

"Here's something else strange," I said to Plossus. "He thinks that the deceased was murdered."

"Murdered?" exclaimed Plossus. "How extraordinary!"

"Now, sir," I said, addressing Viadro. "I saw the corpse. I have been to hundreds of wakes and thousands of taverns, so I have seen all manner of dead men who died in every possible way. This Bastamenti did not have a mark on him. Not a bruise, not a scratch, not a drop of blood. How could he have been murdered?"

"Well," began Viadro. "It could have been poison."

"Well said, signore," said Plossus. "What say you to that, Feste?"

I shook my head.

"Young sir," I said. "I will endeavor, by a series of proofs that will withstand the scrutiny of the highest of philosophers and the lowest of fools, both of whom are sitting across from me at this very moment, that this merchant could not have been poisoned."

"I believe he just called you a fool," commented Plossus.

"All right, Fool," said Viadro, automatically pouring himself another cup. "Proceed."

"Primus," I began, holding up one finger. "His room was undisturbed by the throes of the recently poisoned, nor was there any sign of drink or food that could have been the vehicle of such method."

"He could have taken poison outside of the room," objected Plossus.

"Exactly!" agreed Viadro.

I held another finger. "Secundus, if he was poisoned outside his room, then it would have had to have been when he dined. But he dined at your embolum with all of you. Someone would have seen it."

"He could have stopped on the way home," said Viadro, shifting uncomfortably on the bench.

"Exactly!" agreed Plossus.

"There's no place to stop," I said. "Not a single establishment in between his home and the embolum. No, sir, he had his evening meal and came straight home, walked unaccompanied up to his room, closed the door, barred it, and lay down to his everlasting sleep."

"How do you know all this?" asked Viadro. "You weren't there. This is just idle gossip."

"Sir," I said indignantly. "This is no ordinary, cheap, everyday, secondhand gossip. This is the freshest of gossip, from firsthand observations. It is completely reliable. Bashti died alone in his locked room, resting peacefully on his bed. No one went upstairs with him."

"Then what killed him?" demanded Viadro.

"God's will," I said piously, pressing my palms together and casting my eyes upward. "It was his time to depart this crumbling rock."

"He could have been poisoned at the embolum," insisted Viadro.

"That would explain it," said Plossus.

"Where was he sitting?" I asked.

"What?"

"At the table, boy," I said, shaking my head with exasperation. "Who was by him?"

"He was seated in the middle of the bench by the wall, between Ranieri and ... and ..." He stopped, the blood draining from his face.

"Go on," I prompted him.

"Myself," he whispered.

Plossus and I glanced at each other. I refilled Viadro's cup. He barely noticed.

"So the men who had the best opportunity to slip some poison into his drink were a respected merchant who had known him for decades," I said, "and a tippling stripling who accused him at his own wake of being a traitor. Sounds like a motive to me."

"Come, fellow, he's besting you," urged Plossus, whispering in Viadro's ear. "Defend yourself."

"If I had murdered him, I would hardly want to draw attention to the fact," protested Viadro. "I would have kept mum and let him go unmolested to his grave with no one the wiser."

"That is a most excellent point," applauded Plossus. "What say you to that, old man?"

"Are you saying then that Ranieri is the culprit?" I asked.

"No, no, it couldn't have been him," said Viadro quickly.

"Why not?" asked Plossus. "If it wasn't you, then it was him."

"And if it wasn't him, then it was you," I said. "Tell me more about the dead man. Who would want to kill him? And why?"

"He was an informer," said Viadro.

"What secrets are worth killing for around here?" laughed Plossus.

"You'd be surprised," muttered Viadro.

"You're bluffing," I taunted him.

"Now, Feste," warned Plossus. "Be kind to the man. If he says there's something, there probably is."

I leaned my face into his, all sweat-grimed, hideous, white-masked monstrosity. Viadro reared back in alarm.

"Prove it," I growled. "Or you're a hollow, loud-mouthed fool."

We had him. At that exact moment, we had worked on the precise nexus of arrogance, indignation, and inebriation to bring the answer spewing out of him. I knew it, Plossus knew it, and somewhere inside the youth, he knew it.

And so did the man standing behind him.

"There you are," said Ranieri, clapping Viadro on the shoulder. "I've been looking everywhere. We were supposed to dine together."

"I had forgotten," said Viadro, sinking a bit under the force of his hand.

"Well, no harm done," said the older man. "It looks like all you've done is drink. Let me get some solid food into you. Good evening, Fools."

We bowed as he hauled Viadro away.

"So close," I said in chagrin.

"I learn so much from watching you. Anything left in that bottle?" chirped Plossus. I emptied the dregs into his cup, and he tossed them back cheerfully. "Let's get out of here."

We walked back to my place.

"Well, we're getting somewhere," Plossus called from several feet up.

"Please do me the courtesy of walking by my side," I said a bit petulantly, and he swung down from the stilts and shouldered them.

"So, he was poisoned at the embolum by either Viadro or Ranieri," he said.

"No."

"What?"

"Tertius, there is no poison that I know that will take so long to act upon its victim. If he was given it at the embolum, he would have made it to the street, but not all the way home, up the steps, into his room, into his nightclothes, and into his bed."

"Then that was all for nothing?"

"No. There is something there. Something Viadro knows and is scared of revealing, despite his braggadocio."

"And it involves Ranieri. I wonder if he suspects us yet."

"He might just take us for gossips and fools," I said. "But watch your back, just in case."

"I always do. Here's a thought. No one saw anyone go upstairs with Bastiani, but what if someone was already waiting for him in his room?"

I stopped, rubbing my temples.

"Good thinking, my friend," I said. "The murderer accomplished his task, then waited for everyone in the building to fall asleep before making his escape."

"Or her escape," he reminded me. "There's our mystery woman. And a lovely lady lurking in one's chambers may easily tempt one into sampling a little poison unawares. Then she could remove the evidence afterward."

"That would solve the 'how' nicely for my lady wife," I said. "One problem."

"What's that?"

"If she waited until everyone was asleep, she would be leaving too late to pass through the gates to the city proper. Plus, she would have to avoid detection by the local patrols."

"Speaking of which, there've been a couple of Varangians following us since we left the quarter."

"I know," I said without looking around. "It's Will and Phil. You go on ahead. I'll see what they want."

All Varangians are deadly by training, but these two Englishmen were deadly by nature. Philoxenites had found this predilection for violence useful for his own needs. Although I had stayed on the eunuch's good side during my tenure in the city, I always received an apprehensive jolt whenever I encountered them. And I'm a fairly dangerous fellow myself.

I waited for them at a crossroads, standing at a safe distance from anyone who could have been waiting in ambush in a doorway somewhere. Plossus had moved on, but I assumed he had taken a position from which he could keep an eye on me. I assumed that Will and Phil were aware of that as well.

All of this just for a quick conversation.

"Well met, Englishmen," I said.

William, who was large and burly, nodded pleasantly. Philip, who was larger and burlier, spoke.

"The man who pays all of us would like to see you," he said.

"He will," I replied.

"You were supposed to report to him when you found out anything."

"When I find out something, I will," I said.

Philip shook his head. "He thinks, knowing you, that you've already found out something, but that you're holding back from him for your own reasons."

"I haven't found anything that concrete," I said. "Suspicions, mostly."

"He'll like those," said William. "He's a suspicious man himself."

"How urgent is it that I report to him?" I asked.

They looked at each other, amused.

"Do you see us standing here?" asked Philip.

"I do."

"Do you think we waste our time on messages that aren't urgent?" asked William.

"I suppose not. Thank you for taking the trouble. Is it customary to tip you?"

William's face flushed angrily. He took a step forward, but Philip stopped him.

"There are limits, Fool, to our forbearance," said Philip pleasantly. "Don't test them any further."

"My abject apologies," I said. "Tell your master I shall see him in the morning."

Plossus swung down from a nearby rooftop as I turned into the courtyard by my home. Rico's cart and ponies were already tied up in front of it. He and my wife already had dinner prepared when we entered.

"Plossus may have solved your how," I announced.

"Really?" she said.

"He thinks the murderer was already in the room, possibly our mystery woman. She induced him to take the poison, waited for the rest of the building to fall asleep, and left, taking the poison with her."

"After first barring his door from the inside," she said. "How do you account for that?"

"Yes, Plossus," I echoed, turning on the poor boy with my hands on my hips. "How do you explain that?"

He slumped dejectedly onto a stool.

"I had forgotten about that," he admitted.

"As did the great Feste, it seems," said Rico. "Well, I have some small news to share. I was performing down at the Akropolis and saw one of those silky fellows walking by."

"Dark hair, about thirty, watching everything at once?" I guessed.

"That's the one," said Rico.

"Ranieri," said Plossus. "And Feste saw him there yesterday. Why does he keep going to the Great Palace?"

"Were you able to follow him?" I asked.

"Alas, I was in mid-ballad. I could not leave my adoring public in suspense. Besides, I wouldn't have been able to keep up with him on foot at the pace he was going."

"And you, my love?"

"I'm looking into a few things," she said vaguely. "I'll let you know when I have a better idea of what's going on."

"All right. I've been summoned to a meeting with Philoxenites in the morning."

"How much are you going to tell him?" asked Aglaia.

"I'll tell him about the weapons cache, but that we need more time to know who is behind it. We know about Ranieri, but there has to be more to it than him. Tomorrow night, Aglaia and I will go back to Bastiani's room. Rico, will you be our coachman?"

"Certainly, milord," said the dwarf, bowing low.

"Plossus, fetch our horses and get hold of a decent-looking coach. We'll meet back here mid-afternoon."

"I have a suggestion," said Aglaia.

"What is it?"

"I think Plossus and Rico should stay here until this is over," she said. "We don't know how much Ranieri suspects us, but if he does, he may come after us. There's safety in numbers."

"I can take care of myself!" said Plossus indignantly.

"That sentence can be chiseled onto the markers of many a fool's grave," said Rico. "She's right. There are four backs to watch here, so eight eyes will be needed to watch them. Besides, we're coming back here for dinner every night, anyway. You'll eat better with us, boy."

"Then it's agreed," I said. "Only keep the noise down at night. Milady needs her rest more than ever."

"Because God knows when I'll get it after the baby comes," muttered Aglaia.

"I'll be there to help," I protested. She just rolled her eyes and went back to her meal.

When I arrived at the palace the next morning, I was met by Will and
Phil and taken immediately to the eunuch's office. He was standing by
the window, looking across the Golden Horn.

"God's chosen vessel is with his army," he said. "Standing at the
edge of the water, waiting for the enemy to brave the straits. But the
enemy will not do so until they are finished raiding Skutari for supplies."

"How long will that take?" I asked.

"A few days, I think. They have comfortable quarters, room to
exercise their horses, and all the time in the world. In the meantime,
the Emperor will become anxious about being outside the safety of
these walls. He dashed heroically northward, like a little boy charging
the sea, only to scamper back when the tide comes in again. I predict
that the great Alexios will be back in the palace within two days, safe
in the arms of his Egyptian."

He turned back to me.

"Which gives you ample time to tell me what you've learned about
Bastiani's death," he said.

"About his death, very little," I replied. "It may have been from
natural causes, but Lord knows the other silk merchants have been
spooked by it. But I don't know if it's because they killed him, or
because they're afraid the death will draw the attention of some out-
sider."

"And that's it?" he said.

"No. We found a cache of weapons, large enough to arm a squadron
or two."

"That's more like it," he said, sitting. "Where did you find it?"

"In Bastiani's storeroom."

"But he was . . ." he began, perplexed. Then his face cleared. "Someone put them there after he died."

"Yes. But I need more time to find out the full extent of the plan behind all of this. I have the other fools helping me, so we should come up with something fairly soon."

"All right," he said. "However, there is another task that I need you for. Something that just came up."

"What is it?"

He drummed his fingers on his desk, looking back out the window.

"You were right to warn me about the threats to my other conduits to the Venetians," he said. "One of them has disappeared. They say that he fled the city, but no one knows for certain. The other is now too frightened to do anything for me.

"There is a delegation forming at the behest of the Emperor, ready to seek parley with the Crusaders. They'll hurl defiance, make all the appropriate noises, and try and frighten them away."

"That won't work," I said.

"I know it. So, I want you to go with them, then slip off and make contact with your people there. Find out what the Crusaders want to go away. Or what they want to make peace."

"You trust me to do this?" I said, a bit surprised.

"I don't trust anyone in this city," he said bitterly. "But I distrust you less than most."

"Thank you, I suppose. When does the delegation leave?"

"In a few days. I'll send word."

"Very good, milord," I said, bowing. "And milord?"

"Yes, Fool?"

"I distrust you less than most as well."

He laughed, a rare occurrence for him.

"That almost counts as friendship around here," he said. "Now, get out before I change my mind and have you killed."

EIGHT

Fools make a mock at sin.
—PROVERBS 14:9

A clatter of hooves and wheels approached the courtyard. As I looked out our window, an enclosed coach pulled by two horses burst through the entrance, Plossus frantically reining the steeds in. The vehicle stopped just before crashing into the house.

I went out to tie up the horses while Plossus climbed carefully down, staggering as he hit the flagstones. He pulled out a large handkerchief and mopped his brow.

"You could have warned me," he said.

"About what?" I said innocently.

"About what? About this devil incarnate, this four-hooved fiend, this demon in a horse's shape."

"Hello, Zeus," I said, patting the nose of the shaggy gray malevolence that continued to buck in the traces. "Did you frighten my young friend?"

"Frighten?" groaned Plossus. "The beast is the terror of the stables. It took a team of giants to wrestle him into harness. Am I to understand that you have actually ridden this creature?"

"Oh, Zeus is just a sweetheart once he gets used to you," I said. "And he's the fastest thing on four legs in this city."

"That I can well believe," said Plossus. "For he took this carriage down the Mese at a pace that would have left Hermes coughing up dust. Pedestrians scattered, soldiers took cover, and I swear I saw the Bronze Bull in the Forum Bovis leap back to avoid being trampled into pennies."

"Yet you lived to tell the tale," I said. I produced a pair of carrots and gave one to each horse. The second was a sorrel mare who cast a bemused glance in Zeus's direction. "My Lady Hera seems none the worse for the experience."

"Your wife's horse was superb," he said. "She has no equal for equine equanimity. I see now that each horse takes after its rider."

"I'll accept the compliment on her behalf, and forgive the insult on mine," I said. "Nice carriage. Where did you get it?"

"Borrowed it," he said vaguely. "The owner probably won't even notice it's gone until it's already back."

"Good work. All right, we'll see you later."

"Right. Good luck," he said, then he stopped. "I just remembered something I wanted to tell you. I saw one of our wandering silk merchants this morning."

"Ranieri again?"

"No. This time it was our drinking partner of yesterday."

"Viadro? Where did you see him?"

"Staggering around the seawalls near the Petrion Gate," he said. "Below the Fifth Hill. He looked drunk."

"He's been drinking a lot, it seems."

"I said he *looked* drunk," said Plossus. "However, having just seen your masterful performance of last night, I can say with confidence that he was only pretending to be drunk. Badly."

"Really? Any idea of where he was going?"

"He was staggering along the base of the wall, occasionally haranguing a shopkeeper or arguing with a guard."

"Spying out the defenses of that section, perhaps."

"That occurred to me as well," said Plossus. "He got into such a debate with a Varangian at the tower by the gate that several other Varangians had to interrupt their repair work to come separate the two. That's when he turned and saw me watching. I hailed him and walked over to where he was standing, and he started into the drunk act with me. He lacks even a scintilla of your talent, my master."

"Thank you. Did you learn anything from him?"

"No, which was more proof that he was acting. A real drunk would have given up something."

"All right. I don't know how it fits in with everything else, but we'll add it to the puzzle."

I summoned the rest of our band of players from the house. Aglaia was unrecognizable, even to me. She had covered her short auburn hair with a long, curly, raven-black wig and had made her face up according to the fashion of the young and unmarried ladies of the town. She wore a blue silk gown with delicate beadwork across the front and had draped a hooded cloak over everything. She looked at me, then suddenly giggled and flounced like a sixteen-year-old girl.

"I'm convinced," said Plossus in admiration. "In fact, I'm positively smitten."

"Which is why Rico is our coachman," I said. "I need someone who can keep his five wits in one head."

"And here I am," said the dwarf, emerging from the house carrying a horsewhip and an apple. He tossed the apple to Plossus. "Put this on your witless noggin, lad."

"Are you quite sure about this?" said Plossus as he took off his cap and bells and placed the fruit on top of his head.

Rico shrugged, then suddenly cracked the whip in a smooth forward motion. The top half of the apple flew off, leaving the remainder wobbling on Plossus's head. The lad reached up gingerly and removed it, wiping the juice from his hair.

"Nicely done," I said as Aglaia applauded.

"First time for everything," chuckled Rico as he climbed onto the driver's seat and took up the reins. Plossus keeled over in a dead faint, then waved good-bye from the ground as I helped my wife into the carriage.

The horses had watched the exhibition with interest. Zeus looked back at the dwarf sitting serenely with the whip coiled by his side, then looked at me.

"Give us a smooth ride, my friend," I instructed him. "You don't want to make Rico unhappy."

I hopped into the carriage, closed the door, and we were off.

We reached the Venetian quarter as the sun was setting. Rico stopped the carriage about fifty paces from the alley leading to Vitale's house. I stepped out, cloaked but still in motley and makeup, and ran to the front door.

Vitale opened it, then smiled when he saw me.

"It's tonight, isn't it?" he whispered eagerly.

"It is, my good landlord," I replied, handing him some silver. "Now, here is your payment. This buys your silence and no interruptions. You are to remain down here, and you are not to address my master at peril of your wretched hide."

"Is he that close about it?" asked Vitale.

"You will not see him, and you will never see him, or you may never see anything else," I said. "Is that clear?"

"Oh, dear," he muttered. "I'd better go to my room and lie down for a bit."

"That would be the best course," I said and dashed back to the carriage.

A short time later, I emerged as a clandestine aristocratic libertine, escorting a cloaked maid who muffled her giggles with her hands as we entered the building. As we passed by the second landing, I noticed

John Aprenos looking curiously out of his room, but I didn't meet his eye. I heard sawing from that direction.

Aglaia continued the giggling until we reached Bastiani's room. I closed the door behind us, dropped the bar, and listened. Nobody was eavesdropping from the hall.

"It would have been easier if Plossus played the lord," she commented softly. "It would have saved you the quick change."

"I didn't want him playing any more scenes with you," I said.

"You're jealous!" she said in wonderment.

"I am not. I'm just feeling old when he's around. I'm remembering all the things I could do when I was his age."

"I daresay that you can still do just about all of them," she said with a merry look in her eyes. "And by way of proving it, as well as maintaining the illusion we have created, I am fully prepared to make love to you right here."

"Hmm, tempting," I said. "As much as I respect your devotion to authenticity, I'll pass. I dislike getting into debauched characters as an act. I truly don't want to do it in reality."

"Suit yourself," she sniffed. "Keep an ear by the door, good Fool, and I'll have a look around."

Vitale had cleaned up the chamberpot and spread some rushes by the bed, but the room was otherwise as it had been during my first visit. A wick stuck in a dish of tallow burned fitfully and threw off a foul-smelling smoke that became trapped at the ceiling.

"What a dismal existence he had," she said. "I'm revising my opinion. If I had to spend my life in this room, I might consider suicide."

"This was only where he slept," I pointed out. "And made love. He spent most of his time making money at the embolum."

"That such a skinflint could be involved in such a luxurious item as silk is beyond me," she said. "And that any woman would have consented to meet him in such a squalid setting..."

"She was a prostitute. He paid her. Prostitutes don't complain about location. She was probably happy to do it in a real bed for a change."

"I don't think she was a prostitute," she said.

"Why?"

"I have my reasons," she said.

"A woman's reasons?"

"A woman's. And a fool's. You would understand the latter, being a fool, but you've never been a woman."

"As a matter of fact, I once portrayed a courtesan in Toulouse so successfully that—"

"Stop!" she commanded. "Listen to me. A rose once bloomed in a dung heap. I think, odd as it was, that this was love."

"Explain."

She shook her head. "You'll want more than intuition," she said. "I'll have my proofs first."

She walked around the room, opening the cedar trunk and rummaging through it thoroughly, massaging the pallet for any hidden pockets, sniffing the cushions.

"Not a perfumed love, I'll give you that," she said. "There's something missing, I'll warrant."

"What's that?"

"A keepsake. A token of some kind, whether it's a sleeve or a locket or a lovelock. If it was love, then it would be here. But it's not."

"Maybe it wasn't love, then."

She looked at me, a serious expression for a change.

"You do have something of mine, don't you?" she asked sternly.

"I do. I confess it."

She nodded, satisfied. Then she pointed to my right. "What's that?"

I looked. In the corner of the room by the door lay a crumpled heap of cloth. I went over and picked it up.

"Just an old blanket," I said, displaying it to her.

"But the bed is on the opposite wall," she observed, coming over to inspect it. "What's it doing over here?"

"The others probably threw it when they went to help Bastiani."

She looked at the bed critically.

"That bed is the most expensive thing in the room," she said. "Come over and feel the sheets."

I did, expecting the usual coarse linen. To my surprise, they were soft and smooth.

"Well, there are some benefits to being a silk merchant," I said.

"Indeed. The coverlets are equally rich. And they are still here. Why would that ratty old woolen blanket be on this bed? Why, for that matter, would he want a woolen blanket in the middle of the summer?"

She walked over to examine the door. "The hinges were replaced?" she asked.

"According to Vitale."

"But they are affixed to the same spots as the old ones," she said. "So, the door would have swung open in the same direction as where we found the blanket."

"So?"

"Is anyone out there?" she asked.

I listened at the door again.

"No one," I said.

"Very well. Give me the blanket."

She took it and shoved it against the bottom of the door so that it completely blocked the crack at the bottom. Then she unbarred the door and opened it quickly. The blanket was swept against the wall at the same spot where she had spotted it. She closed the door and barred it again.

"That explains how it got there," she said.

I shrugged. "An elegant demonstration, my love, but so what? He kept the blanket at the base of the door to block out the sounds of the hall."

"Or to cover up the noise of his lovemaking," she added.

"In any case, it still doesn't add anything to our shallow pool of knowledge as far as I can tell."

"I wonder," she said. "You didn't notice any letters lying about when you were here?"

"No, but I had less time to search. There aren't any now, but they could have been returned to his family."

"Or his lover could have taken them, along with his keepsake of her," she replied.

"Meaning?"

"Love comes hard to a lonely man," she said. "What if it left him even harder?"

"His lover killed him?" I asked. "But that still doesn't answer how it was done."

"Not that she killed him directly," she said. "But what if she ended the affair? What if she demanded her letters, her tokens, everything that let him have some hope and light in this world without any? She left him alone in that silken bed, and he lay back and died."

"Of a broken heart?"

"Of poison, self-administered," she said. "Something unknown to the Fools' Guild, but effective nevertheless. And all of this nervousness among his friends and colleagues is a reaction to what they think is a murder, when it was only a suicide."

I looked around the room. Apart from the bed, the dominant color was dinge.

"Or maybe the carpenter's thought was correct," I said.

"What was that?"

"That his friends thought it was suicide, but spread the rumors of murder so that he could be buried in consecrated ground. Only they spread them too well and drew the unwanted attention of the Lord Treasurer at a most inopportune time."

"Maybe," she said. She looked around the room and suddenly pulled her cloak tightly around her. "I felt a sudden chill," she said. "Good thing I don't believe in ghosts."

"This would certainly be the place for one," I said, coming over to hold her.

"Do you believe in them?" she asked.

I laughed softly. "Well, my good wife, I saw one once, a long time ago. But it turned out to be something else entirely. Is there anything else?"

"No," she said. "Blow out the lamp. We don't want to burn down the place."

I opened the door so we could see our way by what little moonlight seeped in from the outside, then extinguished the tallow lamp. The smoke, finally gaining an exit, followed us desultorily into the hall.

We crept down quietly. As we passed the door to Vitale's room, I noticed that it was open a crack, but it quickly slammed shut as I turned menacingly in that direction.

Rico hopped down to open the carriage door, sweeping his hat off and bowing as he did so. The ride home was quite pleasant as we snuggled in the dark, watching the city pass by our windows. We were both silent, lost in our thoughts over Bastiani, who died in a room that had about as much light and air as a coffin. They might just as well have left him there, I thought. There wouldn't have been that much of a difference.

NINE

If you wish to know if and when the prisoner will be released or if he has died, follow the directions indicated below and mark well the lines. If you see right and left red vertical lines, he will be released. If you see horizontal lines, count the number. They indicate the years of imprisonment. If they direct you to the side of the [sign], he has died.

—SIGN POSTED OUTSIDE A BYZANTINE PRISON

I was half serious about wanting to make love to Feste in that dim squalor. I had the urge to bring life into a room that was filled with death, especially now that I had new life growing within me. It was hard to believe that a man could spend so many years either in that room, in the embolum, or walking back and forth between them. It was a death of a life, every day of his existence. It was easy to see how he had made his fortune, for he had spent next to nothing on himself. Yet he had managed to find love, somehow. A miser doesn't invest in a solid oak bed with silk coverlets merely to entertain streetwalkers. A lonely man had happened somehow upon a lonely woman, and a romance was born.

She was no prostitute. I was certain of that. I had met her.

The day before we entered Bastiani's room, I went to Euphy's chambers at Blachernae. My jaw throbbed in protest as I returned to the scene of its buffeting, but I clenched my teeth and forced the merriest smile that I could produce. It came out lopsided.

There was a lull in the chattering of the ladies-in-waiting as they saw me come in. The Empress did not deign to gaze upon me. My attempts to interject my brilliance into her conversations were rejected. A chord struck upon my lute died without sequel. Finally, I sat dejected in the corner of the room, watching everything happen without me, feeling sorry for myself.

Sometimes your role catches up with your life. Or is it the other way around?

Nature provided me with an excuse to slip out of the room. It had been a while since my last pregnancy, and I had forgotten what a convenient defense the condition provided for social niceties. I remember more than one tedious state dinner back when I was still a duchess during which I graciously begged some ambassador's kindly indulgence and left as the men all nodded knowingly at my husband. Then I would sneak out to the other wing of the villa, put my feet up, pour myself a cup of wine, bundle myself up in quilts, and read to my heart's content. Some of the coziest evenings of my life were spent that way, alone with my books and my child-to-be.

I didn't think I'd be able to duplicate that experience this time. There are advantages to being a fool, but there were also advantages to being a duchess. You can't have it both ways. I was lucky I had each at different times.

I turned a corner and wandered down the corridor that led to the suites of rooms belonging to the Emperor's daughters and their families. Evdokia had the smallest, an endless source of complaint for her. Everything was a source of complaint for her, when it came down to it. She was an overgrown child who still sucked her thumb when she thought no one was looking. Even her children treated her like a child on those rare occasions when she paid attention to them.

She was sprawled across her bed, picking at a bowl of candied figs, when I knocked gently on her doorframe. She sat up, quickly wiping her thumb on the sheets, and scowled when she saw it was me.

"Well?" she demanded haughtily.

"How is Your Grace?" I asked, bowing respectfully.

"What, my mother's fool is concerned for my welfare?" she exclaimed bitterly. "Or have you come to pick at the scab?"

"I need you to cheer me up," I said.

"Shouldn't the fool be able to amuse herself?" she sneered.

"Actually, I've come to apologize," I said.

"Really?" she said in surprise.

"The other morning, I said that you needed the most sense knocked into you," I said. "I was wrong. The person who truly needed that was me."

"You?"

"Apparently," I continued. "I myself was unaware of this great necessity until the point was roundly brought home right about here." I pointed to my jaw, the swelling still obvious under the makeup. Of course, I had left my whiteface a bit thin there just for the emphasis. She sat forward and touched the place gently. The bitter lines on her face smoothed into sympathy.

"I had heard about this," she said.

"Looking back, it should have come as no surprise that the person with the least sense in the room would be the fool," I said. "But if a fool was that aware of her foolishness, then she would be no fool and therefore in no need of having the sense knocked into her. So, the fool was true to herself and quite taken aback to be so affronted. And yet, I wonder if the Empress's method is the best one for restoring sense to a fool, for if she had hit me any harder, she would have knocked me senseless."

"She used to positively thrash us when we were little," said Evdokia. "We weren't all royal then, so she could do whatever she wanted. Father was off fighting this war or that, and he barely paid attention to us until we were old enough to marry off. Then he saw us as useful commodities."

She stood and walked to the window. Her rooms overlooked the outer wall of Blachernae and the great stone bridge that crossed to the other side of the Golden Horn.

"That's where their army will come," she said. "They'll try and take Galata. If they succeed, they'll try and cross the bridge, and Father will meet them with the Imperial Army and the Varangian Guards, and we will all watch and wave our little silk handkerchiefs, because that's all we silly women know how to do. And then they will make a truce and marry me off to someone suitably noble, no matter how old or decrepit he is."

"You were complaining of not having a husband," I said. "Now, you are complaining of getting one."

"I just want some choice for a change," she said.

"I sympathize."

"Do you?" she said, turning toward me. "You're married to that other fool."

"I am."

"Was that by choice, or did your parents give you to him?"

"My mother died giving birth to me. My father died when I was thirteen. My marriage was of my own making."

"You chose to marry a fool," she mused. "You must love him."

"I do, milady."

"I love a man," she blurted suddenly.

"That is good, milady."

"But he is in prison."

"That is unfortunate."

"And he is married."

"And that is foolish."

[113]

She stepped toward me, her hand raised. Must run in the family, I thought as I waited for the slap, but she paused.

"It is, isn't it?" she sighed, her hand falling to her side.

"Forgive me, milady, but a fool is expected to speak truthfully. That is why people keep us around."

"You are kept around by my mother," she observed.

"I was until this morning," I replied. "Now, I am not so certain of my imperial status."

"Will you let me keep you?" she asked.

"Milady, it is a serious responsibility keeping a fool. You must feed her, clothe her, and allow her to ridicule you several times a day."

"All of that? And what, pray, do I receive in exchange for all of this responsibility?"

"Someone to talk to," I said simply.

"Like a sister!" she exclaimed, her face brightening. "Only nice, like a sister should be."

"If you like," I said. "I never had a sister. But I will be whatever you wish."

"Good!" she cried, clapping her hands. "You shall be my fool. Irene and Anna don't have fools. Won't they be envious when they see me with you! Come, we shall appear in public together. You shall accompany me on my charitable rounds. Tell my maid to have the carriage brought around."

"Very good, milady," I replied, bowing.

It takes a good deal of preparation by a team of servants and slaves for a lady as noble as Evdokia to become charitable. In addition to the driver, there was a brace of Imperial Guards to accompany her, a maid-servant to attend her and keep her makeup and hair intact, and a train of three wagons filled with loaves of bread and other foodstuffs along with enough servants to distribute them. There was one person whose entire function was to shout out praise for the beneficence of milady, so that all within a two-mile radius should know how virtuous and humble she was. And there was me, sitting beside her and pretending to be sympathetic while she prated on.

We rattled down the Mese, citizens scattering before us. At the places we stopped, people gathered in seconds to snatch up the food tossed from the wagons. I noticed that most of the bounty was gathered up by some thuggish-looking men at the expense of those who looked like they actually needed it. I also saw that a number of the ladies jostling each other for the bags of beans and flour looked anything but poor. Silk sleeves poked out of their cloaks, and their shoes were of high quality. Hoarding season had commenced.

I decided not to point out any of this to Evdokia. She was busy basking in her own sun, oblivious to the warning signs around her. I thought for the first time about the prospect of pregnancy during a siege. I had been so caught up with the two events rushing by that I never considered the impact one would have on the other. Hoarding food suddenly seemed prudent, given all that I was going to be eating. I patted my belly to comfort the little one and turned my attention back to Evdokia.

"They really do love me," she sighed happily as her servant led the crowds in inauthentic cheering. "I will be the most beloved empress in history, you'll see."

"Empress? How do you propose to manage that?" I asked. "It seems to me that there are a number of people ahead of you."

"The number is three," she said serenely. "But the secret of becoming an empress is to have an emperor for a husband."

"Your sisters are both married to generals," I pointed out. "You are not only unmarried, but somewhat scandalously divorced from your first husband."

"He was a brute," she said. "The only difference between his love-making and rape was . . . well, I can't think of one. If I sought a little kindness elsewhere, who could blame me?"

"The Church," I said. "Your family. The entire Byzantine Empire. Whichever kingdom you were married into."

"He was King of the Serbs," she laughed. "Such a puny little king-dom, completely without morals or manners. I was happy to get out."

"Yet you remain unmarried," I said. "How shall you become em-press? You can't even take a decent punch from your mother."

"But I'll outlive her, you just watch," she declared. "Even a survivor like my mother has to die someday, and she's old and not getting any younger, no matter how much rouge she slathers on that hard leather thing she calls a face."

"And your sisters?"

"Irene is in disgrace ever since her husband revived his leg injury. Men all over Byzantium are preparing to die for my family, but he won't. He'll never be emperor now."

"How exactly did he hurt this leg?" I asked.

"That's right, you weren't around here then. It was quite funny, really. The floor under Father's bed had rotted through or something. Michael had gone on ahead of Father, and the whole thing collapsed under him. They say he fell three stories, but Father treated him royally after that, like he had stepped in front of an oncoming arrow or something. And Michael's been lording it over everyone ever since. But you can't be a general and then back down from a good fight. Oh, no, the scales have fallen from Father's eyes when it comes to Michael."

"And Theodore Laskaris?"

"He's a good man," she said. "Decent. Honest. Brave. How he ended up in our family is beyond me. But he's such a brave man that he will be right in the thick of battle. Sister Anna is already assembling a team of tailors to make her mourning attire. No, I shall be empress before them. I am certain of it."

"It sounds completely uncertain to me."

She shook her head vehemently. "It has been preordained," she asserted. "One of Mother's best astrologers was brought in one day. He cast her fortune, but then turned and looked at me with such import that I knew we must speak. I invited him to my room. It turned out that there was a rather interesting ritual involved, and after that, he told me that I would become empress."

From the satisfied purr in her voice, I had a pretty good guess as to the nature of this ritual.

"Well, that's good enough for me," I said. "So, who's the lucky fellow destined to be your emperor?"

"You'll see him today," she whispered eagerly. "Our last stop."

The procession wended its way toward the Great Palace complex at the tip of the peninsula. We stopped at the immense doors of the Chalke Prison, just beyond the entrance to the complex. These were wooden doors, hastily installed after the Emperor Isaakios Angelos had the bronze ones removed and packed off to another church that he favored. He then had the building converted from a church to a prison.

Now, he sat somewhere inside the prison he had created, guarded by the same Varangians he had once commanded and favored. That he was still alive and guarded so sympathetically was in large part due to the efforts Feste and I made the previous year.

The warden, a toadie of the Emperor's who the Varangians barely tolerated, came to greet her when we arrived, bowing obsequiously and calling for the keys in a most grandiose manner. He unlocked a massive iron padlock securing a gate at the end of the entryway, and a slave pushed it open.

Where once there had been chapels, there were now large communal prison cells, crammed with a mixture of the politically disfavored and disciples of Father Esaias. I knew more of the latter than the former, thanks in part to my unsavory profession, but also because many of those who had displeased the Emperor had done so before my arrival. I winked at a pickpocket who had occasionally helped us out on some matters, and followed Evdokia down the center aisle.

The status of prisoners rose as one approached the former location of the altar. The cells became less crowded, and I could see that some of them contained some comfortable couches and sideboards laden with roast chickens, bottles of good wine, sweetmeats, and other delicacies. The only thing lacking was light, as oil was a commodity precious above all others. The few lamps that burned marked the quarters of the most influential prisoners.

Evdokia stopped before a darkened cell and beckoned to me.

"Though the Alexios who sits on the throne in Blachernae rules all Byzantium, there is another Alexios here," she said softly. "And he rules my heart, little Fool. My love? Do you hear me?"

And so came my first encounter with Alexios Doukas. I heard him before I saw him, as a deep rumble came from a far corner of the cell.

"Is that you, empress of my heart?" he said, and I was put in mind of the caressing growl of a sleepy lion. "Hold the torch so that I may gaze upon your splendor."

Her servants hurried up with a pair of torches and stood on either side of her while she posed prettily for his perusal.

"Did a goddess of antiquity come to walk among mortals again?" he cried. "Is the very simulacrum of Helen standing before me? I must not look directly upon her, for fear that I may be blinded by her radiance."

"Oh, get on with it," muttered one of his cellmates.

He stepped out of the darkness. I had anticipated a handsome, virile man, one that would cause a young woman to take leave of her senses.

I was surprised to see that the home of the croaking compliments was a decrepit, hairy man of sixty, the coarseness of his beard a match for his rough voice, his hair thick, matted, and greasy. He looked like one of those elderly bears that travel with circuses, jammed into a tiny cage and covered with sores, let out only to dance clumsily about a ring before being whipped back to its jail.

Yet Evdokia looked at him with swoony adoration. She loved him sure, did the little princess, and she eagerly thrust her fingers between the bars for him to bend down and brush his lips across them.

"I've brought you something," she giggled.

"What is it, my pet?" he sighed. "Wine to help me pass this sorrow of long separation? Meat to sustain me when I can't have my fill of your beauteous visage?"

"Something even better," she said. "Music! Come, Aglaia. Put your fingers to your strings."

I began playing softly upon my lute. A look of disappointment flashed across his face, and the momentary frown caused his bushy eyebrows to meet just over his nose.

"But I need no music other than the celestial song of your voice," he said, and she melted against the bars. I kept playing anyway. It's what I get paid to do, and I didn't think her voice was so celestial, unless the dominant sound in the heavens is whining.

"I am in agony," she cried. "Agony when we are apart and agony when I see you suffering behind these cold bars."

"But these are merely earthly barriers, such as mortals may encounter," he replied. "Our passion is greater than any prison. You must be patient, my sweet. Our deliverance will soon be at hand. God's own army has arrived, and one way or another, I shall be liberated. I am sure of it. Until then, you must wait for me and no other besides me."

"And we will be together forever!"

"As long as this heart beats, it is yours," he said, pounding his chest with both hands to make the cliché even more obvious.

This land once produced Hero and Leander, lovers for the ages. To think that it now produced these paragons of corruption: the Emperor's least favored daughter and Alexios Doukas, lover for the aged.

They pressed their faces against the bars and began whispering to each other. Something he said made her blush, a talent I did not know she possessed. Something else caused a wicked giggle to burst from her, but he frowned and she immediately turned serious.

This went on for some time. Finally, she pulled herself away from the cell, with much fervent casting of glances and blowing of kisses. He made as if to weep, standing at the bars and watching her tearfully depart, but I glanced back as we left and saw him standing there, dry-eyed. He caught me looking and quickly turned away.

Evy had a knack for falling for the wrong men. I couldn't see what she saw in this one. It was clear to me that he was using her to try and worm his way back into political favor and freedom, but she was blind to his motives. And to his looks as well. Normally, when she went after a specimen that hideous, there was at least one compensatory factor that was all too obvious. But that wasn't likely in this case, unless she had bribed the warden to allow the two of them some privacy together, which I suppose was possible. Still, he was a hairy beast, and an old one at that. Perhaps at close range he exhibited some allure that wasn't evident to me at ten paces. I decided to maintain that distance in all future encounters.

Evy was unusually somber after her visit to Chalke. My attempts to rouse her from her torpor were met with sighs and stares that went beyond me and across the Bosporos.

"There is so much misery and sadness in the world," she mused.

"Yes, milady."

She started slightly, apparently unaware that she had spoken aloud. "You think I am daft, wanting him, don't you?"

"I am not one to judge, milady. I married a fool."

"Well, I don't care what anyone thinks about him. He is noble of heart, and that is worth all the good-looking young men in the world."

I agreed with the sentiment, certainly. I just thought that it was misapplied as to Doukas.

"You're probably wondering what we whispered about," she continued.

"It is not my place to wonder, milady."

"He was saying that in this time of crisis, I should put aside my selfish pursuit of him and devote more time to the caring of others in any way that I can. Is that not a beautiful thing to say?"

"It is indeed, milady."

"Back to Blachernae," she commanded her driver. "Charity begins at home, Aglaia."

"Very good, milady. Will you be needing me further today?"

"No, little Fool. Your company has been most supportive. Will you be my fool again tomorrow?"

"If you wish it, then I will."

I leapt down from the carriage at the Forum Amastrianum. I was curious about the mystery woman that Feste and Plossus had seen. I thought that a woman might reach another woman better than any man could do. In fact, I thought I could do most things better than any man could do, but that's me.

I wandered along the seawall by the Golden Horn, passing the Mitaton Mosque. This was set aside for the Moslem traders who stayed in their own quarter, which was west of the Venetians. I stopped by a spice merchant of my acquaintance and picked up a little local gossip. I came away with nothing more useful than a small box of cinnamon, which he gave me at a friendly markup.

The faithful were being called to prayer, unrolling their mats and facing east. A woman in front of me joined them, and as she sank to the ground I heard a tinkling of bells. I glanced at her ankles, which had become exposed despite the heavy black cloak she wore to conceal them, and saw the source of the sound: tiny bells around her ankles. It was the Egyptian flutist who shared the Emperor's bed when he desired it. It never occurred to me that she was religious at all, but the present circumstances were enough to put the fear of God into anyone.

I had directions to the woman's house from Plossus. The Fifth Hill was one the steeper hills in the city, and the winding roads that cut through the lower slopes quickly had me sweating through my motley. I found myself winded, and only then I remembered that walking in this summer heat was not the best thing for a woman in my condition.

I tried to remember what it was like when I was having my first two children. I had a vague sense that I didn't do anything active while pregnant in Orsino's villa. I wasn't allowed to do anything. I was carried everywhere and propped up with cushions whenever I sat. As a result, I nearly lost both my children and nearly died in the process.

Well, this one would be different. My little fool needed her exercise, and Lord knows that my training for the Guild had put me into the best physical condition of my pampered life. I took a deep breath and marched up the hill.

The houses, placed anywhere there was room, were a jumble of odd angles, frequently underpropped to prevent them from sliding right off the hill. Our unknown lady was more fortunate. There was a momentary plateau, as if the road itself had paused to rest and gather itself before attacking the summit. From here I could see that I was close to the monastery of the Church of the Pammakaristos, a modest but beautiful structure of brick and stone. The brick and stone had been hauled up the hill by slaves so that monks could pray to God—and for the emperor who owned the slaves. I suppose the monks thought that by living closer to heaven they wouldn't have to pray so loudly. Or maybe they just liked the view.

I located the stone wall and iron gate that shielded the lady's house from the rare passer-by. I wanted Plossus's stilts, but lacking the height to see over the wall, I sank to a bug's level and tried to peer under the gate.

It was a pleasant dwelling, a two-story marble structure with a simple colonnade in front, giving ample shade while allowing the breezes through. There was an elderly gardener tending to a patch of vegetables.

"Ho, good sir!" I called. He didn't react, choosing to continue weeding a plot of beans.

"Gentle gardener, there is one at the gate who needs watering," I said. "I feel myself wilting as I speak. Would you give comfort to a weak pilgrim?"

He moved on to an herb garden, watering it liberally.

"He's deaf," said a woman's voice.

I looked toward the house and saw her standing at the front door, looking out from the shade.

"Then, good lady, may I make the request of you? I am on my way to visit my brother, who is a monk at the monastery above us, but I misjudged the distance and need to refresh myself before I continue."

She hesitated, then turned back toward the house. I thought that she was ignoring me, but she came out moments later with a full bucket and a ladle. She came to the gate and unlocked it.

She was cloaked and veiled, even in this heat. I thought of the first time I set eyes on the woman who would eventually marry my brother. Olivia had been in mourning for her own brother at the time, but had so taken to mourning that she had made it a thing of beauty. This woman, on the other hand, slumped under the weight of her garments. When her hand emerged from the cloak to pass me the ladle, I saw a wrist that was practically a bone picked clean.

I drank, then handed the ladle back to her.

[123]

"God bless you, lady," I said. "Will you have something of mine in return?"

"I ask nothing of pilgrims," she said.

"No payment, lady," I said quickly. "And forgive me for the offense of the implication. But may I sing something for you, or entertain you in some other fashion? I see that you are bereft. I know not whom you lost, but I am sorry for it, and would bring you some comfort."

"Your words are comfort enough," she said. "I thank you for them. Now, we are even. Go in peace."

"They say you are a gentlewoman," I said. "May I know your name, so that I know whom to pray for?"

"Will you pray for me?" she said, surprised. "Why should you?"

"Because you gave me water," I said. "Because you grieve. And because I think that you fear for your life."

She stepped back and tried to close the gate, but I had already stepped forward into the interior yard.

"Why are you here?" she cried.

"I wish to help you," I said. "You are alone here. That old man couldn't stop even someone so weak as me. For whom do you grieve, lady?"

"It does not concern you. Go away."

"Was it a husband? I know what it is like to lose a husband."

"My husband lives," she spat.

"A brother? I have a brother, and I once thought him lost forever. It was the darkest day of my young life."

"No. Go away, please."

"A lover, then," I said softly, and she stood stock still. "I have hit the mark at last. Well, a lover's loss is painful, milady, especially when the marriage left over is loveless. This is where jesters become profoundly useful, in my experience, whether for song or for story, or even

[124]

just sitting and listening. Will you avail yourself of my services, lady? You'll find me reasonable for a fool."

"Is that what you do?" she said scornfully. "You seek out those in sorrow and prey upon them? You are like a carrion bird, Fool, feasting on corpses."

"No, lady," I said. "I do not feast on the dead. I provide sustenance for the living."

"Then seek your fortune elsewhere, Fool. I am not among the living."

"You feel that way in the midst of your sorrow," I said. "But people have this funny way of surviving in spite of themselves. It is our nature to want to live. Are you killing yourself, milady? Are you starving yourself to death? I saw more bone than flesh in that wrist. It runs against the fashion of this city to be so thin."

"Who are you?" she asked. "You are visiting no brother. You have come here to plague me."

"I have come here, but only to help," I said. "I do not know your name, but I know the one you mourn. And I know he lies beneath the ground with a purple kerchief in his hand."

She backed away from me, trembling, raising that bony hand to point at me.

"Stand back!" she hissed. "What are you? How could you know that? You have been conjuring with my life, you witch!"

She turned and fled inside, slamming her door behind her. The gardener stood and approached me, holding his hoe menacingly.

"You had better leave," he said. "I don't know what you said to her, but I saw her face."

I bowed and backed out of the yard. He closed the gate and locked it.

I still didn't know her name. I had gone to see a woman to satisfy myself that she was neither a whore nor a witch and had instead been accused of being a witch myself. So much for the sympathy of one woman for another.

I walked slowly back down the hill. I didn't know whether to laugh or to cry. I did a little of both, as I recall, but I forget in what order.

ᴱTEN

When the emperor of Constantinople learned of it, he sent good envoys to ask them what they sought there and why they were come there . . .

— ROBERT DE CLARI,

THE CONQUEST OF CONSTANTINOPLE

This was all very well and good, but there was still a war to worry about. While we were concerned with an insurrection from the Venetian quarter, we still needed to find some way to bring about a reconciliation between the Crusaders and the Greeks, no matter how absurd a prospect that may have seemed. While the Venetian fleet remained firmly ensconced at Skutari, we spent the next few days running around the city, gathering information, sounding out prospects from different quarters and interests, and generally doing what the Guild expected us to do.

Blachernae was relatively calm. The focus on the oncoming war had set aside most of the internal rivalries, even among the squabbling sisters.

"And Evdokia has truly taken her beau's advice to heart," said Aglaia on the evening of the last day of June. "She's been quite the angel of mercy, making bandages, donating her jewelry to raise money for provisions, even volunteering to care for her brother-in-law when her sister needs to rest."

She was keeping up the constant chatter while I dithered about the room, packing my gear. I had received a summons that afternoon. We looked up from a quick meal to see Will and Phil standing at our threshold. Despite being in full armor, they hadn't made a sound climbing our stairs.

"I don't recall inviting you in," I said, rising to my feet.

"I don't recall giving a damn," replied Phil.

My three colleagues rose as well, hands inching toward weapons, wondering what angle of throw might put a dagger anywhere useful.

"Look, Will," said Phil. "They think we want to fight."

"Aw, how cute," said Will. "Four fools, armed in motley. That stuff won't even keep the breezes out."

"It's quite comfortable in summer," said Plossus. "Try it sometime."

"No one is fighting anyone," I said. "They're just messenger boys. Never kill the messenger. Especially when he's bigger than you."

"True enough," said Phil cheerfully. "The message is this: You are to join a delegation to the invaders. Bring your horse and meet at the Imperial Wharf tomorrow at dawn."

"And when I get there?"

"Talk to your contacts," said Phil. "Get the story as to what they really want. As our mutual friend knows, any man has a price."

"Unless he's a fool," added Will.

Then they left, laughing at their own jokes. Always the mark of an amateur.

So, I packed while Aglaia blathered on about one thing or another, finally driving me to the point of exasperation.

"What, my dear wife, has put you into this senseless volubility?" I asked.

She looked at me, hurt.

"I was only trying to distract you," she said.

"Do I need distracting?"

"Maybe not," she said, "but I do."

I sat next to her on the bed.

"You've been moody ever since we left Bastiani's place," I said. "What is on your mind?"

"Let's see," she said. "There's a war, and you're about to ride off into the thick of it. Could that be it?"

"I'm going with a delegation to parley," I said. "There'll be no fighting."

"You're going in as a spy," she replied. "You're in such an ambiguous position that either side might decide to kill you. It's dangerous."

"Of course, it's dangerous. Half of what we do for the Guild is dangerous, and the other half is acrobatics and juggling sharp objects. You knew that."

"Yes, I knew that."

"And in the sixteen months that we have been husband and wife, we have both walked knowingly into deadly situations. What makes this one any different?"

"That we are no longer just husband and wife but father and mother as well. That changes things. At least, it does for me. Doesn't it for you?"

"I don't know," I admitted. "I guess I hadn't really thought about it."

"Then think about it now!" she snapped. "You need to learn about being a parent, Feste. Let me teach you something. The hardest thing a mother will ever do is tell her child his father is dead. And I am speaking from experience, as you very well know."

She waited for me to say something, but I was silent.

"We're fools," she continued. "I joined the Guild willingly, knowing what was entailed. I wonder now if you joined our marriage the same way."

"What would you have me do?" I asked. "Run away?"

"Is suicide part of your mission?"

"Sometimes," I said.

"You bragged about having a knack for surviving," she said, looking away. "You rejoiced when we came to this city that I was with you to watch your back. Now, you don't think enough about surviving, and you go where I cannot. This is not what I married you for and not why I decided to have your child."

I slipped my dagger into my sleeve.

"I have no choice," I said. "If we don't bring about some kind of truce, then many will die."

"Many will die anyway. There will come a point where you will recognize that you cannot stop what is happening. When you do, I want you to recognize that you do have a choice. And then I want you to choose me."

"Over the Guild's directives?"

She shrugged. "I gave up everything in my life to be with you," she said. "When will it be your time to return the favor?"

"Did you tell your first husband all of this when he rode off on the Third Crusade?"

"Yes," she said. "He chose to ignore my wishes. Called me a silly girl for worrying about it. Then he left me and I sat at home worrying about him for the next two years while raising a child and running a city. That did wonders for our relationship."

"We're fools, and we're here. I can't just up and leave in the middle of everything."

"There's always everything, and you're always in the middle of it, no matter what you do. Can't the Guild put us somewhere that will only require us to juggle and make bad jokes instead of risking our lives? At least, until our child is grown? What do they do for other couples?"

"Frankly, there aren't that many. I have no idea what the Guild policy is. Look, let me get through the parley. It shouldn't be much trouble. Then we'll talk about this some more."

"I'm tired of talking," she grumbled. She lay down, her back to me.

I closed my bag and curled up next to her. I reached around her waist and patted her belly.

"I want to see this one grow up, too," I whispered.

"Then make sure that you live," she said.

"I'll do my best," I promised.

Before dawn, I arose and walked up to a stable near the Rhegium Gate. Only the stable's farrier was up, heating up his charcoal for the day's shoeing.

"Feste himself," he said when he saw me. "You'll be wanting Zeus, I hope."

"The god incarnate," I replied. "Let him be brought unto me."

He picked my saddle from a hook on the wall and threw it to me.

"Bring yourself unto him," he said. "I don't go near that beast when I don't have to."

I lugged the saddle over to Zeus's stall, wondering what exactly I was supposed to be getting for my stabling fee.

"Good morning, sire," I said cheerfully as I entered his stall.

He was staring at his hay balefully but perked up when he saw the carrot in my hand. He snatched it away in a blink, leaving only a trace of orange on my fingertips, then looked at me expectantly. I held another carrot in front of him, then pulled it away.

"First this," I said, showing him the saddle. He deigned to let me strap it on him, then refused to budge until I gave him the promised fee. I led him outside and mounted.

The Imperial Wharf was at a landing by the Golden Gate, jutting into the Sea of Marmara. The boat was a small galley, and I could feel my land-loving steed tense as he saw it. The sight of other horses being led into its hold assuaged him somewhat, but he would allow no one other than me to touch him.

[131]

After securing him in the makeshift stall that had been rigged in between the rowers' benches, I went up on deck to meet my new traveling companions.

There were the expected high toadies of the Emperor, some officers from the Imperial Guard, and one interesting choice, Nicolò Rosso. He was a Lombard and an experienced courtier. He was frequently called upon when foreign diplomats visited Blachernae, more often than not to smooth over some gaffe of the Emperor. He was a confident man with an elaborate mustache that required constant maintenance. As the oarsmen pulled us away from the landing, he stood in the prow, trimming it carefully while a servant held a mirror before him. He saw my reflection and arched an eyebrow at it.

"I heard you would be joining us," he said. "I'm not sure that I understand why."

"I'm not sure that I understand either," I said. "Perhaps the Emperor thought some entertainment would help things."

"If you can tell a joke good enough to stop a war, then you will earn your place in Heaven," he said. "If not, I suggest you leave the negotiating to your betters."

"I'd be happy to," I said. "But if you decide you need me, give me a yell and I'll dance in and do a few routines."

He sniffed and went back to his grooming.

I saw no point in entertaining the high and mighty, so I spent our crossing cheering up the oarsmen down in the hold. It made the time pass for all of us and gave me a chance to work with a drummer. A steady beat does wonders for a song.

We arrived at the Asian shore at a mercantile dock that had been skipped by the Crusaders. An Imperial Guardsman immediately brought his horse onto land, mounted and galloped north to bring word of the proposed parley. The rest of us stretched our legs, careful not to stray too far inland in case a hasty getaway was needed.

"Mind you," said one of the oarsmen, "if they send some galleys after us, we're captives right away."

"They won't bother," said another. "We're small fry. Why chase minnows when there's big fish swimming inside the city walls?"

The Imperial Guardsman returned around noon. We had safe passage to Skutari and would camp on the grounds of the palace that evening. They would hear the parley in the morning.

We brought our horses and supplies up from the hold. Zeus required three carrots before assenting to carrying me. He was angry about being cooped up in the hold. The galley left, with the understanding that they would meet us at Skutari on the morrow. That would also give them a chance to assess the Venetian fleet from up close.

The entire party consisted of twenty men, including servants and one fool. The journey wasn't long—Skutari was a league north of Constantinople, and we had landed maybe half a league south. Yet it seemed like an eternity as we passed one burning farmhouse after another.

About halfway there, a man suddenly leaped out of some bushes and frantically waved his arms. The soldiers in the party immediately drew their weapons.

"Wait!" cried the man, and we recognized him. It was Michael Stryphnos, sans horse, sans armor, sans army.

"My dear Lord Admiral," said Rosso. "Whatever are you doing? When we last saw you, you were leading five hundred knights across the straits. Are they also hiding in the bushes?"

"We were taken by surprise," blurted Stryphnos. "One of their patrols came upon our camp and scattered us. I must report back to the Emperor."

"And where are your men? Are they following you into retreat?"

"I don't know," said Stryphnos. "Let me have a horse."

"You had five hundred horses," said a captain with the Guard. "Are they now learning French commands?"

"Give me a horse, I command you!" shouted Stryphnos. "I have influence in Blachernae."

"Not anymore," said Rosso.

The man looked despairingly about at our party, finally settling on me.

"A fool rides while an admiral walks?" he protested.

"An admiral is supposed to be on a ship," I said. "Why don't you—oh, that's right, you don't have any more."

He stormed up to me.

"Give me that horse," he said.

"He's mine," I said. "Or I am his. I'm never sure what the relationship is. But he will carry no rider but me."

"Get down, Fool, or I will have your head!" screamed Stryphnos.

"Do it, Fool," commanded Rosso. "I want to see what happens."

"Certainly, milord," I replied, and swung myself down from the saddle. "Now, my Lord Admiral, you must place your foot in the stirrup, thus—"

"Get out of my way," he snarled, shoving me aside. He vaulted onto Zeus, which might have been impressive if he hadn't previously lost his armor, and seized the reins. The next moment, he was flying through the air. He landed in a particularly prickly bush, screaming in pain and frustration.

"Nice aim, old fellow," I said, slipping Zeus a pair of carrots. He snorted at the naval posterior, then held still as I mounted him.

Stryphnos finally extricated himself from the bush and shook his fist.

"The Emperor will hear of this!" he blustered.

"Yes, you really should mention it during your account of how you let yourself be taken by surprise and ended up losing five hundred knights and horses," I said. "The affront to your dignity caused by my steed should be of the deepest concern to the Emperor. Constantinople is that way. Try not to sink any more boats on your way home, my Lord Admiral."

Our party resumed its northward journey, not without casting a few smirks behind us.

"You have made an enemy there," commented Rosso.

"I doubt it," I said. "He has no more power. I would bet that he doesn't even try to go back. I wonder how many Crusaders it took to rout his troops?"

"How did you get your horse to do that?"

"I don't get him to do that. He does it on his own. When I first saw Zeus, I was told that only a fool would ride such a creature. We've been together ever since."

An hour's ride brought us to the palace at Skutari. This was a summer palace, a place for parties and assignations amidst the cool breezes from the north. It was not built to withstand a siege, the reason being that if an army of Turks or Arabs had pushed this far through Anatolia, it was high time to flee to the safety of the walled city across the Bosporos.

The palace was a modest building with only a hundred or so rooms. The grounds, normally home to exotic birds and perfumed plants, were filled to the bursting point with one pavilion after another, the bright cloths surmounted by competing standards. Atop the tallest tower of the palace flew the flags of Montferrat, Champagne, and Venice.

The Crusaders, unlike the troops under our brave Lord Admiral, knew a little bit about maintaining a watch. As our party approached the palace gates, mounted patrols of Flemish knights in full armor appeared at our flanks to escort us in.

"And they're riding our horses," a Guardsman observed bitterly. "Rubbing our faces in it."

A nobleman stood at the gate, wearing an outlandishly plumed hat that he doffed with great ceremony as we entered.

"Hail, noble vassals of the usurper!" he greeted us in langue d'oc.

"Hail, oath-breaker and excommunicate," replied Rosso smoothly in the same tongue. "And how is your esteemed mother, Charles?"

"Nicolò?" laughed the other. "I should have known they would send you. My mother is as ornery as ever, thank you. Come, we have a tent and food prepared."

We were taken to a corner of the grounds where an ornamental fountain still burbled merrily in a grove of cedar. A meal was laid out on an oaken table.

"Enjoy your repast, gentlemen," said the Frenchman. "We have found the local provender to be quite tasty. We hope you will as well."

"We are overwhelmed by your hospitality," said Rosso dryly.

"Imperial silver," said one of the guardsmen, holding it up for inspection. "And look at the food. They're wallowing in the spoils before they've even won."

"Bravado, my friends," said Rosso. "Ignore it. No doubt they are eating scant portions themselves, but they want to put on a display for us. I suggest that you take advantage of it."

He sat at one end of the table and dug in. I followed him. I had a sinking feeling that lavish meals were not going to be too frequent in the near future, so I should grab what I could get while I could get it. One by one, the others joined us. We ate in silence—it didn't seem to be a good time for jesting, so I let it alone.

When we were done, I picked up my lute and rose.

"Where are you going?" asked a guardsman.

"He's going to wander the grounds and play his lute," said Rosso sagely. "Isn't that right, Fool?"

"Precisely," I replied. "Good evening, gentlemen."

I strummed gently as I walked, occasionally plucking a particular phrase of four notes. The soldiers camped on the grounds varied greatly in rank and nationality, but I noticed that the closer I got to the palace, the higher the rank. The commanders, I assumed, were inside the palace itself.

As I passed by the far end of the palace, a knight stood abruptly and looked in my direction. I did not look at him but continued to stroll along. I played the signal phrase again and waited for a response.

The response I got was not the one I was expecting. He drew his sword, screamed, "Bastard! Where is she?" and charged.

My response was to flee. Fortunately, it isn't difficult to outrun a man in armor. I quickly sought out a group of soldiers roasting a side of beef over a fire made from some ornamental trees recently chopped down.

"Excuse me, good sirs," I begged them. "Your comrade has taken offense at the sight of me for reasons I know not. I know my face is not the comeliest, but that shouldn't be cause for taking my head off."

"Strange," said a captain. "Does he know you?"

"No, sir," I said.

"Bastard!" screamed the knight as he staggered toward me.

"I am certainly not that," I protested.

"Feste!" he screamed.

I stared in shock. He came into the light and put his visor up.

"Sebastian!" I exclaimed.

"The same, Fool," he growled. "Prepare to meet your maker."

"Wait!" I cried, darting behind the soldiers who were now laughing at my plight. I kept them between us. It became a ridiculous little game as I dashed in and out. Finally, he ran out of breath, giving me an opportunity to get a better look at him.

There was a time when he and my wife could pass for each other, but that was long ago. Their shapes had taken different paths since then, thanks to drink in his case and childbirth in hers. Still, those were her eyes looking out from that visor, and the same auburn hair. But the expression on the face I saw now was far from the loving one I was used to seeing.

"What is this about, Count?" asked the captain.

"This fool carried off my sister," panted the Count. "He has despoiled her honor. Now, honor demands an accounting."

"Sounds reasonable," said a soldier, and I suddenly found myself pinned between two of them.

Sebastian raised his sword and slowly advanced.

"Good Count," I pleaded.

"Save it," he barked.

"Would you make your sister a widow?" I cried.

He stopped.

"Or your unborn niece fatherless?" I continued. "Sir, I have loved and honored your sister as much as any man in this life. You know me, Count. Have you ever known me to do anything as tawdry and despicable as to bring one such as her to shame? I swear to you that we are man and wife in the eyes of God, the Church, the law, and the world."

"My sister has married a fool," he said in astonishment. "Where is she now?"

"She is in Constantinople," I said. "She is a jester and is fool to the Empress Euphrosyne."

"She's a fool and carrying a fool's child," he wondered. "And you say that you haven't brought her to shame?" He raised his sword again.

"Count Sebastian!" shouted a man behind him. The Count whirled to see a gaudily dressed man with a lute slung behind him. He was a plump fellow with long, flowing hair, meticulously curled about his shoulders. But he held a sword with the confidence of a man who knew how to wield one.

"This fool, dear Count, is a member of the party sent from Constantinople to negotiate terms," he said. "He is, therefore, protected from any molestation. I believe beheading would come under that heading."

"He is negotiating nothing," said the Count. "He is a common fool."

"Then you dishonor yourself in taking a fool seriously," said the man. "Lay down your sword, or you will have me to contend with."

"You're not wearing armor," said Sebastian. "It would not be a fair contest."

"No," agreed the fellow. "But the advantage belongs to me, my dear Count. Or are you unaware of my reputation?"

Sebastian peered more closely at the fellow, then quickly dropped his sword.

"This isn't over," he said to me.

"Nothing ever is," I replied. The soldiers released me.

"Come, Fool," said my rescuer. "I will escort you back to your companions."

I bowed, and we walked away, side by side.

He sheathed his sword and swung his lute around to his chest. Then he played the inverse of the four-note phrase that I had been playing.

"And what name are you using nowadays, Theo?" he said softly.

"Call me Feste," I said. "Your timing, Raimbaut, was impeccable as always."

"But of course," he said. "Tarry a bit by my tent. There is music to be played, and I think that you will recognize the other musicians."

Raimbaut de Vaqueiras in the abundant flesh—a stout fellow in a time of need and one of the most renowned troubadours in the Guild. He had been a fixture at the courts of Orange, Provence, and, for the last decade, Montferrat, where he had become the bosom companion of Boniface. Saved his life on more than one occasion and risked life, limb, and lute following the Marquis into one reckless adventure after another. Raimbaut was in his late forties now, and he pruned the gray from his ringlets fanatically.

Music sounded from within a tent at the rear of the palace. Raimbaut lifted the flap for me to duck under, and there, strumming by candlelight, were Giraut, Gaucelm Faidit, and my old friend Tantalo.

"Look what I found," said Raimbaut. "Had to save his neck from separation once already tonight."

"About time you got here," said Tantalo. "We were getting ready to draw straws as to who was going to swim across the straits to contact you. Have a seat, Theo."

The music kept on while the conversation took place. Raimbaut sat by the entrance, raising his voice in song whenever someone came within earshot of the tent.

"How are things in the city?" asked Tantalo.

"Gearing for siege," I said. "What did you expect?"

"No uprisings on behalf of the child?" exclaimed Giraut. "How disappointing. Young Alexios guaranteed that the city would fall from within the moment his presence became known to it."

"Well, Alexios will have to rethink his position," I said. "The city isn't even aware that he's part of all this. They just think it's a feeble attempt at conquest, and the idea seems to be rallying them. The Emperor has never been more popular than he is right now."

"You mean we've come all this way on the word of a boy, and the Greeks don't know he intends to be their emperor?" chuckled Raimbaut. "How droll!"

"Terribly funny," said Tantalo. "We may all die laughing in a few days."

"What will it take to make the army go away?" I asked.

"A hypothetical question, or are you asking on behalf of someone?" asked Raimbaut.

"You have the ear of Montferrat. We can reach the Emperor. Unofficially, I have been asked to find out what it will take to bribe a Crusade."

"The boy on the throne, and all the money he promised," said Tantalo. "And I don't think that there's enough money in the city to equal his promises."

"But that's nonsense," I said.

"Then there will be war," said Gaucelm sadly.

"What will happen if the troops realize that the Greeks just aren't interested in putting the boy on the throne? Won't that mean something?"

"Maybe," said Tantalo. "But how do we convince them of that? We can't just accept testimonials from a visiting fool."

"Proclaim the boy to the city," I suggested. "Have them display him on a ship, and tell the people who he is. There will be a crowd on the Akropolis anytime you go by. You'll see what kind of reaction he'll get, and that should remove the wool from the eyes of your soldiers."

"Interesting idea," said Tantalo. "Raimbaut, bring it up with Boniface."

"Done," said Raimbaut. "But I'll put it in terms of trying to raise the populace in revolt. He'll like that."

"Is there anything else?" asked Tantalo. "We can't be away from our patrons for too long."

Quickly, I sketched in the events in the Venetian quarter.

"Curious," said Tantalo. "What does that have to do with us?"

"You're with the Venetians," I said. "Who are their contacts in the quarter?"

"I don't know," he confessed frankly. "The Doge plays his own game and doesn't share even half of what he knows with his allies. As far as

I've seen, there has been no contact with the quarter since our arrival, but it's likely that anything that was arranged was done so beforehand. We'll keep our ears open."

"Very well. Play on, my colleagues, and perhaps we'll give a joint performance after peace comes back to the land."

"I hope that we won't have to wait too long," said Giraut.

Raimbaut walked me the rest of the way back to my camp.

"I fear the worst," he said. "Too many soldiers have endured too much for too long just to walk away without a battle. Peace is the least thing in their thoughts."

"Work on them, Raimbaut. We'll see what happens."

I was not present at the morning's parley, but I heard about it as we rode to the dock afterward. Rosso brought the Emperor's puzzled concern over the arrival of the Crusaders and his offer to help provision them for their journey to the Holy Land. Conon de Bethune spoke for the Crusaders, venting poetically tinged defiance. Rosso reminded them of the Pope's renunciation of the Crusaders and his assurances to the Patriarch that he did not want this conquest. Conon declared that they were God's own army and would prevail.

"And they believe that," marveled Rosso as we boarded our galley. "The ease of their battles reinforces that belief at every step. Do you know how many it took to rout Stryphnos and his five hundred? Eighty knights! They cut through the camp like a hailstorm and achieved total victory without losing a man."

The trip across the Bosporos was quick and quiet. They let us off north of the Golden Horn so that Rosso could ride immediately to Blachernae. We passed by the Galata Tower, ducking under the great iron chain that barred entry into the harbor, then crossed the great stone bridge at the rivermouth.

I went straight home to reassure Aglaia that I was still alive. She flung herself into my arms, weeping unreservedly. I told her of my adventures.

"Oh, and your brother sends his regards," I said. I confess that I secretly enjoyed the look of amazement produced by those words.

ELEVEN

*"Whoever could get hold of this youth," said the mar-
quis, "would be well able to go to Constantinople . . .
for this youth is the rightful heir."*

—ROBERT DE CLARI,

THE CONQUEST OF CONSTANTINOPLE

"Sebastian's a Crusader?" she said in shock.

"In the thick of it, spoiling for a fight. So much so that he tried to pick one with me."

"You didn't hurt him, did you?"

"No, dearest. And, by the way, he didn't hurt me, either."

She paced the room, ignoring me.

"He must have really gotten on Olivia's nerves this time," she mused. "Otherwise, she'd never have consented to his leaving."

"He didn't hurt me, either," I repeated.

"I can see that, husband, so don't belabor the point." She stopped, snapping her fingers. "Olivia must have a new lover. Of course, that's it. She sent him off to give herself a clear field."

"Entirely possible. Just like David and Uriah, only she's David."

"Could she want him dead?" she wondered. "Olivia's not that cruel. There's no reason for it. She already has the regency. She has nothing to gain from his death."

"It may be simply that he wanted to go," I said. "He missed out on the last Crusade. Perhaps his ambition to have some adventure overwhelmed any opposition at home. Or that he nobly volunteered to lead the tribute the town owed Venice so that someone else could stay home. Whatever the case may be, he's here."

"The idiot," she murmured. "He'll throw himself into the van and get himself killed." She turned to me. "We've got to stop this."

"Ah. Now that your brother's involved, you don't mind me risking my life."

"That isn't fair!" she protested.

"You objected to my risking it for people I don't know. Many of them, I suspect, are someone's brother or father. Or even father-to-be, although they've taken so long getting here that the only fathers-to-be are probably cuckolds. Still, I was prepared to risk my life stopping this war before I knew your brother was involved. I don't object to continuing on."

"Because this is what fools do," she said slowly.

"Yes."

"All right, lesson learned," she conceded. "I thought that we had left the master-pupil part of our lives behind."

"Everyone needs a refresher course once in a while," I said. "Even me. I'll try to temper my suicidal tendencies with cares toward impending fatherhood. Fair enough?"

"Fair enough."

"What's been happening here?"

"Today was the Feast of the Robe of the Holy Mother over at the Hagia Soros. It was the first time that I had seen that particular relic. Kind of a ratty old thing, but I suppose it's seen better days."

"Although not Biblical ones. That was one of the fake relics brought back by Constantine's mother."

"Well, don't tell Euphy. She takes it very seriously. She practically flattened the Bishop in her haste to take over the ceremony. She held the robe over her head and launched one prayer after another calling upon the Holy Mother to smite the enemies across the waters."

"Mary never struck me as the smiting type."

"Never underestimate the wrath of a woman. All the other ladies joined Euphy, of course, and great was the weeping and gnashing of teeth thereof."

"Sounds like quite a party. Well, despite my longstanding fear of wrathful women, I'm going to chance taking you to bed, if that is agreeable."

She held out her hand.

"Every opportunity left to us, say I," said she.

A pair of Varangians pounded on our door in the morning. This didn't worry us, as Will and Phil wouldn't have bothered with the courtesy. It was Henry and Cnut with an altogether different sort of summons.

"Come on, Feste, you've been challenged," called Henry from the courtyard when I looked out the window. "Throw on your motley and grab your lute. The honor of the city is at stake."

"But I haven't eaten yet," I protested. "And why should I be up before noon?"

"No sympathy here," said Cnut. "We've been up since cock's crow. But perform well, and you shall eat and drink on our company's coin for a fortnight."

"A week, boy, a week," Henry corrected him hurriedly. "But make haste, Fool, and give your lady a kiss from each of us."

"How many of you are there?" called Aglaia from our bed.

"Just the two of us, Mistress Fool," replied Henry.

"Then fetch more Varangians, good Captain, for two kisses is inadequate payment for parting us! I demand a company's kisses."

"A squadron now, and another when I return," I said. "I won't be leaving the city's walls today."

I made good my payment, threw on my motley and makeup, slung my lute around my neck, and joined our friends. We took off at a quick march toward the Akropolis.

"Who has called me out?" I asked, tuning my lute on the run.

"Well, it wasn't you specifically," said Henry. "The Crusaders have sent ten ships floating by the seawalls. They are parading some puny boy back and forth on the deck of the Doge's vessel and are proclaiming him Emperor. And some overdressed minstrel on the prow is demanding the best voice in the city to engage in a singing duel. Naturally, we thought of you."

"I'm flattered."

"Well, Alfonso, that troubadour friend of yours, left town, so you were the next best choice."

"I'm less flattered than I was before. But should I be Constantinople's champion? I'm not even from here."

"Neither are we," said Cnut. "But we'll die defending these walls just the same. All you have to do is sing."

We ran through the Great Palace and climbed a ramp to a tower near the lighthouse. It was a hot, clear day on that third of July, and I could see all the way across to Chrysopolis and Leander's Tower. About fifty yards out was half a tithe of the Venetian fleet, the *Eagle* and another of the great roundships along with a gaggle of smaller vessels filled with archers.

On the raised foredeck of the *Eagle* stood the young Alexios. It was the first time I had ever seen the lad. He inspired neither awe nor confidence, being merely a beardless boy with barely enough strength to support the armor he wore. A servant stood surreptitiously by to steady him on the rolling vessel. I doubted that the youth would ever lift a sword himself in the promised battle, and the crowd gathering on the Akropolis behind me seemed much of the same opinion. That section of the city actually rose higher than the walls defending it, and the masses had their first good view of their putative conqueror.

The *Eagle's* bowsprit extended a good fifty feet beyond the bow. At the very tip of it sat Tantalo in his best checkered tunic and cape, his feet dangling some sixty feet over the water.

There was a blast of trumpets and drums, and a herald stepped forward and bellowed, "Behold, citizens of Constantinople, your true Emperor, Alexios, son and rightful heir of Isaakios the Second, who was basely deposed by the Devil who now pretends to the throne!"

"What's he talking about?" said a man on the rise behind me.

"That's Isaakios's boy," replied his companion. "They're saying he should be Emperor because of what happened to Isaakios."

"But that was years ago," objected the first. "The boy took his time, didn't he?"

"Had to grow up first."

The second man cupped his hands and yelled, "We don't want any Venetian boy prostitutes on the throne. Send him back to the Doge's bedchamber."

This brought hoots of laughter from the Greeks as well as guffaws from the Varangians posted on the seawalls.

It was hard to read the expressions of the Crusaders from so far away, but Alexios seemed to sag a little. The officers surrounding him remained stoic, but the regular soldiers and sailors seemed surprised, even dismayed. They had been led to expect cheering, perhaps an immediate armed uprising. Instead, jeers and catcalls greeted them, their first taste of how daunting a task truly faced them. They had already seen the size and strength of the fortifications around the city. The idea of actually storming them had been suppressed by the hope that they wouldn't need to, but now it was foremost in their minds.

Then there was a brief chord, and we looked back to see Tantalo standing easily at the tip of the bowsprit, lute at the ready.

"Have you brought your champion, Greeks?" he called. "I espy motley amidst the armor. Is a fool the best you could find in this vast city?"

"The best fool in all Christendom," I shouted back. "Shall we match wits in song?"

"With that voice?" scoffed Tantalo. "A nightingale will not consort with a crow."

"Yet when the battle is over, the nightingales lie dead on the field while the crows hop about, pecking at their eyes. I am for you, signore. My gage is in my hand." I held up my lute to the cheering of the throng behind me.

"A *tenso*, is it?" cried Tantalo, using the old troubadour word for these trials by song. "Very well, I accept."

There was cheering by the Crusaders, albeit without the enthusiasm of the home crowd. Tantalo had a distinct advantage in this contest. He had had his entire journey to prepare for it, while I would have to improvise my offering on the spot in whatever style he chose. I waited, hoping he would pick a verse that I could match easily.

He began.

"O Greek,
I speak
Of your prospects which are bleak.
You face a foe
On fields of woe
With an army oh so weak.
Your fleet won't float.
Your very fittest boat
Is far from young
And now has sprung
A mighty leak.
If you take the field

[149]

Then you soon shall yield
For the shield
That you wield
Is antique.
By sword and drum
In Kingdom Come
Your future you will seek."

He finished with a flourish and looked at me expectantly.

"Bastard," I muttered.

"He's good," said Henry begrudgingly.

"Is it too late to send for Alfonso?" I asked.

"Come on, Feste," urged Cnut.

I stepped to the edge of the tower, trying to get the interior rhymes together as I struck the opening chord:

"My word.
I've heard
Of lyrics less absurd
From drunken boys.
And braver noise
From the roisterings of a bird.
The field is yours;
We'd rather stay indoors,
And watch you fall
Before this wall.
That is assured.
Enjoy your final meal,
And then come sup on steel,
'Til you feel
That this zeal

Is cured.
You praise your boat
Because it can float.
Well, friend, so can a turd."

Howls from the Varangians. Henry clouted me so hard on the back that I would have gone over the edge of the tower but for Cnut's quick grab.

Not exactly a proper troubadour sentiment from either of us, but this wasn't a musical tournament at Fécamp or the Courts of Love—it was a declaration of hostilities. And I was a fool, not a troubadour. The higher Tantalo would go in his songs, the baser would be my reply.

Tantalo bowed to me from his perch.

"Well sung, Fool," he shouted. "We'll call it a draw for now. The challenge will be renewed when Alexios sits on the throne."

"He sits there now," I replied.

"I like that," he said. "You ask no quarter, and you give none, as we say in Venice. Well, I must bid you farewell. As Odysseus said to the Cyclops, remember my name!"

A rock sailed over our heads, splashing well short of the *Eagle*. Others followed, the crowd surging forward with glee and vituperations. The fleet's oars bit the water as the aspiring Emperor was hustled below decks. The ships pulled slowly away, back to the safety of Skutari.

Only rocks were thrown. No one facing a siege was about to waste a vegetable.

"All right, Cnut, I'm going to feed this poor fool," said Henry. "Keep an eye to the north, lad. If you see more than ten ships, sound the alarum."

We walked down the ramp as the watchmen relayed their calls from tower to tower, up and down the seawalls.

"Your opposite has a good voice," commented Henry as we walked towards the Hodegon bastion where the Varangians were quartered.

"One of the best," I agreed.

"You know him?"

"We've crossed paths a few times," I said.

"Was one of those times two nights ago?" asked Henry.

"Why do you want to know that?" I asked.

"I have no great objection to dying in battle," he said. "But I like to know that it was for something worth dying for."

"I thought soldiers just followed orders," I said.

"And who gives you yours?"

"I'm not a soldier, Captain, I'm an entertainer. I don't get orders, I take requests."

We entered the garrison and raided the larder.

"My point being," continued Henry with his mouth full, "that if there are secret negotiations toward a truce, but the powers that be still want to put on a good show for the locals, then I'm not a soldier anymore. I'm also an entertainer."

"Lord knows there's no honor in that."

"No offense, Feste. So, what's going on?"

"There's no truce, Captain."

"Any prospects on the horizon?"

"There's nothing on the horizon except Venetian ships."

"Then war it is," he said, satisfied.

"What do you think of this boy, Alexios?" I asked.

"What's he to us?" he said. "We've sworn an oath to the Emperor."

"As you did to Isaakios before him."

He was silent, swishing the ale around in his cup and watching the whorls.

"We were in the city when that happened," he said. "He was in Kypsella. By the time word came, there was nothing we could do."

"You could have honored your oath," I said. "Rose against his usurper."

"Another pointless battle," he said.

"How so? I'm not disagreeing with you, but why did your oath mean so little then?"

"Because Isaakios had been blinded," he replied. "We were told that according to local custom a blind man could not sit on the Byzantine throne. We had therefore been absolved of our oath to Isaakios."

"Who told you that?" I asked.

"The leaders of the garrison then were Will and Phil," he said. "I believe that you know them."

"The sources of some of my more interesting requests," I said dryly.

"I thought as much. They've done quite well for themselves since persuading us that passivity was honorable." He drank his ale. "To the Emperor," he muttered.

"To the Emperor," I echoed. "What do you think of him? Just between us."

"How do I know it stays just between us?"

"I give you the word of a fool."

He rinsed his cup in a water barrel and put it back on the shelf.

"I've heard things about you," he said.

"What sort of things?"

"That you play a different game than the rest of us."

"A jester plays many kinds of games. You've known me for a year, Captain. What do you think I am?"

"Someone who has saved some lives," he said.

"A worthy virtue."

"And ended others," he added.

I shrugged.

"But the others were worth ending," he concluded.

"Then still virtuous, if not exactly worthy," I observed.

"They say you saved Isaakios. Is that true?"

I nodded.

"Do you visit him often?" he asked curiously. "He's in the Chalke Prison now."

"I know. I see him about twice a moon, with the knowledge and blessing of the Emperor. Brotherly love or guilt, I know not which."

"A captain of the Varangians can't pay social calls like that," he said. "Next time you visit, tell him that Henry wishes him well."

"I will," I promised.

He picked up his helmet. "And, in answer to your question, the Emperor can go hang himself for all any of us cares." He put the helmet on and left.

I rinsed my cup and ambled across the Augustaion, trying to gauge the mood of the citizens. For the most part, they were chattering away. The sentiments I picked up were unremittingly anti-Venetian, and the return of Alexios did not impress them the slightest. He was perceived as a puppet of the Doge, although the reality was that more than one hand pulled his strings.

There were two Alexioses and one throne, I mused. If neither went away, then there would be war. The old one would not leave, and the young one could not. And that was Ranieri cutting across my field of view and interrupting my train of thought.

I had my cloak on in a trice. He had not marked my motley, fortunately, and in the great throng of people in constant motion it was not hard to follow him unobserved.

He was heading back to the Great Palace but veered to the right before reaching the Chalke Prison by the entrance. He cut over past the public entrance to the Hippodrome. As he did, a small, pale rabbit of a man came through a small grove of mulberry trees, looking around nervously. I hung back, watching some grooms exercising a group of racehorses in a paddock nearby. The two talked briefly. I saw a small pouch emerge from Ranieri's cloak and a small wicker box handed over in exchange. Then the two separated, Ranieri walking behind me as I chatted with a stableboy, my hat concealing my face. The rabbit went into the building that once housed the old baths of Zeuxippos.

Once again, I found myself with two men to follow, only this time there was no Plossus to help me. I decided to tail Ranieri and check on the rabbit later.

The Horologion showed noon as we passed it. The Venetian walked briskly through the covered portion of the Mese, not even bothering to check and see if he was being followed. I took my normal precautions nevertheless, staying safely back a good hundred paces while checking to make sure that no one was following me.

Yet, for all that, I was to learn nothing further. Ranieri simply entered the Venetian quarter and resumed business at his table in the embolum, chatting casually with everyone in the room, especially Ruzzini. I saw no further transactions with the wicker box he had obtained by Zeuxippos. I watched as well as I could, but hanging about looking from the outside was risking discovery. I gave up and left.

First order of business upon my return home was the second part of my payment of kisses to my wife, which left us both breathless and giddy. It was my turn to cook, and as the others arrived, I filled them in on the events of the morning.

"A wicker box?" wondered Rico. "About how big?"

"The size of your hand, my friend," I said.

He held his palm before his eyes.

"Not a document," he said. "Too little to be a spice of any value."

"A jewel," guessed Aglaia. "Or a ring."

"A seal of office," offered Plossus. "Useful for forging orders and sowing confusion during the upcoming war."

[155]

"That sounds promising," I said. "And that would make sense for someone working in the Great Palace. There's mostly governmental offices there now. Anyone know what Zeuxippos is used for nowadays?"

"Never been there," said Rico. "Hasn't been used for baths in decades."

"I thought it was a museum," said Aglaia.

"No, I think it's now a factory of some kind," said Plossus. "But I have no idea what they make there."

"Well, we'll have to investigate further. I don't know if this has anything to do with Bastiani's death, but we haven't much else to go on."

"If only we knew who the Crusaders' contact in Venice is," mused Aglaia.

"No hope of that from our colleagues," I said.

"How is that?" she asked.

"Because of what Tantalo said after the *tenso*."

"Yes, I wanted to ask you about that," said Plossus. "What were his exact words again?"

" 'You ask no quarter, and you give none, as we say in Venice,' " I quoted. "Then he said, 'Well, I must bid you farewell. As Odysseus said to the Cyclops, remember my name!' "

"The first part is obvious," said Plossus. "He used 'Venice' and 'quarter' in the same sentence. But does that mean that we were supposed to find someone named Odysseus there?"

"Or Ulysses?" asked Rico.

"Maybe a man with one eye," suggested Aglaia.

"We can stop the search before we start," I said. "Odysseus did use his own name when he and his men rowed away from the Cyclops's shore. But Tantalo is rarely that obvious. As the story went, before he escaped from the monster's cave, he had told him that his name was Nobody, so that when the blinded creature called to his fellows and tried to tell them what happened, he told them that Nobody had done this to him."

"And so they left him, laughing," remembered Aglaia.

"Yes. I think what Tantalo's trying to say is that nobody is the Crusaders' contact in the Venetian quarter."

TWELVE

Nos fom austor et ylh foro aigro, e cassem los si cum lops fait mouto. (We were hawks and they were herons, and we chased them as the wolf chases the sheep.)
—RAIMBAUT DE VAQUEIRAS, "EPIC LETTER"
(TRANS. JOSEPH LINSKILL)

The fleet kept to Skutari the next day. I wanted to speak with Philoxenites again, so I joined Rico and my wife on their walk to Blachernae.

"If there is no Crusader contact in the Venetian quarter, then what exactly are we looking for?" asked Aglaia. "And don't tell me Nobody. That was a tired joke when Homer used it."

"Sing to me, Muse, of the wrath of Enrico Dandolo," intoned Rico. "No, it lacks the poetic ring. I'll leave the balladry to Raimbaut and company. Maybe they can turn this farce into something pretty."

"Bastiani was still an informant," I said. "That's frequently reason enough. Something is going on there. That weapons cache tells us that."

"But that may just be for defending the quarter," said Rico. "We haven't found any conclusive evidence of a plot, let alone a murder."

"Shall we give up?" I asked.

Aglaia shot me an astonished look.

"I've never heard you say that before," she said.

"I bring it up as a possibility. One death goes unexplained. The world won't come to an end."

She sighed. "Let's continue. I think that there's something there, although I don't know what it has to do with us."

"Rico?"

He shrugged. "It passes the time."

"An enthusiastic endorsement. Very well. We'll go on."

When Rico and I came to the throne room, the Emperor was seated on his sawhorse while his servants wheeled him around an enormous model of the city and its surroundings. His generals, minus Michael Stryphnos, looked on intently.

"Ah, Feste!" he called when he noticed me. "I heard of your noble exploits facing down the fleet. Well done, Fool. Here's gold for you."

He tossed me a small pouch. I bowed.

"But all he did was sing," commented a general.

"He stood tall and defeated his man," barked the Emperor. "He's the first hero of the war. Maybe I should make him my commander."

"The men won't follow a fool," protested the general.

"Not another one, anyway," I said.

"Well, back to work," said the Emperor. "Where will they make their landing? What's your guess?"

"They won't attack the seawalls," said Laskaris. "There's no room to land at either the straits or Marmara. The Golden Horn is blocked by the chain. That leaves either the north shore or south of the city. My guess is north. It's an easier landing."

"So, that's where we'll wait for them," said the Emperor. "Archers, crossbows, and Varangians at the beach, and petrarries set up on the stone bridge. If we have to fall back, we'll make our stand there."

"What about the Imperial Guard?" asked their commander.

"The Imperial Guard guards the Imperial Person," said the Emperor. "You stay with me. Do we have the Pisan and Genoese representatives here?"

Two men stepped forward and bowed.

"Gentlemen, your fortunes are tied to my own," said the Emperor. "If we prevail, there will certainly be no more Venetian trade in this city. You would find that situation advantageous, would you not?"

They agreed, bowing some more.

"So, we need your help in preserving our empire. Say, five hundred men in armor apiece. And don't tell me you don't have armor. I know what goes on in the quarters as well as any man. Hm?"

"We will be happy to defend our quarters against attack," said the Pisan representative.

"Oh, no need for that," said the Emperor. "You've got that lovely high seawall covered with Varangians protecting you, not to mention the chain across the harbor. No, I'm going to send you somewhere more useful. Get your men together and await my orders at the Galata Tower."

The representatives looked at each other uneasily, but bowed and left without any protest.

"How is the mood of the city?" asked the Emperor.

"They have rallied behind you as they have never rallied before," said Philoxenites smoothly. "They have every confidence that you will drive the invaders back into the sea."

"Good, good," said the Emperor, pleased.

He went back to his battle plans. Philoxenites nodded to me and left. I followed him.

"What do you think of his tactics?" he asked me when we reached his offices.

"I'm not a general," I said.

"Neither am I," he replied. "Neither, I think, is he. It's the plan of a timid man, not a hero."

"Heroes die," I said.

"Sometimes. But sometimes they achieve victory. I have my doubts that the Emperor will manage the same. The citizens are wondering openly how he managed to let the navy dwindle so badly, and the news about the five hundred knights lost won't stay secret for long. The morale could drop like a stone in a moment."

"Therefore what?"

He closed the door.

"How was your meeting with your contacts?"

"We met. I suggested that they break the news to the troops that the boy had no support in the city. His reception at the seawalls should have confirmed that nicely."

"Yet they still may come," he said. "Did you learn anything else?"

"One thing I wanted to tell you," I said. "There is no Crusader contact in the Venetian quarter."

"What?" he exclaimed. "Impossible. Bastiani himself was one."

"Or at least that's what he wanted you to think," I said. "A ruse to obtain your patronage, perhaps."

"Maybe," he said. "But there must be someone inside waiting for the Doge's orders."

"I have seen Ranieri acting oddly," I said. "I followed him to the Great Palace yesterday."

"Interesting," he said. "Where did he go?"

"He met with someone who came out of Zeuxippos," I said. "I don't know the man."

He looked at me and started laughing.

"Fool, you disappoint me," he said. "Of course he met with someone from Zeuxippos. It houses the Imperial Silk Factory. Why wouldn't a silk merchant be going there?"

Chagrin and disappointment. One of the few leads I had, shot down in an instant.

"Well, you've solved that mystery," I said. "It doesn't get me any closer to finding Bastiani's murderer."

"That may no longer be a priority," he said. "I may need you to contact your friends again. I want you to sound them out about that final possibility we once discussed."

"Which you don't want to say directly anymore."

"No."

"And how am I supposed to contact them? I can't travel to Skutari without the aid of an Imperial galley, and they all seem to be busy at the moment."

"I wouldn't worry about that," he said. "I have a feeling the Crusaders will be meeting you halfway."

Plossus burst into our room the next morning, shouting, "Something's happening!"

We threw on our motley and dashed up the steps to the roof, from where we could see over the seawalls. The mangonels were in action, launching huge stones over the Golden Horn.

We could hear trumpets and tabors sounding from the fleet in the distance. The horse transports were approaching the Galatan shore, towing the giant transports behind them. The smaller galleys were swarming with archers, with more on barges pushed ahead of them. They soon began launching one volley of arrows after another, quickly clearing the beach.

The mangonels mounted on the ships joined in, launching stones at the Greeks and their allies. As they did, huge ramps lowered from the sides of the horse transports into the shallows, and armored knights, already mounted on their steeds, were led into the waves, lances held high.

All around us, the rooftops and towers were packed with Constantinopolitans, watching with fascination as the morning sun reflected off the gathering armor.

"I can't see," muttered Rico irritably.

"Half a moment," said Plossus, and he dashed downstairs. He soon returned, carrying his stilts, and handed one to me. We clasped hands and pulled ourselves up, bracing against each other. Then we reached down with our free hands and pulled the dwarf up to our shoulders.

"Much obliged," said Rico.

"What about me?" protested Aglaia.

"You're pregnant," said Rico. "Shut up and let me watch the show."

"Here come the Greeks," said Plossus as they marched toward the beach to the accompanying cheers of the city.

"Here come the Crusaders," said Rico, as the horsemen lowered their lances and charged the oncoming army.

"And there go the Greeks," I said.

The prospect of imminent skewering proved too much for the Emperor. He turned and fled, the Imperial Guard trailing him, the archers and crossbowmen panicking as they were left unprotected. Shields, swords, and armor were discarded in their wake as they were chased all the way through their abandoned pavilions. The Crusaders cut down dozens, stopping only at the approach to the stone bridge when a hail of bolts from the crossbowmen greeted them.

The Varangians tried to hold firm, abetted by the Pisans and Genoese, but the rest of the Crusaders had landed by this point. They drove the defenders through the Jewish enclave at Galata until they were forced to retreat into the tower itself. So many pressed to get in that the doors could not be closed. Before the tower was finally secured, the Crusaders killed dozens, and more were crushed to death by the frenzy of their comrades seeking refuge. The Varangians inside the tower finally drove the Crusaders back by hurling stones from the top, and the doors were barred from within.

The rooftop audience was silent. With the exception of the Galata Tower, the Crusaders had taken the entire north shore of the Golden Horn up to the stone bridge, inflicting many casualties on the defenders. They had done it in less than an hour.

They spent the rest of the day setting up camp and unloading siege engines. The entire shoreline of the harbor was dotted with standards and pavilions. I marked where Boniface erected his pavilion near the Jewish quarter. I figured the troubadours would be nearby.

We brought our midday meal up to the rooftop and ate there, watching the activity across the way. Four fools, eating in silence.

"What next?" asked Aglaia when we had finished. "Will they attempt to take the bridge tomorrow?"

"There won't be a bridge tomorrow," Plossus pointed out. We looked in that direction. The Greeks, under the cover of the crossbowmen, were frantically destroying the bridge, heaving the stones into the mouth of the harbor.

"The next nearest crossing is several leagues up," I said. "I don't think they'll risk sending their army that far from the mangonels. They'll probably spend a few days moving them within closer range of the city."

"Looks like we'll be in range then," said Aglaia.

"They'll be going after the walls and the gates," I said. "They won't waste stones on houses. What do you want, Will?"

The others turned to see the two Varangians standing on the roof behind us.

"We're losing our touch, Phil," said Will. "They heard us coming."

"Good view from here," observed Phil. "We were in one of the towers by the Genoese quarter. You could hear the Imperial Guard screaming in terror all the way from the other side."

"But our boys stayed and fought," said Will proudly. "That was Rolf's squad keeping them busy. Good man, that Rolf. We're going across tonight to join him."

"Good luck," I said.

"You're missing our point," said Phil. "*We* are going across."

We looked at each other a bit uncomfortably.

"How many of us is we?" asked Rico.

"Just Feste and us," said Will. "Reinforcements are going to sneak over to the tower after sundown. Our job is to get Feste to the Crusader camp on the way."

"And how am I supposed to get back?" I asked.

"You know, the topic never really came up," said Phil. "But I guess a clever fellow like you can figure something out."

"A clever fellow would not go in the first place," said Aglaia, looking at me pointedly.

"I guess I'm not that clever," I said.

"Sundown at the main Pisan wharf," said Will. "Do you need anything? Weapons? Disguises?"

"Just a large wineskin," I said.

"A wineskin?" said Phil, smirking. "What for?"

"You don't think I would do this sober, do you?"

"At sundown, then," said Will, and they left.

"How are you going to get back?" demanded Aglaia.

"I'll figure something out, despite my deficiency of wit," I said. "If I have to, I'll just keep going north and take the next bridge up."

"What if we're under siege by then?" she asked.

"They don't have enough time or men to surround the entire city," I said. "I'll loop around to the far end and come in near the Golden Gate."

"When's the last time you ran that far?" said Plossus.

"The last time there was a war coming up behind me," I said.

As night fell across the Golden Horn, a squadron of Varangians and I slipped through a gate in the seawall and quickly filled a dozen long-boats.

We were shielded from observations from the opposite shore by a Pisan roundship that had been idled by the raising of the chain. The

Varangians had chosen this point for crossing because there was a shallow dip on the Galatan side that would give them some concealment as they broke for the tower.

The oarsmen propelled us across the Golden Horn quickly. Will, Phil, and I were on the second boat. The squadron leapt to the shore and vanished, cloaks around their armor and cloth over their axe-blades to prevent them from reflecting any moonlight. The moment the last man landed, the boats took off and returned to the safety of the city.

My two escorts peeled off from the main group and motioned me toward a small city of pavilions that had sprung up during the day.

"There's a patrol about a hundred paces away," whispered Phil. "We could probably distract them for you."

"On the contrary, let me distract them for you," I said.

"What makes you think you can do that?" asked Will.

"Just give me the wineskin," I said.

They shrugged and handed it to me. I took a long gulp, then splashed a little on my face and motley. Not the first winestain on the latter, and I prayed silently that it wouldn't be the last.

"See you after the war, gentlemen," I said, and I climbed up the slope and started staggering in the direction of the pavilions.

A normal man who tries to sneak into an armed camp will be discovered and executed as a spy. A fool, on the other hand, is a harmless creature, as we all know. Especially a drunken fool bellowing a sea chanty at the top of his lungs,

"*Fare thee well now, milady, my ship leaves at dawn.*
I knew when I paid thee that I soon would be gone.
Though the weather may be stormy,
And I know you adore me,
The sea lies before me, and I must sail on."

A patrol was upon me in no time, a well-armored sextet with Flemish colors.

"What the hell are you doing?" demanded their leader.

I stared at him stupidly. "What the hell does it sound like I'm doing?" I said. "I'm singing.

"We'll travel to Outremer where Our Savior was born.
Then we'll carry silks and leathers from the great Golden Horn,
To the country of Isis,
And we'll come back with spices,
And maybe the price is too low—we'll sail on."

"Stop that," he said. "What are you doing here?"

"I'm singing!" I shouted. *"A good man stays pious—"*

"I said, stop that," he interrupted me. "Why are you singing here?"

"I live here," I said. "What are you doing here?"

He stared at me.

"You live here?"

"In Estanor," I said. "Over there. I took a room with a Jewish family. I've been drinking, and I need to lie down on my own bed. Want some?" I pulled the wineskin from my shoulder and offered it around.

"Search the fool," he commanded. "If he has no weapons, let him go."

Two of his men frisked me, and I started giggling.

"Please, stop," I gasped. "I'm ticklish."

They were grinning, but finished the job.

"Nothing, sir," said one.

The officer was looking at me carefully.

"Aren't you the fool who sang at us from the walls?" he asked.

"I am, sir," I said, puffing out my chest proudly. "And I've been drinking on that glorious exploit ever since."

"Then you are with the enemy," he said.

"No, sir!" I protested vehemently. "When the Greeks pay me to sing, I sing for the Greeks. When the Crusaders pay me to sing, I sing for them."

"And who are you singing for now?"

"Myself, sir. Sometimes a fool has to assert his independence.

"A good man stays pious, and so does his spawn.
He'll keep to his faith though the mouths of Hell yawn.
That kind of behavior
May gratify Our Savior,
But this side of the grave you're going to have to sail on."

"Tell you what, Fool," said the officer. "The payment for passage is that you sing a verse for the glorious Crusaders who stand before you. That will cleanse you of the taint of singing for the Greeks."

"A fair price, and may the good Lord bless thee for it," I said.

"Tempests will toss me, and the Fates change the tide.
And pirates and cannibals are along for the ride.
So drive back the invaders,
And hang high the raiders,
But if you call them Crusaders, then God's on their side."

"Not the most pleasing sentiment, but close enough," he said. "Pass, Fool."

I saluted them, and staggered on. When I was safely beyond them, I fished my dagger out of the wineskin and slid it into my sleeve.

A low whistle came from a tent as I passed through the camp. The flap opened, and I saw Tantalo beckoning to me. I ducked under.

My colleagues were all there. Giraut had a bandage wrapped around his head, and Gaucelm's left arm was in a sling. They looked grimy and pale in the flickering light of the single candle in the center of the tent.

"Well, you've been busy today," I observed.

"Shut up, Theo. We're not in the mood for banter," said Raimbaut. "What do you want?"

"I carry a proposal," I said. "A possible solution."

"You had one the other day," said Giraut. "It didn't work."

"This one might. It has the benefit of stopping Alexios's claim to the throne while allowing the Crusaders to be faithful to their oaths."

"Let's hear it," said Tantalo.

"The boy's claim is through Isaakios. The Crusaders are here to overthrow the Emperor in support of that claim."

"And to gain as much loot, territory, and trading concessions as they can from this mission of mercy," said Tantalo.

"What if Isaakios was restored to the throne?" I asked.

"What if pigs fly?" scoffed Raimbaut. "That's not going to happen."

"But what if it does?" I persisted.

They glanced at each other.

"What are you talking about?" asked Giraut quietly. "An assassination?"

"That would just enrage the Greeks," said Gaucelm. "They wouldn't go along with Isaakios just because the Emperor's dead."

"I'm not talking about an assassination," I said. "I'm talking about the legitimate restoration of Isaakios with the support of the city."

"You're talking nonsense," said Raimbaut. "You have no way of arranging that."

"But if I did?"

"Then Alexios would defer to his father," he said impatiently. "Now, let's leave the dreamworld, shall we, Theo?"

"What is the matter with all of you?" I asked.

"Theo, we appreciate all the efforts you've made," said Raimbaut. "But this war cannot be stopped."

"You've given up," I said.

"We tried everything we could, Theo," said Tantalo dejectedly. "And we failed. That happens sometimes."

"But then you try something else," I said.

"Theo, I don't think that you thought this through entirely," said Raimbaut. "Let's look at the situation. What is your goal?"

"To bring about peace," I replied.

"Laudable," he said. "And if that isn't possible, what then?"

"To resolve this conflict with the least possible amount of bloodshed," I said, chafing a bit under his interrogation.

"Admirable," he said. "And if that isn't possible, what then?"

I was silent. The expressions ranged from defeat on the faces of Giraut and Gaucelm to pity on Tantalo to triumph on Raimbaut.

"What then, Theo?" repeated Raimbaut. "You never took the next step: assuming there will be a full-scale war, who shall be the victor?"

"The Guild—" I began.

"The Guild said nothing about that!" he shouted furiously. The others tried to hush him, but he ignored them and continued. "Consider the situation of four poor troubadours, stranded with an outnumbered army, starving and desperate. Troubadours don't just sit and watch battles from a safe distance like jesters. We're soldiers. Remember the story of Taillefer, who marched into the Battle of Hastings while juggling swords and singing heroic lays? That is our fate. We either win or we die. Given that particular range of choices, forgive me, Theo, for wanting to win."

"And if you win, the Crusaders take the traditional three days of rape, slaughter, and pillage," I said. "Does your fate encompass that pleasurable prospect as well?"

"Of course not," he said. "But, God willing—"

"How dare you invoke His name on behalf of this infernal enterprise," I said coldly. "You've forgotten why we're here, Raimbaut. You're despicable. You've been with these avaricious idiots so long that you've become one of them."

"Easy, Theo," cautioned Tantalo.

"Do you go along with this decision?" I said, turning to him. "You're the one in charge."

"We took a vote," said Gaucelm weakly.

"A vote?" I said derisively. "Was it unanimous? Three to one? Do the four of us in the city get to vote, too? Wait, I forgot. You can't raise your hand when you're dead."

"It was unanimous, Theo," said Tantalo. "If there was any other way—"

"I've brought you another."

"But you can't do it," he protested.

"Perhaps not," I said. "But I am going to try, anyway. At least, I'll die knowing that I'm no traitor."

Raimbaut drew his sword.

"No one calls me that," he said.

"Tell him, Tantalo," I said quietly.

"Put up your sword, Raimbaut," urged Tantalo.

"For what? A fool? Doesn't he know who I am?"

"I know who you are," said Tantalo. "I know what you can do. But I know Theo, and you don't. If you take him on, you're dead. If all four of us took him on together, it would be the same."

Raimbaut looked at him in disbelief.

"And I, for one, will not be joining this particular fray," added Tantalo.

"Will you all stop this ridiculous posturing?" said Giraut wearily. "My head hurts enough."

[171]

"Put up your sword, Raimbaut," said Gaucelm. "There's enough blood to spill without adding that of a fool."

Raimbaut rammed his sword back into its scabbard, then stormed out of the tent.

"I'll leave you two to rest up," said Tantalo. "Theo, come with me."

We walked quietly through the camp. Around us, fires were dying down, and soldiers were grabbing what sleep they could. Of those who could not, some prayed, some paced, and some stared motionless to the east, waiting for the first glimmering of sunlight.

"How were you planning to get back?" he asked.

"I was going to head upstream to the next crossing," I said.

He shook his head. "You won't get through that way tonight. They're not letting any civilians out. You had better stay with me. Depending on events, I might be able to slip you out tomorrow."

I agreed, reluctantly. I was worried about being caught on the wrong side of a siege. The wrong side being defined as whichever side my wife wasn't on.

Tantalo's tent was near the Doge's pavilion.

"Did Dandolo actually come ashore?" I asked.

"He was the first one to leap from the ship," he said, shaking his head in wonder. "Blind or not, ninety or not, he led his men."

"Greed and folly make leaders and followers," I said as we entered the tent.

"Any luck on that murder you're looking into?" he asked.

"No," I said. "Thanks for telling me about Nobody."

"Actually, since our little songfest, I picked up a bit of information," he said.

"What?"

"Unfortunately, I came in at the tail end of a conversation, but I overheard one of the Doge's advisors referring to the Venetian quarter, and the Doge said, 'Don't worry, the Silk Man will take care of it.'"

"The Silk Man? And that was all?"

"I'm afraid so," he said. "And I was wondering if it was your dead man. They wouldn't know about that here."

"Maybe," I said. "Well, it's something, at least. Thanks."

"Better get some sleep while you can," he said. "Things will be a bit busy tomorrow."

I stretched out on the ground, my lute beside me.

"Do you really think that you can topple the Emperor by yourself?" he asked.

"Not by myself," I said. "But I have an idea and some interesting allies."

"I hope it's enough," he said. He started putting on his armor as I drifted off.

I snapped awake shortly before dawn as trumpets blared around me. Tantalo was already at the opening of the tent, sword in hand.

"They're attacking from the tower!" he cried. "Get out!"

I grabbed my lute and ran with him, then pulled up short.

The reinforced squadrons poured from the tower and charged the camp, while archers launched arrows from the top. But the Crusaders were prepared and were already counterattacking from both the north and the south.

Which left me in a bit of a quandary, since I was cut off from escape on all sides. There was nowhere to go but back toward the Golden Horn, and I had no idea how bad it was between here and there. But with arrows and stones landing perilously close, I saw no reason to tarry.

"I'm off," I said. "Take care of yourself."

"And you. Nice work at the *tenso*, by the way. I wanted to tell you that."

He put on his helmet and charged into battle.

The Varangian sortie had limited effect on the invaders and proved disastrous to the defenses of the tower. The axe-bearers had charged too far out and could not retreat safely. Troops under the colors of Amiens managed to fight their way between them and the tower, cutting them off.

Some of the Varangians tried to hack their way back but were cut down. The rest realized their situation and decided to make for the Golden Horn, while the Crusaders came at them from every angle.

In other words, the battle was heading right toward me. So much for sitting and watching from a safe distance.

I had hoped that there would be boats waiting to rescue the troops, but the city had been taken by surprise by the sortie from the tower. The first stones from the seawalls began crashing down indiscriminately in the center of the battle. Several longboats were beginning to pull away from the Pisan wharf, but I didn't think there would be enough time for me to wait for them. It was a five-hundred-yard swim, one I could make under normal circumstances, but arrows were raining from all directions.

Then a crossbow bolt struck just by my foot, and I panicked. I looked north and saw nothing but Crusaders. South of me, the great chain was swaying gently across the mouth of the harbor. The section nearest me was about ten feet up, except for where a large boulder jutted out of the ground.

Well, I've walked across ropes that were a fraction of the width of those huge iron lengths. I ran to the boulder, gathered myself, and leapt high, getting one hand on the lower part of a link. I pulled myself up until I could get my other hand on the top and swung my body onto the chain.

A number of Varangians saw me and tried to duplicate the feat, but their armor weighed them down. Those that reached the chain couldn't climb on top and resorted to pulling themselves hand-over-hand across the harbor. Several of the longboats peeled away from the wharf and made for them. Meanwhile, the Crusader archers and crossbowmen started directing their missiles at us.

If this had been a typical fool's performance on a rope, I would have danced across, pausing for some casual acrobatics, amazing all with my poise and balance. But this was the performance of a man fleeing death, and I had no scruples about steadying myself with my hands as I clambered along. Some fifteen feet beneath me, the waves were beginning to swell. The longboats reached the chain behind me, and the luckier Varangians managed to drop into the boats. Others missed, and their armor dragged them under the waves and out of sight.

Then I heard a mighty roar from both shores and looked to see the cause.

The *Eagle*, three banks of oars on each side pulling mightily, was bearing down on the Golden Horn. The ship's prow was encased in iron plates, coming to a sharp edge that split the air before it. It was coming right at me.

I jettisoned whatever caution I had left and ran, crouching, the rest of the length of the chain. About thirty feet from the seawall, the chain rose toward its end, fixed in the wall by the Gate of Eugenios. Right as I reached that point, there was a screech from the pits of Hell as metal hit metal. The chain rocked wildly beneath me. I threw myself onto it, holding on for dear life.

The center could not hold. The links split with a thunderous snap, and the two broken ends fell away into the water. I rode my half, swinging toward the city on a crazy trapeze, until the weight of the links hitting the ground dragged it to a stop.

Behind me, longboats and a few pathetic galleys were scattered and broken like kindling, spilling soldiers and oarsmen into the water. The oarsmen made it back to the wharves. The soldiers didn't.

The rest of the fleet followed the *Eagle*, nestling into the wharves on the opposite shore as if they were home.

I pulled myself up the remaining links until I reached the top of the seawall. A group of Varangians were watching the slaughter of their brethren with looks of horror. Cnut was one of them, and he was the first to look down and see me, exhausted and terrified, trying to get over the top of the wall. With one massive hand he grabbed the back of my tunic and hauled me up.

"Feste!" he exclaimed in astonishment.

"Thanks, friend Cnut," I gasped. "Don't worry about my living off your squad this week. We're even."

I looked back to see the Crusaders displaying their flags from the top of the Galata Tower.

They had taken the Golden Horn.

THIRTEEN

A merry heart doeth good like a medicine: but a broken spirit drieth the bones.
—PROVERBS 18:22

When my first husband sailed off with most of the men of Orsino on the Third Crusade, we stood on the dock, weeping copiously, and waved our handkerchiefs until the vessel was a dot on the horizon and our arms were sore. Then I invited the rest of the wives back to the villa for a consolatory dinner. We ended up getting rip-roaring drunk in our efforts to assuage our sorrows and decided to repeat the affair monthly until the men returned. When our steward died and I took over managing the affairs of the town, these dinners became informal town councils, and I daresay that we women ran the place better than it had ever been run.

When my second husband rowed across the Golden Horn, I did not stand on the dock, waving my handkerchief. I was angry at him, even though I knew his motivations were of the highest and that I would have done the same. But, after a sleepless night alone in our bed, I once again sought the company of women. This time, however, we had no control of our situation. A pity. Once again, I think we would have done a better job of running things.

Wine still had its place, fortunately or unfortunately. Euphy had started drinking before sunrise, and by the time I arrived was well into her third or fourth high dudgeon of the morning.

"Turned and ran!" she cried, flinging a gold goblet at the assorted ladies. "That's the Alexios I married. A coward. A frightened deer, fleeing at the first sign of a lowered lance. He lost the city yesterday, ladies. We might as well start throwing ourselves off the walls, like the women of Troy, to avoid dishonor." She pulled out a dagger from the folds of her robe and waved it around as the women ducked and scattered. "By the Holy Mother, I swear I will use this on the first Frenchman who dares to lay a lustful hand on me. They're all rapists. There's not a female, young or old, who they won't hesitate to violate, and all thanks to my husband, who can't even find safety in numbers. Where's my goblet?"

A maidservant dashed to retrieve it and handed it to the Empress, trembling all the while. Euphy filled it from a pitcher by her throne, sat down, and drank the wine in one gulp.

"I wouldn't have run," she muttered. "I know the responsibilities of leadership, even if I'm merely a woman. I may not have been to the purple born, but by God I know how to wear the mantle better than anyone who has ever sat on this throne. Or on his!"

She refilled her cup and emptied it in seconds.

"Has he returned?" she cried.

"Yes, milady," said a guard.

She heaved herself off the throne, jammed her crown crookedly on her head, and threw her cape haphazardly over her gown.

"I will go to him," she announced grandly. "Attend me."

She lurched out of the room, guards and maids scrambling into place behind her. I didn't join them. My charge was Evdokia, who even as Euphy left was tying on her own cloak, watching her mother disdainfully.

"Look at that," she muttered to me. "She didn't even fix her makeup and hair before going to see Father. It's one thing to inspire a man to go to war; it's quite another to scare him into doing it."

"Helen of Troy in reverse," I said. "Men will fight their way out of a besieged city to escape her."

She clapped her hands to her mouth to stifle a shriek of laughter.

"Let us go on our errands, Fool," she said, still gasping.

Her wagons were waiting. I noticed that there was less bread than on previous expeditions. To be expected, I suppose, but the appearance of generosity was maintained.

"I've never seen my mother so out of control," she said as we drove down the Mese. "She's becoming quite useless. It wouldn't surprise me if Father has her locked up for the duration of the battle, just to buy him some peace and quiet."

"There's plenty of peace and quiet when one flees danger," I commented.

"He didn't exactly endear himself to the city, did he?" she mused. "Now he's in seclusion, Mother's going mad, and my sisters are in a crying competition. Oh, well, I guess it's up to me to rescue the family reputation."

We came to a square, and were quickly surrounded by citizens. To my surprise, she stood in the chariot and addressed them.

"My good people," she began. "These are times of danger. I want you to know that no matter what happens, I shall not flinch at performing my duties."

"Is that what you call your father's conduct? Flinching?" shouted a man from the back of the crowd. There were angry murmurs of assent.

"My father will do as he sees fit," she replied calmly. "But remember that I have the blood of emperors running through my veins from both sides of my family. I vow before all of you that I will not be moved from this city, and that when the last man is gone, I will be at the walls myself, defending our empire or dying in the attempt."

There actually was some cheering at this. She waved to the wagons containing the food, and the guards began throwing loaves to the masses.

"I think that went rather well," she said smugly as we left.

"Indeed, milady," I replied. "I wish you luck defending the walls."

"It won't come to that," she laughed. "But it sounded awfully brave, didn't it?"

She repeated the distributions as well as the speech at a few more locations, then we stopped at the Chalke Prison. The Varangians there were openly grumbling about being held back from battle to maintain guard duty. I wondered if they would let the prisoners out to fight if things got that desperate. And I wondered which side the prisoners would take if that happened.

Once again, I lent the plucking of my lutestrings to the amorous whisperings of Evdokia and Alexios Doukas. He nodded his head approvingly several times, no doubt finding the defeat of his imprisoner to be good news.

When we left, Evdokia released me for the remainder of the day. I started walking up the Mese toward home, but as I passed the Moslem quarter, I heard the shouts of men in the distance and the mangonels on the seawalls launching their stones.

I hurried to the walls, but there were soldiers blocking the approach. I was by the shop of my friend, the spice merchant, so I ducked in.

"What's going on?" I asked him.

"I don't have a good view from my roof," he said. "Someone said they're fighting by the Galata Tower."

"Dear God," I whispered.

Feste had said that he would cut north and go around to one of the gates on the other side of the city. I calculated how long it would take for him to reach the next crossing after the stone bridge. He was quick, especially over short distances, but his leg still troubled him under the best of circumstances. I knew I couldn't expect him for several hours, at least.

And these were not the best of circumstances.

I walked out of the shop. My eyes blurred, and I realized that I was crying. I fell to my knees, reached inside my tunic to grasp the silver cross that had once belonged to my mother, and prayed.

Around me, others were also falling prostrate. It was the call to prayer again for the Moslems. I stayed down, wrapping my cloak around my motley and hugging myself like a little girl afraid of an oncoming storm. As I did, I heard a familiar tinkling of bells.

It was the Emperor's flutist again, not far ahead of me. How nice, I thought. We're both praying for our men. Only hers was safe inside Blachernae, and mine was somewhere outside the walls.

I waited while the prayers continued around me, not wanting to disrespect the locals by rising in the middle. I watched the flutist some more. Praying next to her was a man who seemed to be a sailor by his dress. He was a swarthy, bearded fellow, with a livid scar slicing through the beard on the left side of his jaw. He wore gold hoops in both ears and a green, embroidered sash over his blouse. His left hand was missing two fingers. I noticed that in particular as he used it to slide a note over to the flutist just as the prayers ended.

She took it without glancing at him, secreted it under her cloak, and quickly walked away.

Well, I knew where she was going. I followed him until he disappeared inside a boarding house that I knew catered to sailors on short duration. I didn't see if he met with anyone, so I decided to move on. Probably a tryst, something to keep her occupied when the Emperor didn't require her services.

I wanted to see what was happening across the Golden Horn. Our own roof was just a bit low for me. I remembered the Monastery of the Pammakaristos at the top of the Fifth Hill. It should afford even a short person like me adequate viewing of the opposite shore. Maybe I would even be able to glimpse a certain motley mixed in with the armor.

When I reached the top, I found a large crowd staring silently across the waters. I angled my way through to a good vantage point. To my shock, all I could see was the Venetian fleet clustered against the Galatan wharves.

"When did this happen?" I asked a monk who was standing nearby.

"Within the past hour," he replied. "It's God's punishment."

"But what happened to the troops at the tower?"

"Dead, captured, or scattered," he said. "They were surrounded and cut off. I haven't seen many come back."

He's a survivor, I thought. That's what he kept telling me. I won't worry about anything. Nothing's accomplished by worrying. I'll just wait. And not worry.

"Right," I muttered, trying not to burst into tears again.

I turned away and found myself looking right into the face of Bastiani's lady. She had been watching me the entire time.

"Milady," I said, bowing briefly.

"What are you doing here?" she asked. "You're not following me. You were here before me."

"My husband is somewhere over there," I said briefly. "I don't know whether he's alive or dead right now."

Something in her face softened. For the first time, she seemed to live.

"Is he a soldier?" she asked softly.

"No, lady. He's a fool, like myself." I hesitated for a moment, then took a chance. "Milady, he was at the funeral service for Bastiani. He had been playing at the embolum and went to the church after. He is the one who saw you place your handkerchief in Bastiani's hand. It was

[182]

no witchcraft on my part, and I am truly sorry for the fright I caused you."

She perused my face. I had no idea what kind of picture I made. I'm sure the tears had streaked my whiteface and left it a shambles.

"Do you love your husband?" she asked abruptly.

"More than life," I replied.

"Do you have children?"

I patted my belly in response. She bowed her head.

"You are fortunate," she said. "I hope for your sake that he is alive."

"Thank you, lady."

"Why did you seek me out the other day?" she asked.

"We are looking into the death of Bastiani," I said.

"Why you?"

"We are fools," I said. "Sometimes fools can find out things that others cannot."

"For example?"

"For example, we found you," I said. "Will you speak with me?"

She looked out across the seawalls. Already, the Venetians were beginning to unload the machines of war from their ships.

"We seem to have plenty of time on our hands," she said dryly. "Why not? Come to my house."

It did cross my mind as I accompanied her that I could have been walking into a trap. For all we knew, she was Bastiani's killer. But my instincts spake otherwise. She was in deep mourning for him, and that was not the demeanor of any killer I had ever seen. There was no need for her to maintain that as a sham for the casual observer. Few knew that Bastiani even had a lover, and none knew her name. In fact, I still didn't know her name.

Of course, she could have been mad. It wouldn't hurt to be careful. I casually made sure the daggers I kept in my sleeve and collar were loose enough to get in a hurry. I missed having my sword, but it was too conspicuous to wear in the city streets. Fortunately, a large part of my tutelage under Feste was mastering the art of throwing objects of varying shapes and sizes.

She led me back to her home, past the deaf gardener, who was quite surprised to see us together. When she opened the door, mice scampered out from the front hall.

The furniture was covered with cloths, while the floors were covered with dust and dried leaves. I followed her to the rear of the house. The kitchen was the first room that showed any sign of use. She threw a log onto the embers that still glowed in the fireplace, and blew on it until it caught.

"I'm heating up some gruel," she said. "Would you care for some?"

"Yes, thank you," I said. "Are you alone here? Besides the gardener, I mean."

"Yes," she said. "I no longer have the funds to maintain this house the way I used to. I've started selling a few pieces of jewelry to keep myself alive, but so many others are doing the same that I can't get much for it."

"Bastiani was keeping you?"

She turned upon me furiously.

"I was not being kept!" she shouted. "I am not some whore preying on a lonely merchant."

"Forgive me," I said hastily. "I meant, he was helping you?"

She collapsed into a chair suddenly, her fury abated.

"There's a fine line between the two, isn't there?" she said ruefully. "Yet when two people love each other, then *keeping* is the wrong word. *Helping* is the wrong word."

"What is the right one, lady?"

"I don't know anymore," she said. "Do you believe that love is a sin?"

"No, lady. But it can lead to sin as well as anything I've ever seen."

She was silent as she ladled the warm gruel into two bowls. She slid one to me. I waited. She nodded and popped a spoonful into her mouth.

"Quite safe, Fool," she said. "That's what you were worried about, wasn't it?"

I shrugged. "He was poisoned somehow. You had the opportunity. But I don't think that you did it."

"Thank you for that," she said. "Why don't you think so?"

"One woman's faith in another."

"You don't think women are capable of murder?"

"Of course they are capable," I said. "But a woman who murders a lover does not behave the way you do. How came you to be lovers?"

"I came to him, seeking to sell some tapestries. My husband had been away for some time, and I was getting desperate. Camilio was very kind. He gave me a good price and insisted on escorting me back here. And then we started seeing each other secretly. He was married, too, but his wife was in Venice, and he was a lonely man. He said that I was all of the colors of the rainbow in an otherwise gray world."

"A pretty sentiment," I said. "Didn't you fear discovery?"

"No one in the quarter knew me," she replied. "No one on the Fifth Hill knew him. The circles of gossip did not intersect. We both shut the world out when we were alone, and we shut it out even more when we were together."

"Why do you think he was murdered?" I said.

"I don't know that he was," she said slowly.

"What do you think happened?"

"I thought that he killed himself," she said briefly.

"Suicide would have been a sin to a Venetian," I said.

"So is adultery," she replied. "No doubt he is in Hell, and I am going to my grave without seeking absolution to make certain I can join him there."

I shivered. "These are terrible thoughts, lady. You are still young. There is life to be lived."

She gave a bleak bark of laughter.

"I am young, destitute, and still married to a man who doesn't want me," she said. "What prospects of happiness are left to me?"

"Why do you think Bastiani killed himself?" I asked.

"Toward the end, he was becoming more and more nervous about something," she said. "He said something about his ship coming in, then would laugh quietly. He told me that he'd soon be able to take us away from here to someplace we could be together."

"And?"

"And I said no," she said. "When I was faced with a choice between happiness and duty to a vow I never wanted to make, I suddenly became a coward. I saw the path of my life in a vision, the road to Paradise stretching out before me. But I somehow knew it was an illusion. I said no. Bowed to conformity, even though I had certainly paid it little heed to date. I left him that night. He was distraught. He closed the door and barred it behind me. And the next morning, I found out he was dead."

She started weeping. I took her hand.

"Lady, I cannot tell what the right choice was," I said. "But surely he would have left a note of some kind if he had killed himself, some explanation to his friends and family, or to you."

"Maybe," she said dubiously.

"Did he have any keepsake of yours?" I said. "Some token of your love?"

"A ring," she said. "An emerald set on an enameled cross on a ring of gold."

I shook my head in puzzlement. There had been no ring in that room. I would have to ask Feste if he noticed it on the body. Of course, it could have been stolen or lost.

Thinking of Feste reminded me that I wanted to find out if he was back by now. I rose.

"Lady, I would like to be of more comfort to you," I said sincerely. "Will you let me visit you again?"

"I don't know," she said. "It was good to share this with someone. With a woman. I doubt that I could have faced a priest."

"Then as a representative of the sisterhood of bereft women, I absolve you," I said. "Take care. I still don't know why Bastiani was killed, but I will find out."

"I hope that your husband returns," she said.

I thanked her.

"And I pray that mine does not," she said softly.

"Amen, lady," I said, and I left her there.

It occurred to me about halfway down the hill that I still didn't know her name.

"Greetings, Sister Fool," said a man's voice when I reached the bottom.

I turned to see Father Melchior walking toward me. I bowed.

"Well met, Father," I said.

"Indeed, Sister, for you have saved me the last portion of my journey."

"You were coming to see me?"

"You, or your husband. Father Esaias sends word that he made enquiries on behalf of Feste. No prostitute visited your late merchant."

I had forgotten that Feste had asked them to look into that. I thanked Father Melchior for the information.

"There's another matter," he said. "Father Esaias feels that we should confer at the church. Where is your husband?"

"He went across the Golden Horn last night," I said briefly. "He hasn't returned yet."

And then this murderer in monk's garb placed his hand on my shoulder. "Be comforted, Sister," he said. "He's a hard one to kill. I prophesy a long life together for the two of you."

"Thank you," I said, disconcerted but grateful. "One or both of us will be there. While you're here, tell me this: do you know a Moslem sailor, missing two fingers on his left hand, with a fearsome scar cutting a swath through his beard?"

He chuckled, a bit grimly. "I know him," he said. "But I am not at liberty to reveal what I know. If Father Esaias wills it, you will learn more tonight."

"Until later, then," I said, and he glided silently away.

I stopped at home. No sign of Feste—or of the others, for that matter. I didn't want to sit around waiting, so I went back to Blachernae.

No sooner had I entered the Empress's throne room when a shriek rent the air. Euphy, who was seated on the throne with a cold cloth pressed to her head, started, and guards came rushing in from all directions.

"Are they here?" cried Euphy. "What is happening?"

Irene dashed in, wailing. For once, it sounded authentic.

"He's dead!" she cried. "My husband is dead! Oh, Mother, what shall become of me?" She threw herself onto her mother's lap, weeping.

Euphy stiffened momentarily, then recovered and patted her daughter on the back.

"So, he really was sick," she said. "I had my doubts. Forgive me."

"He was recovering," cried Irene. "I thought he might ride to battle soon. It happened so—" She stopped suddenly and turned pale. "Where is she?" she hissed. "Where is that little tramp?"

"Who?" asked Euphy, perplexed.

"Evdokia!" shouted Irene.

Her sister came in, removing her cloak.

"I'm here," she said calmly. "What's all the fuss about?"

Irene strode toward here.

"He's dead," she said, choking.

"Michael's dead?" exclaimed Evdokia. "Oh, Irene. I am so sorry."

"He was alive until I let you start nursing him," spat Irene.

Evdokia looked shocked.

"What are you saying?" she said. "You've been telling us that he was at Death's door ever since the fleet showed up. And now that he's finally passed on, you're blaming me?"

"You little bitch..." Irene said, starting toward her.

"Daughter, cease," commanded Euphy, rising to her feet. Irene's fear of her mother stopped her in her tracks.

"I'll have no more of this," Euphy continued. "It's giving me a headache. Irene, you have funeral preparations to make. You had better get started if you want to give him a proper burial. Would you like me to have it announced that he died heroically in battle? It would help us in finding you your next husband."

"Mother!" wailed Irene.

"Get going, girl," ordered her mother, and the new widow fled.

"Shall I go with her, Mother?" asked Evdokia primly.

Her mother looked at her with an expression that was difficult to read. Yet I thought there was some recognition in her as she looked at her youngest daughter. Even some pride.

"No," she said thoughtfully. "My guess is that she won't accept consolation from anyone in the family right now. You'd better sit here with me, Evy."

"As you wish, Mother," said Evdokia, and she pulled up a small bench beside the throne and sat by her mother.

The resulting tableau was a caricature of a mother and daughter together. It sickened me, and in my condition, quite a few things did. I slipped out before anyone realized I had been there in the first place and went home.

Feste was lying on our bed when I arrived. I took one look at him and threw myself on top of him, holding him for all I was worth. He held me weakly, then lay back again.

"Are you injured?" I asked.

"No," he said. "Just exhausted. There were crossbows, Aglaia. Hundreds of them. I ran."

"And you made it!" I shouted triumphantly.

"Please," he said, wincing.

There was a clatter up the steps, and Plossus burst into the room.

"Is it true?" he cried. "They're talking about it all over the city."

"Is what true?" I asked.

"Shut up, boy," muttered Feste.

"They're saying that he ran across the great chain like a squirrel across the treetops," said Plossus breathlessly.

"He did what?" I exclaimed.

"Shut up, Plossus," barked Feste.

"And that he stopped in the middle, pulled out his lute, and sang an insulting tune to the oncoming ship!" continued Plossus.

"That part isn't true," said Feste quickly.

"But the first part is?" I shouted. I went over to my chest, opened it, pulled out a crossbow, and leveled it at my husband. "I swear by the First Fool, Our Savior, that if you try to go to the Crusaders one more time, I'll kill you myself, just to end the suspense."

FOURTEEN

The cistern contains: the fountain overflows.
WILLIAM BLAKE, "PROVERBS OF HELL"

One may be frightened by the same event twice: once when it is actually happening and a second time when you look back and realize that it was far more dangerous than you first had thought, now that you've had some time to reflect upon it. Or, if you don't reflect upon it but have a wife who is more than willing to do so while pointing out the numerous flaws in your intellect, character, foresight, and so forth. I did as any man would do under the circumstances—I mumbled apologies, swore that I would never do anything like this again, and begged her to leave me alone for a short while so that I could catch up on my sleep.

She left me reluctantly, and I did manage to get a brief nap. I woke shaking to find her holding me tight, tears coursing down her face, and thought more seriously about honoring my oath to her.

Plossus and Rico joined us for dinner. Aglaia caught us up on her information, and I told them of my encounter with the troubadours. My companions looked at me with dismay.

"How could they?" said Plossus. "I could see Raimbaut caving in like that from what I've heard about him, but all of them?"

"They became too isolated from the Guild," speculated Rico. "Sing the songs of the warrior long enough, and you start to believe you're one as well."

"In all fairness, they don't believe there's anything more that they can do," I said.

"But they gave up too soon," said Aglaia. "Without even finding out what we're going to do."

"Right," I said. "It's time. Let us go meet with our crooked allies."

We walked toward Father Esaias's church as the sun set. Rico was intrigued by the death of Michael Palaiologos.

"I never thought little Evy had the nerve," he said. "Do you really think she poisoned him?"

"I think it, Irene thinks it, and Euphy thinks it," said Aglaia. "But no one can prove anything. It's good riddance as far as Euphy's concerned, and I think she's realized that she underestimated the capabilities of her little girl. She's beginning to take her into her bosom more and more. But she's having her food tasted, just in case."

"What about Anna?" I asked.

"She's telling her husband to stay in the thick of battle. It's safer for him than staying home."

We reached the church and stayed with Father Esaias through dawn, discussing the merits of various plans until we settled on the one we thought had the best chance of working. Rico and Aglaia were needed at Blachernae, so Plossus was selected to be our liaison to the underworld.

"Makes sense," he observed as we staggered back to our place to grab a few hours sleep. "I can run faster than you."

"Not if there's a crossbow pointed in my direction, you can't," I said.

The gates of the city were shut and barred, except for one the public used near the Golden Gate. The traffic through this one was a continuous flow away from the city, as the populace began sensing the depth of the incompetence of their ruler.

The Venetians regularly sent ships patrolling around the city, just out of the reach of the defenders' catapults. There was no military purpose for this. There was no Imperial Navy left to contest them. But it was a constant, floating taunt, and it did not wear well on the Greeks.

The city, with much of its daily commerce shut down, took to the roofs, watching with morbid fascination the preparations across the Golden Horn. The machines of war were being assembled on the decks of the larger ships, and carpenters swarmed over the bowsprits, extending them further and hammering planks and railings along their lengths.

Meanwhile, the main body of the Crusader army moved up the harbor to the remains of the stone bridge and began the arduous task of rebuilding it.

The Greeks could have engaged them there. Taking a bridge is one of the most costly efforts in warfare, yet the Emperor didn't even bother sending archers to pick off the French peasants who were doing the heavy lifting in the hot sun. Their noble lords supervised them from the shade of their gaily decked pavilions, a safe distance away.

And, an even safer distance away, Emperor Alexios the Third sat on his throne and fretted.

"It was a strategic retreat, can't anyone besides me see that?" he whined.

"Just an advance in the other direction, that's all," said Rico.

"And the rest of your plan, Your Majesty?" asked a general, warily.

"Do you question me?" shouted Alexios.

"I do not question you, sire. I asked a question of you," replied the general.

"Simplicity," said Alexios. "Let them bring the battle to the walls. They will lose so many in the attempt that they'll be powerless to resist us in the end."

The generals looked at each other.

"Then you mean to let them cross the bridge unopposed?" asked the first general.

"Well, you haven't done such a wonderful job of opposing them so far, have you?" said Alexios. "Barely able to protect the Imperial Person, much less the rest of the city. But the walls will protect us."

"And what of your people outside the walls?" I said, sitting by Rico and strumming my lute.

"Their fault for choosing to live outside the walls," said Rico. "We can't save people from their own stupidity."

"Precisely," agreed the Emperor, patting the dwarf on the head. "The farmers will come through all right. They always do. A few fields get burned, some peasant women violated. A small price to pay for the safety of the Empire."

"Whatever's left of it," I muttered.

I stood, bowed, and left. Philoxenites collared me in the hallway outside.

"He's falling apart," he said. "He lost all support in the city when he ran. Everyone saw it happen."

"Yet relying on the walls to repel the Crusaders isn't the worst idea I've heard," I said.

"Strategically sound, but politically insane," he said. "There's as much danger from within the city as without. The people want action, not retreat."

"You have always been a man of the people," I observed.

"What did you find out from your friends?" he asked.

"That my proposal would probably have the desired effect."

"Now, you realize that for me to have any part of this plan would be treason," he said quietly.

"But I, on the other hand, have no loyalties," I said. "Or is it treason for me as well?"

[194]

He smiled. "I'll let your conscience be your guide on that point."

"And your conscience?"

"I have none," he said. "Now, before you put whatever plan you have into action, I ask one more thing."

"What?"

"Talk to Isaakios. I cannot, and it would be dangerous if even one of my men sees him. See if he'll be up to the task before you go ahead and restore him to the throne." He walked away, then turned. "If this works, there'll be something in it for you."

"And if it doesn't?" I asked.

"I'll do my best to get you out of the city alive," he promised.

I didn't go see Isaakios right away. I was still hammering out the details of our plan with Father Esaias. I also didn't want to have the former emperor sitting in prison with this new hope in his breast. The old fool might babble the secret too soon to the wrong ears and would find himself strangled within hours.

When some free time presented itself, I decided to satisfy my curiosity as to Ranieri's visits to the silk factory at the Great Palace. He was up to something, no matter how innocent the ostensible reason for these trips. I covered myself once again with my cloak so as to pass as an everyday citizen and waited outside his home one morning.

He arose at dawn and went to the embolum, as usual. I spied through the windows from across the street but saw nothing out of the ordinary within. He spoke to Ruzzini for a few minutes, then spent the rest of the morning making entries in a large ledger book, occasionally rising to check on bolts of green and yellow silk that were being carried into his storeroom.

Around noon, he left and headed toward the gate leading to the rest of the city. I trailed him from a safe distance, but he never looked back until we reached the covered portion of the Mese. I quickly ducked into a stall and haggled halfheartedly with a paper-seller, but resumed the chase as soon as Ranieri entered the Augustaion.

He went as he did before to the grounds outside of Zeuxippos, but the rabbity man wasn't there. Ranieri waited, looking around impatiently. Finally, he walked to a door at the side of the building, opened it, and went inside.

I crept up to the door and listened but couldn't hear anything. I opened it cautiously, peered inside, and was met with a faceful of steam for my troubles.

The part of the building that once held the baths was ideal for the silk operation that currently occupied it. The water was heated beyond the bathing level until it boiled, and the steam that rose from it enveloped frames holding stacks of wooden trays, which in turn held the cocoons of the silkworms. The steam softened the protective casings and allowed the silkworkers to begin the delicate process of unraveling the luxurious threads that became the fabrics of the rich.

As the steam billowed about the room, I felt the sweat pouring through my makeup. I walked between the stacks of trays on narrow planks over the boiling baths, taking care not to go plunging over the sides. Unfortunately, it was the distraction of maintaining my safety that brought me up face to face with my quarry before I realized it.

"Why are you following me?" Ranieri demanded.

"I, sir? No, sir!" I riposted. "I am as surprised to see you here as you are to see me."

"You followed me from my home this morning," he said. "And watched me in the embolum. You're a spy of some sort."

"Why would anyone want to spy on you?" I asked. "Sir, you mistake me. I came here to meet a friend for lunch. What could you possibly be doing that would be of interest to anyone?"

"Certainly nothing that would be of interest to a fool," he said.

"Why, sir, a fool has nothing but interests," I rattled on. "So much to see, so much to learn. It is only men with true callings who can stay with only one occupation. You, sir, are a silk man. Where else would you be but here?"

"True enough," he said slowly. "I come down here often to discuss shipments. Not that it matters to you."

"No, sir, of course not," I said. "No doubt there was a shipment in that tiny wicker box you received outside when I saw you here the other day."

He flinched, then recovered quickly. "That was merely a gift from a friend, Fool. A token of gratitude for my business."

"Then your friend must be grateful indeed, sir," I said.

"Why is that?"

"For he is standing behind you with another token of his gratitude."

He turned and saw the rabbity man standing some feet away, holding another small wicker box in his hands. He looked at Ranieri uncertainly. Ranieri turned back to me.

"You should be careful where you stand, Fool," he said pleasantly. He nudged the board I was on with his toe so that it rocked gently. "The footing is a bit unsteady. One false step, and they would be serving boiled jester for dinner."

"Actually, sir, a fool is usually served as dessert," I said, bouncing lightly on the board. Then I launched myself into a backflip, landing on the board behind me. "Sir, just the other day I ran the length of the great chain. These planks are good road by comparison. Care to dance?"

He looked at me, fingering the hilt of his sword.

"What do you want from me?" he asked.

"I have some questions," I said. "Somehow, I think that you may be able to answer some of them."

"Why should I?"

"No reason," I said. "But it is curious that when given the opportunity to allay my suspicions, you choose instead to increase them."

"And what do I gain by satisfying this strange curiosity of yours?"

"My thanks," I said. "And perhaps my influence."

"How far does that extend?" he asked.

"I have friends in high places and low," I said. "You'd be surprised."

He grinned suddenly. "All right, Fool. I'll chance a meeting with you. But nowhere public."

"There are private places to be found in this city."

"There are indeed. You know the Cistern of the Columns?"

"Off the Mese near the Hippodrome."

"Exactly. Meet me inside at sunset, and you will be satisfied."

I bowed and stepped carefully the rest of the way back to the door.

"It's a trap," said Plossus when I told him about it at luncheon.

"Probably," I said. "But the fact that he's willing to set one means there's something he's trying to hide. He must think that we know more than we do."

"What do you want me to do?" asked Plossus.

"Go on ahead. Find a good observation spot, and make sure that he goes in alone. I'll pass by toward sunset. If there's anything amiss, signal me. If anyone goes in after me, he's yours."

"But what if he plans to take you by himself?"

"Let him try," I said.

He paused and turned as he reached the doorway.

"I thought you promised your wife you wouldn't be getting into any more of these situations," he said.

"I promised her I wouldn't go across the enemy lines," I said. "But this is taking place at home."

"Dead is dead, wherever it happens," said Plossus. "See you there."

As the sun began to set, I walked from the Forum of Constantine to the neighborhood north of the Hippodrome. Under my cloak I held

[198]

a small lantern with three sides blocked so that the light from the candle within shone in only one direction. I also had an unlit torch thrust into my belt, and the usual deadly precautions within easy reach.

The entrance to the cistern was at one end of a small square. As I approached it, Plossus passed me, dressed in everyday garb, and muttered, "Ranieri went in a little while ago, alone. I haven't seen anyone else go through the entrance all day."

"Thanks," I said.

The cistern was underground and filled from pipes that ran from some source I did not know. They say it dated from the time of the Emperor Justinian, which was why it was in the oldest part of the city. When it was full, it provided water to drink and douse fires during times of siege. But it had not been filled yet, another of the Emperor's oversights in planning.

It was a popular site for travelers. Even the locals did not weary of descending the steps from the small building that marked the entrance. You emerged in a sculpted cavern with hundreds of columns, supporting arches and brick ceilings some thirty feet up. The columns were in regular rows, rising from ornately carved bases. To think, all that elaborate decoration in an underground vault that was meant to be flooded.

There was still about a foot of water present, and when I lit my torch, the light bounced off the ripples and played across the ceiling. I sloshed slowly through the cistern, listening for any sign of another living soul. It was a beautiful place, but every column could conceal an attacker, so beauty was the last thing on my mind.

"Fool," called Ranieri softly from my right.

I turned, and he stepped out from behind a column a hundred feet away, holding a lit candle. Though he had whispered, the echoes sent the sound bouncing to my ears as if he was standing next to me. I started in his direction, but he held up his hand.

"I can only trust at a distance," he said. "Especially now."

"Fair enough," I replied.

"You have questions, I believe," he said.

The light flickered off his face, giving it a slightly demonic cast. The eyes, in particular, picked up the flames. Had I wanted someone to play the Devil, I could not have picked a better actor or setting.

"Tell me what's going on," I said.

He shook his head. "Too general, Fool. Ask me something specific, and I'll decide whether I can answer or not."

"All right. Why was Bastiani murdered?"

Whatever he was expecting me to ask, this wasn't it. The question took him off-guard, and he frowned.

"I was unaware that he was murdered," he said carefully.

"But you suspected it."

"I thought it possible," he said. "The condition of his body, the expression on his face—it did not strike me as a natural death."

"Were you friends?"

"I wouldn't say that," he said. "We had business dealings together."

"Profitable ones?"

"Sometimes, sometimes not."

"Any profitable enough to kill for?"

He was smiling again.

"Truly, Fool, I was not anticipating this line of questioning," he said. "A tawdry little matter of murder and money when great events are happening around us?"

"You expected me to ask about the weapons you have stored in the embolum?"

"I thought you might know about that," he said. "Were you our mysterious ambassador from the fleet?"

I bowed.

[200]

"I thought as much," he said. "Especially when you didn't stick around to make contact."

"Who was the contact?"

"Well, as for that," he began, and something glinted in the darkness behind him. The candle fell from his hand, and in the brief instant before it was extinguished, I saw his head fall from his body.

I immediately hurled my torch in that direction, but saw nothing. As the torch doused itself in the water, I stepped onto the base of the column by me, then leapt onto the one to my left and held my breath.

All I heard was the slight lapping of the water. Then, footsteps sloshing through the cistern. I drew my knife from my boot and slid my dagger from my sleeve. I pressed my back against the column and held the weapons down by my thighs, ready to slash in either direction.

But the footsteps were moving away from me. They were also moving away from the entrance. Then the sound changed from sloshing to steps on dry stone, and in the distance, a door opened and then shut.

There must have been another way into the cistern, not known to the general public. I wondered if Ranieri knew that. But I don't think that he knew the killer was there. The brief glimpse I had of the weapon was enough to show that it was an axe. And I had seen an awful lot of axes over the last few days.

Ranieri had been killed by a Varangian. I was certain of it.

I stood a while longer in the darkness to make sure no one else was waiting. Even one breath taken in that place would have been amplified enough for me to hear it. But there was none.

I pulled the lantern from under my cloak. The candle was still burning. It was a weak flame but would have to suffice. Holding it up in my left hand and with my knife ready in my right, I cautiously stepped toward the late merchant.

Just before reaching the body, I stubbed my toe on something that rolled away a few feet. I recoiled as I realized I had just kicked the poor fellow's head like a football. Keeping the lantern safely out of the reach of the water, I searched Ranieri's body, grunting with satisfaction as I found the wicker box.

There was nothing else to do. I went back to the steps leading to the entrance. Just before I reached them, the reaction hit me and I retched, but I still managed to keep the lantern lit.

When I reached the street, Plossus was waiting across from the entrance.

"Nobody went in," he said.

"Someone went in," I replied. "There's another entrance somewhere. Maybe a well someone dug to reach the water without going over here. By the way, remind me never to drink any water from this cistern again."

We went home, and I told them what happened.

"Do you think Ranieri killed Bastiani?" asked Rico.

"I don't know," I said. "Somehow, I don't think so. He was hiding something, but that didn't seem to be it. And he was killed while we were talking about the Crusaders' contact inside the Venetian quarter."

"Let's see the box," urged Aglaia.

I pulled it from my pouch and placed it on the center of the table.

"Care to do the honors?" I asked her.

She reached forward and gently opened it. Nestled inside was a small, gray, sticky lump about the length of Rico's thumb.

"What is it?" asked Plossus.

"It's a cocoon," said Aglaia. "I'm assuming it's silk, but I'm no expert."

"Hardly seems worth all the fuss," said Rico, examining it. "Sneaking out one cocoon at a time won't even produce enough thread to make a lady's handkerchief."

I took the cocoon and placed it back inside the box.

"So, instead of one murder and an answer, we now have two murders and more questions," said Rico. "Good work, Feste. At this rate, we should wipe out the quarter by the end of the year."

ƒIFTEEN

[N]ever, in any city, have so many been besieged by so few.
——GEOFFROY DE VILLEHARDOUIN,
THE CONQUEST OF CONSTANTINOPLE

The following morning, a rumbling from the north sent us running to the rooftop once again. The Crusaders had finished repairing the stone bridge across the neck of the Golden Horn, and the noise came from the mangonels and petrarries rolling slowly across it.

The army encamped on a hill opposite Blachernae called the Kosmidion for a monastery located there. I do not know who Saint Kosmas was. Perhaps he was the patron saint of sieges.

The Constantinopolitans did not take well to seeing the invaders cross the bridge unopposed. With so many idled by the shutting of the gates to the outside world, mobs formed, merged, split off and reformed like giant globs of oil throughout the city. The Blachernae complex had been constructed with an eye toward invasion from without and rebellion from within. When the surging crowds began bumping up against the interior wall, the Emperor ordered that the gates to the complex be shut to all but those on imperial business.

And fools, of course. Rico and Aglaia were Imperial Fools, and I generally had the run of the palace as well. Only Plossus couldn't get in, but he was needed elsewhere, anyway.

So, as the Crusaders crossed the bridge and the Greek citizens fetched up against the walled-off home of their leader, I laid siege to an invidious bureaucrat.

"What on earth are you doing here?" said Philoxenites testily upon opening his door and seeing me.

"We need to talk," I said.

"I am, as ever, at your disposal," he said with an ironic bow. He motioned me to a chair before his desk, but I chose to stand, remembering a previous time I sat in that same chair, bound with ropes and with a knife at my throat.

"You've been playing with me," I said.

"How so?" he said, folding his hands on the desk.

"By having me followed," I said. "And by using me to flush out Venetian insurrectionists so that you could eliminate them."

"Not a bad plan," he said. "I wish that it was true."

"Did you hear about the body in the Cistern of the Columns?" I asked him.

"As a matter of fact, that little tidbit was just brought to me," he said. "A member of the Vigla patrols the cistern every night around midnight. Usually he comes across amorous couples."

"Well, this fellow didn't lose his head over a woman," I said. "He lost it while he was talking to me. It was Ranieri who was killed, and a Varangian axe that did it."

"What makes you think that?" he asked, leaning back in his chair.

"The only Varangians I know of who are capable of both that kind of stealth and that deadly efficiency are Will and Phil," I said. "No one else in the Varangian Guard could have pulled this one off. You've been having them tail me. But they struck too soon. I was just about to get some answers out of him."

He looked at me with disdain.

"Feste," he said. "It is one thing to play a fool, but quite another to become one. Perhaps you've been playing the role for too long."

"Your meaning, Eunuch?" I asked.

"Will and Phil never got out of Galata," he said. "They are presumed to be dead, not being the types who would let themselves be captured. But they haven't been seen since the battle at the tower."

I looked at him, and he returned my gaze through hooded eyes. I couldn't tell if he was lying or not. He always looked like he was lying, even when he told the truth, so his present shifty demeanor gave me no clue.

"I appreciate your efforts," he continued, "but you are wasting my time. This is the second cockeyed story that you've brought before me, and I am beginning to wonder if my faith in your abilities was misplaced."

"Someone did kill Ranieri," I said.

"Someone did," he agreed. "Apparently with an axe. But there are many axes in this great city of ours, and even Varangian blades may be obtained from the right source. God only knows how many of the guard lose them dicing in back alleyways."

"Maybe that was it," I said dubiously.

"At least you've stirred something up," he said thoughtfully. "They must be close to some course of action if they were willing to risk this. Have you talked to our mutual friend in Chalke yet?"

"No," I said. "I wanted to wait until the time was ripe."

There was a sudden crash, and the room shook slightly, sending an inkpot at the edge of the desk crashing to the floor.

"If you wait any longer, we will be beyond ripe and into rot," said Philoxenites. "Get going, Fool."

The stones that were launched from the Kosmidion were directed at the wall in front of Blachernae, but enough sailed over it into the palace to keep the residents clustered in the interior. The Greeks returned the barrage, but the invaders had the higher ground to their vantage, and their machines kept up the attack in complete safety. The stones mostly damaged other stones and bricks, but one caught a pair of Imperial Guards patrolling the Blachernae wall. Their bodies were retrieved sixty feet away, flattened in their armor.

I strode briskly down the Mese to Chalke Prison. As I crossed the Augustaion, I saw a woman in mourning stop and stare at me. She raised her veil, and I recognized her as Bastiani's lady. Her expression was complicated to read. I could not blame her for despising me for spying on her in her grief, but there was something akin to sympathy mixed with it.

"You survived," she said quietly.

"Yes, milady," I said, bowing.

"I am glad for your wife's sake," she said.

"Thank you, milady."

She lowered her veil.

"Take care of her," she whispered. "If you do not, then my curse will be on you."

I watched her walk away until she was out of sight.

There was a stall where one could get ale near the entrance gates to Chalke, and I decided to avail myself of some fortification. As I paid for my drink, I was hailed from a couple of benches nearby. I turned and saw Tullio, the carpenter, and his mate, John Aprenos.

"It's the fool!" cried Tullio. "Come and sit with us until your cup is empty, and then we shall refill it."

"Alas, I can only promise the first," I said, joining them. "As much as I hate to say it, I have no time for a second today. How are things with you, friend Carpenter?"

He shrugged.

"Business is wanting," he said. "I have tools and skills, but no more wood on which to wield them. I have become just as useless as my friend John."

"Nay," said Aprenos. "I am the more useless one. I will not cede the title."

"I see you found your whore," said Tullio.

"Excuse me?" I said.

"Bastiani's whore," said Tullio, gesturing with his cup toward the north end of the square. "That's the woman you were looking for, wasn't it?"

"I wasn't looking for her, exactly," I said. "And she's not a whore, she's a lady."

"Comes to the same thing," commented Aprenos. "Just a matter of degree in what you pay them."

"You are quite the philosopher," I said.

"Plenty of time to think when the gates are shut," said the huntsman, raising his cup.

"So, what brings the two of you here?" I asked.

"Visiting a mate of ours who got himself locked up," said Tullio. "Made sure he's got a bottle or two to last him in case things get hot around here. And yourself?"

"On my way to do the same," I said, and I drained my cup and tossed it back to the vendor. "Good luck, gentlemen. We'll have another when the war's over. On me."

"We accept," called Tullio as I left.

I entered Chalke without difficulty. With so much idle time forced upon the city, many of its people were doing the things they could not otherwise do, and that included visiting prisoners. The aisles between the cells were milling with people, and the tone of the place was strangely buoyant, almost raucous. I gathered that Tullio and Aprenos were not the only ones to bring in some wine.

The former emperor, as befit his rank, had the largest and most luxuriously appointed cell in the prison. It was the last one on the right, and was one of the few to have an actual bed, rather than a pile of moldy hay or damp ticking. He shared it with a few other political prisoners who acted as an informal bodyguard, a situation winked at by the warden and probably by Emperor Alexios as well. The current emperor was a sentimental man in surprising ways. Having deposed, blinded, and imprisoned his brother, he wished no further harm upon him. A more pragmatic man would have simply had him killed.

I announced my approach with a low whistle, a salute that had long become familiar to Isaakios. He was sitting on the edge of his bed while one of his fellows read to him, but he stood immediately and strode firmly toward me, stopping just short of the bars.

He had been a strong man in his prime, but living in sightless confinement for so many years had by this point worn away much of his frame. His clothes, tattered remnants of rich, embroidered silks, hung loosely on his limbs, and his hair and beard, once a glorious red, were gray and matted.

Yet he still had dignity, even command in his carriage, and this gave me hope that we might actually pull this off.

"Is that you, Fool?" he whispered eagerly.

"Sire, it is I," I replied, kneeling.

He motioned me to my feet.

"Don't waste time on ceremony," he said impatiently. "Tell me what has happened."

"The invaders have rebuilt the stone bridge and have encamped on the Kosmidion."

"Interesting," he murmured. "They must think that section of the wall to be the most vulnerable to attack. My predecessors should have done a better job building it. But they would be foolish to attempt it, nevertheless. They can't possibly sustain the losses they would have in taking it."

"Normally, I would agree with you," I said. "But these are not normal times."

"How so, my friend?"

"Your brother has mismanaged the armies and lost the confidence of the people. He may be content to sit in the palace and wait out the siege, but the city won't have it."

"Won't they?" he chuckled. "About time they came to their senses. So, you think they will rise against my brother?"

"I think it possible," I said. "Which leaves the city wide open to being taken by the Crusaders."

"Unbelievable," he said, shaking his head. "Things would never have come to this state if I had remained emperor."

"There are those who agree with you," I said, and he nodded at the compliment. "And there are those who would have you Emperor again."

He would have stared had he still possessed eyes.

"What are you saying?" he asked softly.

"I have been asked to inquire of your willingness to assume the great burden of rulership again."

"A burden," he said. "Aye, it is that. Does not God have the burden of the world on His shoulders? When it fell upon me to lead this empire, I did so willingly, even though it cost me much care and woe. I am still that man, Fool. I would accept the burden gladly, and bear it lightly. But we are talking of fancies, are we not?"

"Milord, stranger things have happened," I said. "For years, you have lived in terror that soldiers would come through these bars in the dead of night to carry you to your doom. Now, I ask that you listen for these soldiers with hope."

"I swear, Fool, that if you prophesy correctly, you shall live with all that an emperor's generosity may provide," he said.

"I am but a messenger, milord," I said.

"As was the Archangel Gabriel," he said. "Tell them that when the time comes, Isaakios will be ready."

"Then, sire, I will take my leave of you."

I noticed, as I left, that a dark form was stepping away from the front of the cell next to the former emperor's. No doubt he had heard our conversation. I hoped that he was not a lackey of the current emperor.

Then, as a small group of people walked in my direction, I heard a lute playing. I stared dumbfounded as my wife walked blithely between the cells as if she was a strolling entertainer at a garden party.

She marked me as she came to the cell next to Isaakios's. She smiled, her fingers never hesitating.

"My nanny always said I would end up with a man in prison," she drawled.

"Fancy meeting you here," I said. "Quite the romantic setting."

"Isn't it?" she agreed, nodding toward Evdokia, who was preening in front of her beau.

I had seen him before on my visits to Isaakios but had never paid him much mind. I pulled out my flute and joined my wife's music. The additional instrument startled the lovers slightly. Evdokia smiled with delight when she saw me.

"What a surprise!" she squealed. "You didn't tell me that your husband would be joining us, Aglaia."

"I thought that music from one loving couple would be most appropriate for another," said my wife with a straight face.

"How sweet," said Evdokia. "Thank you, good Feste, for taking these pains."

"No pains, mistress," I said, winking at Aglaia. "I take pleasure in playing, mistress."

Alexios Doukas was watching me with a curious expression, his brows furrowed, almost meeting in the middle.

"These two fools are married, my dove?" he asked, his voice rasping as though he did not use it much.

"Yes. Isn't it wonderful?" she said. "Just as we shall be."

He took her hand between his and patted it.

"Soon," he whispered fervently. "It will happen soon. I can feel it in my bones, and I know it in my heart."

And they dropped into a frenzy of whispering. I couldn't make out their conversation, so I gave myself over to the exquisite pleasures of making music with my wife.

It carried through the prison. Quite well, in fact. The acoustics of the one-time church lent themselves to our duet as they had once done to the preaching of the Word. The myriad conversations going on around us faded, and prisoner and visitor alike turned to hear us.

And when it comes down to it, more than anything a fool loves to perform. The setting doesn't matter. The size of the crowd, the level of wit shared among them, the type of coin flying out of their hands into our caps—none of these things matter. Let us but have a reason to perform, and we are happy.

I watched my beloved, her white skin gleaming in the torchlight, the music transmuting her into some rare and lovely sprite, and I thought, this is all that I need. This is all that I want. I thought of her desire to find a place where we could just be fools together and nothing else. Maybe. I had done more than most for the Guild, risked life and damaged limb on many an occasion. Maybe it was time to quit gallivanting about and become a fixed fool in an out-of-the-way county somewhere, trotting myself out for feasts and state occasions, entertaining the children. Especially my own child. We could watch her grow and learn all that we could teach her.

Well, Theo, live through this little escapade first. Then we shall see.

There was a lull in the war for a few days, a calm before the oncoming storm. Broken by the intermittent squalls of sorties by the Greeks, more to harass the Crusaders' flanks and keep them from foraging too far than to actually confront them in combat. However, this meant that the invaders' provisions would be running low. The Greeks were forcing the issue rather than settling down and waiting for attrition to do the job for them.

After Ranieri's death, I had no more leads. I watched the embolum to no avail. Like much of the city, I spent a fair amount of my time on the roof, looking at the Crusaders digging into the hill and constructing earthen fortifications that baked hard under the relentless summer sun.

I was sitting in our room a few days after my talk with Isaakios, moping with a wineskin. Aglaia came in with bread and cheese.

"You would not believe what I paid for this," she grumbled, tossing me a loaf.

"Maybe we should just buy flour and make our own," I said, cutting myself a piece.

"I have no time for baking," she said. "And if you have, then I'm worried about you. You're drinking more than is usual."

I made a show of letting the wineskin fall.

"Better?" I asked.

"It might have been had it not already been emptied," she said. "What's wrong?"

"I'm stuck," I said. "I cannot piece this all together. I can't find the common thread."

"You will," she said. "I have faith in that warped mind of yours."

She sat back, munching away.

"I'm going to need motley for when I'm huge," she commented. "Maybe you could sew me one in your free time. I'd like a suit more like yours."

"Mine?" I said. "It's just one piece sewn onto another. There's no pattern to it. It's all patch. I doubt that there's an original piece of cloth left in it."

"That's what I like about it," she said. "It has character. Oh!"

"What?"

"I've spotted your keepsake," she said. "You purloined my yellow handkerchief and added it to your motley. How lovely!"

"You have found me out, my sweet. Forgive me for stealing from you."

"And it's over your heart, too. I never noticed it in the middle of all of those colors. You're a sentimental fool, and I forgive you."

"Thank you," I said.

Her expression changed abruptly. She frowned, thinking hard, her eyes distant, and I wondered if she had changed her mind about the theft.

"Feste," she said slowly. "I have a riddle for you."

"All right," I said, puzzled.

"What's the difference between motley and a rainbow?" she asked.

"I don't know," I said.

"The color purple," she concluded, and she stood and capered about the room.

"Not your best effort, I think," I said, baffled.

"Don't you see?" she asked. "You've no purple in your motley. I've found the common thread, and it's made of silk!"

"What on earth are you talking about?"

She grabbed the wicker box that I had retrieved from Ranieri's body.

"Tell me, Fool," she said, plucking the cocoon from it. "What garment could you weave from this?"

"From that?" I laughed. "Not even the pinky of a child's glove."

"Wrong, Fool!" she crowed. "You could get thirty gowns from this, a hundred robes, a thousand tapestries!"

"You must be a wondrous fine weaver, Arachne," I said. "How do you do that?"

"What color was the handkerchief that Bastiani's lady placed in his coffin?"

"It was purple," I said.

"Why have you no purple in your motley?" she demanded.

"Well, it's not easy to come by," I said, then I realized what she was talking about.

" 'I may not be to the purple born,' " she said, imitating Euphrosyne perfectly. "Purple silk, Feste. The rarest of dyes, the finest of weaves, so valued that its manufacture . . ."

"Is reserved exclusively for the Emperor," I finished.

"Exactly," she said. "Ranieri wasn't smuggling silk. He was smuggling silkworms. He was going to set up a rival manufacturer. And Bastiani was in on it. He gave his lover that purple handkerchief as a keepsake. He told her that he was expecting to make his fortune shortly."

"But you need more than just the silkworms," I countered. "They have a special diet."

"Mulberry trees," she said. "A particular kind like the ones growing at Zeuxippos. They must be smuggling those as well."

"Wait a second," I remembered. "When Rico hid in that crate during our burglary, he said that it had some kind of ornamental bush in it. It didn't occur to me at the time, but that's an odd thing to find taking up valuable space in a silk embolum."

"I'll bet it was mulberry," she said.

"But is this really something worth killing for?"

"Silk of that quality is worth its weight in gold," she said. "And gold is always worth killing for."

"The carpenter was right," I said. "If it's a merchant, it's probably about money. So, there must be at least one other involved. Ruzzini is the logical choice. He's the top silk man there." I stopped, thinking. "The Silk Man. Could he be the Crusader contact?"

"Maybe," she said. "What do we do about this?"

"If it involves a threat to the Emperor's silk monopoly, I can bring it to the authorities. I should probably talk to Niketas first. It will finally give him a reason to flex his muscles as Logothete."

I flopped onto the bed and hugged her.

"My dear, you are worth more than your weight in gold," I said, and I patted her belly. "And you will be appreciating in value soon, if I am any judge of pregnancy."

"It's good to be appreciated," she said, snuggling against me.

$\mathcal{S}$IXTEEN

Let me tell you here of an outstanding deed of valour.
—GEOFFROY DE VILLEHARDOUIN,
THE CONQUEST OF CONSTANTINOPLE

Niketas Choniates agreed to meet at his office in the Senate before dawn. As I walked down the Mese, there was a glow to my left that had nothing to do with the approaching sunrise. There were bonfires atop each of the guard towers along the seawall, and the flames were strong enough to cast my shadow all the way to the Augustaion. In between the towers, I could see the Varangians patrolling the walls.

A stray unit of the Vigla passed me on their way back to their bastion, a few of them waving as they saw me. Niketas had his servant waiting for me at the Senate doors, and I was ushered quickly inside.

There was another man seated in his office, one I had never met, but who eyed me with a glance that seemed to gather every detail at once. Niketas motioned me to a chair.

"This is Demetrios Gabras," said Niketas. "He is the Keeper of the Imperial Silk. After I got your note, I invited him to join us."

"An honor, milord," I said. "Feste the Fool at your service."

"I've seen you," said Demetrios.

"Have you ever seen this before?" I said, placing the wicker box on Niketas's desk.

Gabras opened the box, looked inside, and frowned. He removed the cocoon and placed it on a white linen square, then took a small, sharp knife and carefully slit it open without damaging its occupant.

The silkworm writhed on the cloth, exposed to the world too soon. Gabras turned it over with the tip of his knife and examined it, then picked out a strand of the cocoon and rolled it delicately between his thumb and forefinger.

"Where did you get this?" he demanded curtly.

"Oh, stop being a bore and put the knife away," said Niketas. "Feste is here to help."

Gabras sheathed his knife.

"Forgive me," he said. "I am upset by this. It was not unknown for my predecessors to lose their heads when outsiders got hold of the Imperial worms."

"Someone saved you the trouble," I said. "I took this off the body of a Venetian silk merchant named Ranieri."

"Ah, the decapitated fellow in the cistern," said Niketas. "I had a feeling that you had something to do with that, Feste."

"I was there, but I didn't take his head off," I said. "Ranieri decided to save his skin by giving up the conspiracy. My guess is that a fellow conspirator removed him before he would talk. Probably the same one who killed Bastiani."

"He was involved as well?" marveled Niketas.

"I believe so, though we'll never know for certain."

"Who did Ranieri get this from?" asked Gabras, holding up the cocoon.

I described the rabbit, and he nodded quickly.

"I know him," he said. "I must report this to the Eparch. He'll have him taken into custody. But the Venetians——"

"Are mine," said Niketas. He snapped his fingers, and his servant came in. "Rouse those useless fellows who pass for guards and have them meet us in front of the building in five minutes."

The servant ran out.

"Are they any good?" I asked.

"I don't know," said Niketas. "They have only had to perform on state occasions. But they march well and dress superbly."

"I'll take this," said Gabras, pocketing the cocoon and the dying worm. He held out his hand, which I took, wishing that he had wiped it first after handling that disgusting little grub. "Thank you, Fool. You will be rewarded."

Niketas put on his official robe and walked with me to the steps. A sleepy and sullen group of guards had assembled, awaiting his orders. He looked over them benignly.

"Good morning," he chirped. "This is one of those rare occasions where you might actually have to earn your pay. We are going to conduct a little surprise inspection of the silk embolum in the Venetian quarter. No rough stuff, but if they resist, use all available force."

"A favor," I muttered.

"What is it?" he asked, turning to me.

"Give me a head start, maybe five minutes."

He grimaced. "I don't think that these fellows could keep up with you at this time of the morning. Go ahead."

Behind me, dawn began to break over Anatolia. I ran toward the Venetian quarter, passed the gate, and charged the embolum, my knife drawn.

Ruzzini was seated alone, his hands clasped before him on the table, his head bowed in prayer. He looked up when I crashed through the doorway, but made no attempt to grab a weapon.

"Good morning, Fool," he said quietly. "Have you come to sing to me again?"

"I think it's your turn to do the singing," I said. "It's over, Ruzzini. If you want any help from me, you had better start talking."

"Talking? About what?" he asked. "And why do I need help, and why should I believe that you can provide it?"

I went around the table, grabbed him by the front of his tunic, and threw him down on the floor. He lay there, momentarily stunned, and I straddled him and put my knife to his throat.

"In just a few minutes, this warehouse will be searched," I said. "They will find silkworms and mulberry trees smuggled from Zeuxippos, and caches of weapons. You will be taken into custody, probably tortured, certainly put to death."

"Death?" he said. "Not for smuggling."

"There are two men dead, thanks to you. I overheard your conversation with Ranieri. I know you were in the conspiracy with him and Bastiani. Ranieri killed Bastiani, and you killed him."

"I killed no one," he gasped. "And neither did Ranieri. We were together the night Bastiani died. There were several witnesses present."

"All Venetians, I suppose."

"Venetians and a captain and several officers of the Vigla," he said. "We were discussing the brawling that's being going on with the Pisans. Ranieri was as surprised by Bastiani's death as anyone. It served us no use."

"Why not?"

"Bastiani had the contacts to get the purple dye," he said. "The silk was important, but that was the other piece of the puzzle. His death set us back months."

"But you panicked and killed Ranieri," I said.

He said nothing.

"I can arrange it for you to live," I said. "I have that power. Ranieri wanted you to kill me, but you killed him instead."

"No," he whispered. "It was Viadro."

"What?"

"You know so much, let me prove it to you," he said. "Let me up." I stood, keeping my knife handy, and pulled him to his feet. He took a key from the desk and unlocked the padlock on Bastiani's store-room, then pushed the door open.

"Look," he said.

I pushed him ahead of me, suspecting a trap. But there was no one in the room. The crates lay shattered, the precious bales of silk tossed about. The weapons were gone.

"Where is he?" I shouted.

At that moment, Niketas entered the embolum, followed by his guards.

"Search the storerooms," he commanded. "Arrest the Venetian."

"Logothete, this is a violation of several treaties," smirked Ruzzini.

"I suppose it is," said Niketas calmly. "So is the invasion. I'll accept the morality of my position for the moment."

"Where's Viadro?" I asked.

Ruzzini shrugged.

"He never took me that far into his confidence," he said grimly. "Smart lad under the circumstances."

Two guards led him away, while the rest commandeered some wagons and began loading them with crates of silk, trees, and small wicker boxes.

"Well, that's that," said Niketas as we walked outside. "Let me wish you a proper good morning—"

He stopped as we heard several crashes in the distance. Distant shouts passed along the wall from watchtower to watchtower. When they came closer, we were able to make them out.

"The fleet's coming across!" came the word from the seawall.

"The army attacks!" came the word from Blachernae.

Niketas looked at me.

"I'd like to talk," he said. "But the time for talking is over. Go, Fool. Take your wife to safety. I must rejoin the Senate."

He left me standing there.

Viadro was out there, I thought. He was leading a heavily armed band of Venetians. Where was he going?

Then I remembered the encounter he had with Plossus, down by the Petrion Gate.

I assumed the other fools had sprung into action the moment the alarm had sounded, which meant that Aglaia and Rico were on their way to Blachernae and Plossus off to alert Father Esaias. I had no troops to marshal and couldn't go running to any soldiers without something solid to tell them. I had no choice. I had to check it out for myself.

It took me less then ten minutes to run the distance to that part of the seawall. Stones went whizzing overhead in both directions, crashing into ships and buildings. People fled the houses near the walls. I cut through them as well as I could. At one point, a stone hit just behind me, smashing into a fish seller's stall and sending his wares flying.

I ran to one of the towers by the gate. Its entrance was guarded by a Varangian, who was watching the stones fly above us.

"What's going on?" I shouted in Danish.

He stared at me.

"They're attacking, Fool!" he said. "Get out, if you value your hide."

I moved on to the next tower and accosted its guard.

"What's happening?" I shouted in Danish.

He stared at me.

"What is the situation?" I said, this time in English.

Still no response.

"Your mother is a whore," I said in Venetian. His eyes widened, and he started to raise his axe. I kicked his legs out from under him and rammed my knife into his throat.

I slipped through the entrance to the tower. Two Varangians lay dead on the floor. Real Varangians this time. They must have been taken by surprise and the Venetian stationed at the tower base in their stead.

The fighting had been fierce inside. The Venetians had the advantage in numbers but inferior armor. Body after body littered the steps, and the blood made it slippery underfoot. I sheathed my knife and pried a crossbow from a Venetian hand, arming it with a bolt from his quiver. I still felt inadequate in my motley. I took another crossbow and worked my way carefully up the steps, holding them both before me.

With every turn came more carnage. I was halfway up the tower before I found a living soul. It was Cnut, his axe bloody, four men dead around him. A bolt protruded from the barrel-shaped armor around his torso.

"Feste?" he whispered.

"How many are left?" I asked, feeling the pulse in his neck. It was weak.

"I don't know," he said, trying to rise. He winced and sunk back down. "We were watching the fleet. We didn't expect to be attacked from within."

"You did well," I said in Danish. "You honor your ancestors."

"I failed to hold the tower," he said. "I can never look my comrades in the eye again."

"Nonsense," I said. "Rest, Cnut. I'll be back."

I left him and continued upward. The fighting had been fiercest at the top of the tower. When I reached it, crossbows at the ready, only one man still stood. He was tying something to the edge facing the Golden Horn.

"Signor Viadro," I said.

He turned slowly, and smiled when he saw me.

"Hello, Fool," he said. "Isn't this a glorious sight? Come and look."

I pointed a crossbow at him, and he moved away from the tower's edge. Beyond him, a large flag caught the breeze and fluttered merrily.

It was the winged lion of Saint Mark, the same silk flag that had been on the wall of the embolum.

"A flag?" I asked. "Is that all this was supposed to be?"

"A flag and a tower," he said. "A tower on the seawall where the shore is narrow. We were to accomplish that one simple task, and we did. You came too late, Fool. Look beyond the flag."

I did. One of the giant merchantmen was heading straight at us, the extended bowsprit projecting far beyond the bow, reinforced by planks and ropes into a flying bridge, covered with soldiers, three abreast. It rose and fell with each pull of the oarsmen but was high enough that the end of the bridge was level with the top of the tower.

"We take this tower," said Viadro dreamily. "And use it to take the next. And the one after that, then a gate between them, which we will open, and so we shall take the city. No army has ever conquered Byzantium from without. Until now."

"You're the Silk Man," I said.

"I am," he said. "The only one in all the Venetian quarter capable of this. The others were too cautious, too greedy. Too old."

"Why didn't you kill me at the cistern?" I asked.

"Ranieri wanted me to kill you," he said. "I knew that wouldn't prevent your colleagues from finding out about his petty smuggling. I went along with him to see if he would be loyal enough to Venice to keep my identity secret. But he was more interested in protecting his business. I knew he would give me up. So, I killed him." He held up an axe. "These work quite well, once you have a little practice with them."

"And Bastiani?" I said. "Why did you kill him? How did you kill him, for that matter?"

He frowned. "I didn't kill him. I still have no idea how it happened. I was wondering if you could explain it to me."

I motioned with my crossbow.

"Drop the axe," I said.

"I don't think so," he said, smiling again.

There was a roar from behind me. I whirled, trying to bring the crossbow into line. Cnut charged past me, his axe high over his head. Viadro started to bring his up, but the Dane had the momentum. He brought his weapon down in a fearsome blow and split the Venetian from his head down to the middle of his chest.

Cnut wrenched his axe free, then stared out at the approaching ship.

"Come on, lad," I said, pulling at his arm.

"Get help," he said. "I'll hold them off as long as I can."

"Don't be an idiot," I urged him. "You can't take them on by yourself."

"This is what we do," he said calmly. "Will you fight by my side?"

"I don't think so," I said.

"Then you're of no use here. Leave. Pass me those crossbows if you aren't planning on using them further."

I handed them to him. He raised one, timed the rising and falling of the bowsprit, and calmly picked off the knight at its tip.

"Go, Feste," he said. "Give my love to your wife."

It may have been the reminder that I had promised her I would try and live through this that sent me flying down the steps. It may have been the absolute futility of trying to hold the tower with only a wounded Varangian and a fool. Or maybe it was the arrival of the first bolt shot from the oncoming ship that did it.

I burst out of the tower calling for help, but the other towers were already engaged, the guards launching every conceivable missile at the Venetians. The ones on the ground were busy carrying more stones to the mangonels on the walls. Every officer I could find shook me off and continued barking orders at his own men. Then I heard shouts in a different language. The end of the bowsprit was lashed to the top of the tower, and the Venetians were swarming across the narrow flying bridge and into the heart of the Byzantine defenses.

Well, the defenders could see the situation for themselves now. No reason for me to hang around anymore. I ran from the walls as fast as I possibly could.

I turned when I reached the Mese and jumped onto a rain barrel and then onto a nearby roof. From there, I watched throughout the day as the battle raged across the seawall. One tower after another fell to the Venetian assault, just as Viadro had predicted. The Petrion Gate was taken and opened, and the invaders fanned out through the neighborhood, occupying the recently abandoned buildings. The bulk of the Greek forces were at the land walls, I found out later, dealing with the Crusader army, leaving mostly Varangians, Pisans, and Genoese to combat the Venetians here. The appearance of the invaders actually inside the city took much of the fight out of the defenders. So disheartened were they that by noon the fight was taking on the appearance of a rout. The Venetians occupied fully a quarter of the seawall by the Golden Horn, and Blachernae would soon be within their reach.

Then, without warning or explanation, they withdrew. I watched, astonished, as one by one the hard-won positions were abandoned and the Venetians streamed through the Petrion Gate back to their ships. Cheers erupted from the remaining defenders and the few citizens foolhardy enough to stay and watch.

But the fleet struck one more devastating blow as they fell back. Flames suddenly shot from the buildings nearest the gate. The same winds that had propelled the fleet across the Golden Horn whipped the flames across the city like a rider urging on his horse on the home stretch, and the same men who had been holding back the invaders with steel fled before this new onslaught.

The Fifth Hill caught the brunt of the fire at first. I jumped down from my observation point and grabbed a wheelbarrow. Together with a Varangian who had come on the scene, I manhandled the rain barrel onto the wheelbarrow, then we trundled it up the Mese toward the flames.

The fire was already climbing the lower reaches of the hill, leaping from roof to roof with the ease of an acrobat. We spilled the contents of the barrel from a small promontory onto a burning rooftop below us. There were cries from the top of the hill, and we turned to see the monks of the Monastery of the Pammakaristos beckoning to us.

"There's a cistern there!" shouted the Varangian.

We pushed the wheelbarrow up to the top of the hill. The monks were swarming around it. I thought of an anthill that had been roused by malicious children with flaming twigs. The monks were organized, thank Christ, and had seemingly every bucket on the hill either filled or waiting to be filled. We filled the barrel and wheeled it back down the hill until we met up with the fire once again. We upended the barrel, then went back up again.

We repeated the process over a hundred times, working well into the night. It was backbreaking work. I have heard soldiers after a battle, boasting of how they held some hill against an enemy onslaught. Well, we held the Fifth Hill against the fire, fellow fools. The line of houses below the promontory burned down, leaving a band of scorched ground between us and the rest of the flames. The fire spread to the valley between the Fifth Hill and Blachernae but met up with the Blachernae wall at one end and a crowd armed with buckets from another cistern at the other end. Finally, having nothing more to consume, it died out.

I realized, as I sank to the ground in utter exhaustion, that I had lost all track of time, not to mention what was happening in the rest of the world. And that bothered me, because somewhere in the middle of the fire's path was our home.

$\mathscr{S}$EVENTEEN

[T]he emperor of Constantinople, Alexios, sallied forth from the city . . .
———ROBERT DE CLARI,
THE CONQUEST OF CONSTANTINOPLE

I watched out the window as Feste left for his meeting with Choniates. I wanted desperately to go with him and see my theory validated, but Niketas was his contact, not mine. He looked tired as he trudged into the early morning gloom, and it was more than the unnatural hour. He had set his cap and bells at an immense task when he came up with the plan to forestall the war, and the thoughts of failure and the ensuing slaughter weighed him down more than any length of chain could have done.

I turned my hands to baking bread, just to see how it would go. It had been a long time since I had performed this simple task, and the resulting dough was a bit lumpy, but it felt good to knead while the city slept around me.

I set the loaves aside to rise, then took the remaining flour and mixed it with some chalk that I had pounded to a fine white powder. My bag of whiteface was running low. I had stocked up on kohl and rouge before the siege, fortunately. They were hard to find at the moment, among other useful things. I scrubbed my face clean, then applied my makeup. I had just finished the green diamonds under my eyes when I heard the first crash and the shouts from the seawall.

Plossus and Rico sprang from their cushions, weapons drawn, blinking uncertainly. We dashed up to the roof, Plossus carrying his stilts. He gave Rico a boost up to his shoulders, then jumped up to the footrests.

"What's going on?" I called.

"The fleet's coming across," said Rico. "I expect the army is doing the same."

"Let's go," I said.

We ran back down through our rooms. I glanced at the rising dough with regret, but there was no time. Maybe I could bake it later.

Plossus took off to find Father Esaias while I roused Rico's donkeys. Rico brought his cart around. We hitched the sleepy beasts up quickly, and with a flick of the dwarf's whip, we were riding to Blachernae.

People were already gathering at the inner walls, shouting for information, demanding action. The Imperial Guards were out, shoving the crowd back and clearing the entryways. They allowed us to pass through, the gates closing behind us, muffling the shouting.

Normally, I would go straight to Euphy's chambers, but I wanted to know the situation with the Emperor first. So did Euphy, as it turned out. She was already up and in full regalia, regaling her regal husband with one unwanted opinion after another until he finally stood and shouted for his guards to remove her bodily from the room. Two came up and looked at her uncertainly as her hand went to her waist. She raised a small dagger in the air.

"This arm for Byzantium!" she cried. "If you will not be man enough to face the enemy, then I shall step forward—"

At a furious signal from Alexios, the guards caught her from behind, wrested away the dagger, and dragged her off, still screaming.

"At last, some peace and quiet," muttered the Emperor. "Someone tell me what's going on out there."

"The attack is on two fronts," said an officer. "The army is trying to take the Blachernae wall with scaling ladders with little success."

"I should think not," said the Emperor. "And the other front?"

"The fleet is attacking near the Petrion Gate. We think they mean to try and take Blachernae from that direction."

"A good plan," pronounced the Emperor. "They'll try and proclaim my nephew from the palace. Well, how goes the defense?"

"Excellently," asserted the officer. "In fact, we have already taken prisoners."

"Have you?" exclaimed the Emperor in delight. "Are they here?"

"Yes, sire."

"Let me see them at once," he declared.

A pair of Frenchmen, stripped of their armor, were led in. Despite many wounds and bruises, they stood proudly before the Emperor.

"Excellent deportment in defeat, I must say," said the Emperor, inspecting them critically. "How are you, gentlemen?"

They looked at him and said nothing.

"Oh, dear," he said. "I forgot they don't speak Greek. Fetch the Imperial Interpreter, somebody. So, where were these fine fellows taken?"

"At the base of the tower below Petrion," said the officer.

"Well done, well done," said the Emperor. Then he frowned suddenly. "At the base of the tower, you said?"

"Yes, sire," said the officer, a bit nervously.

"But the base of the tower—do you mean to tell me that the Venetians have gotten inside the seawalls?" shouted the Emperor.

The other officers in the room looked pointedly at the one who had been doing all the talking.

"Take this oaf out and get me someone who knows what's really going on!" shouted the Emperor. "Get reinforcements down to Petrion. Good God, I am surrounded by incompetents."

"Hand-picked by yourself," muttered Rico.

Twenty minutes later, a runner from the Varangians came in.

[230]

"Well?" said the Emperor heavily.

"My lord, the Venetians have taken the Petrion Gate," he said. "They occupy four towers, and are working their way along the wall in both directions. We are trying to retake the towers, but they have crossbowmen everywhere and the height to their advantage. More knights are holding the gate itself, and they say that the Doge himself has come ashore."

"And the Crusader army?" asked the Emperor quietly.

"Attacking Blachernae with scaling ladders and siege towers," said an Imperial Guardsman. "We are holding them there for the moment. But if the Venetians work their way up the wall to Blachernae, they could join forces and take the palace."

"And if they do that, they'll stick a crown on my nephew's head and proclaim him," concluded the Emperor. "And they'll be able to defend it from the inside. Curse my royal ancestor for building it on a hill. All right, the immediate danger is from the Venetians. Do we have enough men to drive them off the walls?"

"Most of the troops are committed to the land walls, waiting to attack," said a general. "If we pull them away, that weakens the defenses."

"Sire, the people are calling for an attack," said Philoxenites, who had been listening off to the side the whole time. "They are demanding leadership."

"Leadership," mused the Emperor. "They want their Emperor to act like one, is that it?"

Philoxenites bowed.

"You are their father," he said. "They are your children. They need your protection. If you fail to provide it..."

"Then they'll find a father who can," said Rico.

Alexios looked at the dwarf, startled. Rico returned his stare evenly, his arms folded in front of his chest.

"Have you turned against me, little Fool?" said the Emperor.

"You have turned against yourself, Great One," said Rico. "Now, it is time for you to return to yourself."

The Emperor placed his hands on the edge of his throne and forced himself to his feet, wincing.

"Fetch my armor," he said. "Saddle my horse. The Emperor will ride to battle."

"But, sire..." started a general.

"Nothing to fear," said Alexios. "We have to attack the army. They're outnumbered, so they'll have to send for help. The Venetians will have no choice but to leave the walls and reinforce them. Then we can retake the gate and the towers. Let's go."

He staggered off to his bedchamber as servants came running with his armor.

"You know, that's not a bad plan," commented Rico.

I nudged him and pointed. The flutist was taking advantage of the commotion to slip out the side entrance.

We gave her a short lead, then cut through the soldiers and servants dashing about and went through the same doorway. She was nowhere to be seen.

"Split up?" suggested Rico.

"No. Let's stick together. She isn't likely to be leaving the palace just yet."

From behind us, soldiers were shouting, "The Emperor rides! Make way for the Emperor! Victory to Alexios Angelos!"

"Think he'll pull it off?" I asked.

Rico shrugged. "Self-interest is a powerful motivator," he said. "At least he's finally understanding the situation. Whether that means he'll take the bull by the horns or run for his life, I don't pretend to predict."

"Let's go find the Egyptian," I said.

We decided to search the section of the palace overlooking the landwall, thinking that she would be looking for a window with a good view of the battle. The palace unfortunately had plenty of those, and it was some time before we spotted a door slightly ajar that led to a storage room on the uppermost floor. I pushed it open gently and saw her watching intently as wave after wave of Crusaders were driven back by rocks, arrows, and boiling oil.

"Mind if we join you?" I asked.

She jumped at the unexpected intrusion, then shrugged uncertainly. She pretended as usual to not understand much Greek. I stood next to and slightly behind her at the window while Rico closed the door and leaned casually against it.

From this vantage point, we could see the entire field of battle. The Crusaders were so intent on their immediate objective that they didn't notice the gates opening about a league to the west of us. It took the cheers of the onlookers in the city to alert them to the Greek army pouring onto the plain, and they pulled back from the walls and wheeled into battle formation with surprising speed.

"They are well trained," I said. "I think they'll give us quite a battle even if the numbers favor us, don't you?"

She nodded in a agreement, then stiffened as she realized I was speaking in Arabic.

"You speak my language," she said.

"A tutor from my youth," I said. "He taught me his language and mathematics. I remember the mathematics, too. Would you like to hear me add something?"

"*Salaam alekhem*, lady," called Rico, grinning at her.

"What do you want?" she asked.

"That depends on what happens out there," I said. "Let's watch. Oh, please, don't leave yet. I must insist upon your company."

I had my knife at the small of her back. I knew that I had the advantage of her. One of the problems with wearing as little as she did was that it left her no means of concealing a weapon.

We could see the Emperor riding at the head of his army as the city cheered him on. The Crusaders had six divisions. The Greeks filled the plain.

As the Emperor and his troops rode forward, the Crusaders pulled back to the palisade they had constructed. Everyone from heavily armored knights down to the cooks' boys wearing pots tied across their chests for protection was ready to kill for Christ. Some horsemen peeled off toward the Golden Horn, and soon the Venetian fleet began appearing off to the right. The men on the ships came to shore and quickly joined their fellows on the Kosmidion.

All that stood between the two armies was the Lycos river. There were several bridges across it, and the rest was easily fordable. There was a hush as the city waited for the Emperor to lead the attack. I held my breath, knowing that one of two things would happen, and that if we had guessed wrong, then I would become a murderer before the day was out.

The Greek army inched forward, agonizingly slow. Another hundred paces and they would be in bowshot. Then fifty paces. Then thirty.

Then they stopped.

"What is he doing?" she whispered.

"Deciding," I said.

Those of the Crusaders who were still mounted feinted toward the Lycos, then withdrew. The Greek army stood there. Suddenly, a single division of Frenchmen charged in an unwieldy bulge, closing the distance between the two armies.

And the Greeks pulled back. In orderly, purposeful fashion, they marched back to the military gate from which they had emerged, the Emperor at the lead.

The citizens watched from the rooftops in stunned silence. Then a single, strong voice burst through the stillness.

"The Emperor flees!" he shouted. "Coward! Down with Alexios!"

The cry was picked up and repeated up and down the walls, and reverberated across the Mese and through the city. It became a steady roar of rage and disappointment.

I recognized the first cry, of course. Plossus was in fine voice today, and all of his Guild training paid off. He had timed it perfectly and projected it well, and the rabble-rousers we had recruited from Father Esaias did their job fanning the flames. The resulting revolt might have happened anyway, but even the driest tinder needs a spark.

"Why do they denounce him?" protested the flutist. "Can't they see he only brought the army out to decoy the Venetians away from the seawall?"

"My fellow entertainer, I am surprised at you," I said. "First law of pleasing the public is to give them what they want, whether it's performing or warfare. Displease your audience, and you'll be run out of town."

"He won't leave," she declared.

"He will if you persuade him to leave," I said.

She looked at me, her eyes narrowed down to slits. "That's why you're here with a knife at my back? To ask me this? Why should I?"

"Because he'll listen to you," I said. "And because it will suit your masters as well."

"What are you talking about?" she asked.

"I've been following you, you know," I said. "Ever since I saw you hook up with that captain in the Moslem quarter. You're a Saracen spy, milady, and I've got the goods on you."

"Who will believe you?" she scoffed.

"Quite a few people," I said. "But I'm not interested in denouncing you. I want you to work your seductive charms on the Emperor and get him to leave town. I don't think he'll need a lot of persuading. And it will be in your interests."

[235]

"You see, lady, we figure that with Alexios off the throne, the Crusaders are going to have to remain here a while just to help the new regime settle in," explained Rico. "And since your masters have been doing whatever they can to keep the Crusade from coming to a theater of battle near them, you'll come out smelling like a rose."

She looked back and forth between the two of us.

"Who do you work for?" she demanded.

"We're just fools," I said. "We work for no government and no church."

"And if I refuse, you denounce me," she said.

"No, lady," I replied. "If you refuse, then we report how, in your despair over the public cowardice and shame of your Emperor, you threw yourself from this very window to your death."

"It will be a magnificent recounting," said Rico. "I shall be weeping copiously for your loss."

"I won't," I said.

She glanced out the window, estimating the height in her mind and not liking the result.

"And if I denounce you instead?" she asked.

"Listen to what they're shouting down there," I urged her. "If they storm Blachernae, do you think that the Emperor's concubine will be spared?"

"Excuse me for a moment, ladies," said Rico. He slipped out the door. Seconds later, we heard a thud and a clatter of armor. He came back in.

"Well?" I asked her.

"All right," she said. "I'll persuade him."

I sheathed my knife, relieved. Rico opened the door for us, bowing as we passed by. There was an Imperial Guardsman lying in a heap nearby. The flutist looked at him, then back at the dwarf.

"Did you do that?" she said, impressed.

He bowed, grinning broadly. She walked away, shaking her head.

"Think it will work?" he asked.

I shrugged.

There were cries of panic from the side of the palace facing the city. We ran to a balcony and watched in horror as we saw a great fire climbing the Fifth Hill and surging across the valley before us. Below us, we saw the Emperor and his retinue gallop into the courtyard. The Emperor started barking orders, and servants and soldiers scattered in all directions.

"I'd better get down there," said Rico. "To think, Julius Caesar gained this empire by crossing a river, and now Alexios has lost it by not crossing one."

"And that makes all the difference," I said, watching the flames finally die down just short of the Blachernae wall. "Do you know what I was thinking just now?"

"What?" asked Rico.

"That I had set aside some bread to bake this morning."

He looked out at the expanse of smoldering embers that had until recently been our neighborhood.

"I think it's probably done by now," said the dwarf, and he left me on the balcony, wondering where my husband was.

EIGHTEEN

He who had been blinded was ordained to oversee all things.
—NIKETAS CHONIATES, *O CITY OF BYZANTIUM*

Night fell, but no bonfires lit the seawall. There was nothing left to burn. Around me, citizens roamed through what was left of the neighborhood, salvaging what they could from their homes. Thieves flitted through the shadows, sifting the ashes for anything of value.

I sat on a low wall by the monastery, watching it all like a hawk. Or more like a vulture. Then I glimpsed a strange sight: a royal procession emerged from Blachernae, consisting of chariots, wains, and Imperial Guards.

When an Emperor merits a triumph in this city, he enters through the Golden Gate amidst cheers and banners, and everyone lines the streets and cheers him on. I guess one would call this little parade a defeat. No one came out to watch Alexios Angelos skulk out of the city. No one except for a tired, sooty fool.

The Emperor was leaning back in a large chariot, a quartet of stallions pulling it along, their hooves wrapped to muffle his departure. His legs were propped up on cushions, and the flutist was kneeling by him, massaging his feet. Irene sat behind them, looking tearful and resigned.

"Hail, sire!" I called as they approached.

He motioned to his charioteer to slow down, and I trotted alongside.

"Well, Fool, I must bid you farewell," he said. "You will be one of the people I shall miss."

"You are most kind, milord," I said. "But you have a musician by your side to give you comfort."

"That I do, that I do," he said, stroking her hair. She managed to smile at him while at the same time shooting me a look of pure hatred.

"Now, this isn't surrender, mind you," he said.

"Of course not, milord. Who could think that the Emperor would surrender his empire?"

"Exactly," he said, subdued. "The Empire is wherever I am. Divine Providence has seen to my survival."

"You are truly blessed, milord."

"Yes," he said, brightening. "Blessed. That's the word. I still reign, have troops to command, money to pay them, my musical treasure for companionship, and a newly marriageable daughter, eh, sweetheart?" He reached back to pat Irene's knee. She cringed and buried her face in her hands. He turned back to me.

"She'll get over it," he assured me. "Not the first husband she's lost. But I'm saving her for an alliance somewhere. Daughters are quite handy when it comes to that sort of thing."

"Your wife, milord?" I asked.

"Where?" he cried in alarm, looking over his shoulder. Then he regained control of himself. "Well, yes, my wife. Need to leave someone here to run things for me, don't I? What she always wanted to do. I'll leave the city to her. And Laskaris. I always liked him. Capable fellow. I'll make him my heir someday if Irene can't catch me a better one."

Irene started wailing.

"Oh, do stop that, the journey's going to be long enough as it is," he muttered. "Well, Fool, thank you for all the funny stories and songs. Good luck. And if you see my wife, give her my regards."

And he rode off, chuckling to himself.

I watched the wains go by, guards escorting them on both sides. They must have taken every surviving horse in the army. Then, as I was about to turn and leave, I saw a pair of donkeys pulling a familiar-looking cart.

Rico reined his animals to a halt when he saw me.

"Just where do you think you're going?" I demanded.

"I think they said Develton," he replied. "That's somewhere up north, but they're going the long way round. Don't want to risk any inadvertent encounters with a real army."

"What are you doing?"

"Someone has to keep an eye on him," he said. "Do you know what's in those wains? Most of the Imperial Treasury. I saw them loading it. He's down, but by no means out. He has an army, gold, and Irene, and with those three things he can make a lot of mischief still. As soon as we get settled, I'll get word either to you or the Guild."

I looked at him, not knowing what to say.

"Come on, Feste," he said. "I'm the Emperor's Fool. It makes sense."

I grasped his tiny hand and held it for a moment.

"Take care of yourself," he said gruffly. "Give my love to that wife of yours, and good luck with the baby. And teach Plossus how to cook a decent meal before I get back."

"We will," I promised.

He flicked his reins, and the donkeys followed the wains down the Mese. I watched them until they turned at the Forum Amastrianum and disappeared.

I was hungry. I couldn't remember when I had last eaten. I rummaged through my bag and found some dried fruit and some nuts, which I wolfed down, following with the dregs from my wineskin.

I picked my way through the rubble, trying to figure out where our house once was. Eventually, I found the ruined walls outside the courtyard, and stepped over the stones that had made up the archway at the entrance.

The house itself was a pile of charred stones and ashes. I stirred through them, finding only a few copper pots, and even these were twisted and deformed by the conflagration whose fading heat I could feel even now through the soles of my boots. I stood where I thought our bedroom had been, where our child had been conceived. I wished the bed had survived. What I wanted to do more than anything at the moment was sleep.

" 'Twas the heat of our passion that caused all this," said Aglaia lightly as she came up behind me.

I turned around and pulled her to me.

"You live," I whispered.

"So I do," she said, and she kissed me hard to prove it.

"Looks like we lost everything," I said when we finally separated.

"Things, Feste," she said, wrapping her arms around me. "We lost things, not everything. Things can be replaced. And speaking of things that need replacing, Philoxenites wants you back at Blachernae."

"He does? Why?"

"To help replace the emperor."

"I don't want to be the emperor."

"Why not? At least we'd have somewhere to live. Come, Fool."

She led me toward Blachernae.

The throne room had been stripped of its finery. The remaining bureaucrats milled about, while some I recognized as senators peeked into the imperial bedchamber as if they were gawking tourists.

Niketas Choniates came up to me and shook my hand warmly.

"Well done!" he whispered. "I don't know half of it, and I suspect that's the half I don't want to know, but well done, Feste. And you, Mistress Aglaia. If there's anything I can do—"

"We need a place to stay," she said bluntly. "We were burnt out of ours."

"You shall stay with me," he said firmly. "And that other fool as well. It will be a vast improvement over my usual dinner companions. Now, go over to the eunuch. We have work to do."

Philoxenites was leaning against the far wall, watching everyone. He grimaced when he saw me.

"You look like hell," he observed.

"They have fires there, I think," I replied.

"You're friendly with that Varangian captain, aren't you?" he asked.

"Henry," I said. "Yes, I am."

"Get him here as quick as you can," he ordered. "Smooth things out with him on the way. I've sent for the other captains already. Euphrosyne and Laskaris are trying to assert their authority. We need Isaakios on the throne by dawn."

"I'll meet you back here," I said wearily.

I left Aglaia with Nik and trotted out of Blachernae. There was a ramp going up to the top of the seawall. I climbed it and ran along the top, glancing out at the fleet as I did. The Venetians had anchored for the night, but they kept long torches projecting from the sides of their vessels to prevent any low boats or rafts from floating up by them under the cover of darkness.

The Varangians at the walls and towers had been up as long as I and had been in heavy fighting to boot. They looked close to death but kept up the watch while teams of laborers repaired the damage to the Petrion Gate. It was here that I found Henry, supervising the work. He looked at me bleakly as I approached.

"You're wanted at Blachernae," I said.

He spat. "Who wants me?" he asked. "Who is left there with the authority to tell me what to do? Who should order a captain of the Varangians by using a fool as an intermediary?"

"You swore an oath to an emperor once," I said.

"And that emperor has betrayed us all. That oath no longer binds us."

"Not that emperor," I said.

He looked at me. "What are you talking about?"

"Please come with me, Henry. I am appealing to you as a friend, not as an intermediary."

"There is no place for friendship here," he said. "Cnut's dead. He was as good a friend and as valiant a soldier as any man could be, but he's dead nonetheless."

"I know," I said. "I'm sorry. Come with me, Henry. There isn't much time left."

He picked up his axe and gave orders to one of his men, then walked with me to Blachernae.

The assembled captains of the Varangian Guard gathered in the office of Constantine Philoxenites. Six burly axe-bearers stood suspiciously on one side of the room. On the other sat the fat, bald eunuch. Between them was a fool, sitting on the windowsill, wondering why he was still here.

"My good friends," Philoxenites began.

"We're no friends of yours," said one of them.

"No fancy words, no appeals to our sense of duty if you don't mind," said another.

"Very well," said Philoxenites. "The usurper has fled."

"Usurper?" scoffed Henry. "You called him Lord until a few hours ago."

"To my everlasting shame," said Philoxenites, hanging his head. "I acted dishonorably. Now, I seek to make amends. I do not intend to turn this city over to that French-loving boy. But the people of Constantinople will not have any of Alexios's heirs on the throne. That leaves only one solution. We must restore the Emperor Isaakios to his rightful place."

There was shock and anger in the expressions of the captains. Henry stepped forward.

"Let me get this straight," he said. "We forswore our most sacred oath to Isaakios on your representation that the Greeks would not allow a blind man to rule them. Now, you're telling us that we should put him back on the throne, just like that, and forget all about the oath and the renunciation and the oath we swore to the man you now call a usurper. Do I understand you correctly?"

"Oaths are just formalities, Captain," said Philoxenites.

"Not to Varangians!" shouted Henry, and the others nodded.

"All right, Captain. You have convinced me that our actions dishonored you. Obviously, reparations must be made."

"You're trying to buy us off?" asked Henry in disbelief.

Philoxenites shrugged.

"We cannot change the past," he said. "We can only make amends. Will you let a matter of honor stand between you and the safety of this city?"

"We don't give a rat's ass about this city," said Henry. "We fight for honor."

"Honor alone?" exclaimed the eunuch. "If only I had known from the beginning that there was no need for paying you."

Henry glowered, his fingers playing along the handle of his axe.

"What shall it be, Captain?" asked Philoxenites. "How shall honor be placated?"

Henry held up his forefinger. "One," he said. "There will be no oath sworn to the Emperor."

"Done," said the eunuch.

"Two," said Henry. "We protect Blachernae from now on. What's left of the Imperials will be under our command."

"Agreed."

"Increase our pay by half again as much."

"I'll have to see what's left in the Treasury," said Philoxenites. "If there's enough, I will see to it."

"Four," said Henry. "When Isaakios dies, the Varangians are consulted as to who becomes Emperor."

Philoxenites smiled. "As you are being consulted now, Captain. I agree to your terms, and here is my hand in pledge of it."

I have seen Varangians take on ten times their number with less reluctance than Henry displayed in shaking the eunuch's hand. But the deal was struck, and soon after, I found myself walking with him at the head of a Varangian company back down to Chalke.

"Bargains made at night will seem dearer in the light," he muttered. "My old grandam used to tell me that when she took us to market. I wish she were here now. She was a greater battle-axe than any I've ever carried."

"You had better give me yours right now," I said.

"Why?"

"If you're going to start telling jokes, then the fighting will fall to me perforce."

"I am too weary for both jokes and fighting, Feste."

"Then let us keep a peaceful silence until we come to our journey's end, my friend."

Past the great Horologion we marched. Too dark to see the hour. I sensed that the city lay awake around us, tossing and turning on the uneasy ground on which it rested. We turned right, through the gates to the Great Palace, and banged on the doors of Chalke Prison.

It was some time before they opened. A sleepy servant of the warden's looked at the axes gleaming in the torchlight and woke up quickly. He tried shutting the doors, but Henry belied his declaration of weariness by seizing him by the throat and tossing him into the street.

The Varangians burst through the entryway with me following at a safe distance. The warden came out with several prison guards behind him. He took in the scene with surprise.

"What is the meaning of this?" he shouted.

"We have come for Isaakios Angelos," said Henry. "Be so kind as to turn him over to us."

"I see," said the warden, nodding sagely. "The Emperor is finally having him executed. I can't say that I'm surprised. I never understood why he let him go this long."

Henry began laughing, his comrades joining in. The warden relaxed and sat behind his desk, a pinched smile being his sole contribution to the general merriment.

"I'm afraid you have it wrong," said Henry when it subsided. "Isaakios is being restored to the Byzantine throne. Alexios has fled. Now, turn him over so that we might escort him to Blachernae."

The warden looked around, still smiling, thinking he was the butt of some joke. But the smiles had vanished from the faces of the axe-bearers. Slowly, the bureaucrat turned pale.

"By whose authority is this?" he choked out. "Let me see the orders."

"Very proper," said Henry. "Quite correct. Let me see, where did I put them?" He patted his armor with his hands, searching. "Ah. Here, this should satisfy you." He held his axe high over his head with both hands, and with a swift blow he cleaved the desk neatly down the middle.

"That is my authority," said Henry. "Just open those gates, will you?"

The warden looked at the splintered remains of his only piece of official furniture. The prison guards stood back and nodded to their brother Varangians. The warden looked around the room and realized he was alone. He stood, pulled his keys from his waist, unlocked the padlock, and shoved the door open, then turned and beckoned to Henry to enter.

"You had better come with us, hadn't you?" said Henry, gripping the warden's elbow. "There's more use for those keys now, isn't there? Lads, fan out."

His men spread through the prison as if it was the sort of thing they did regularly. The prisoners woke with the noise and pressed against the bars of their cells, silent. They didn't know whether the soldiers meant freedom or execution.

Henry, the warden in tow, and I walked to the last cell. Isaakios sat on the edge of his bed, his hands folded in his lap.

"I hear armor," he said. "Soldiers. And keys. That would be the warden. And the jingling of bells on a cap. Is that you, Feste?"

"It is, sire," I said.

"Are these the soldiers of hope of which we spoke, Fool?"

"They are, sire. Will you come with us?"

He stood.

"Soldier, give me your name," he said.

Henry knelt.

"Sire, I am Henry, Captain of the Varangians at the Hodegon Garrison."

"I know you," said Isaakios. "You were with me at the Double Column last year. And, if my memory serves, you were a strapping young Englishman who came to the guard when I still had eyes and a throne."

"Your memory is correct, sire," said Henry. "We cannot restore your eyes, but we can restore your throne."

Isaakios hesitated. "My brother," he said. "Does he live?"

"He fled the city a few hours past," I said. "The Crusaders will resume their assault in the morning. The people cry for your leadership."

"Do they?" asked Isaakios. "Well, then I must not disappoint them. Warden, put your keys to use."

Henry shoved the warden forward, and the cell was opened. Isaakios drew himself up and stepped with authority through the door. When he reached the aisle, he turned and faced us.

"There are several others here who I would have released," he said. "They are my supporters, and I will need faithful men to serve me. They are all in the four cells next to mine. Alexios Doukas, are you awake?"

"If this is not some heavenly dream to see you out of your cell, sire," cried the bushy-browed lover of Evdokia.

"Good," said Isaakios. "You have been the source of much good advice since I have been here. I need a new chamberlain. Are you willing?"

"With all my heart, sire," said Doukas.

"Warden," said Isaakios.

"Sire," squeaked the warden, dropping to his knees.

Isaakios turned to us and smiled.

"He learns quickly, does he not?" he said. "Warden, I may yet decide not to have you killed. Now, open those cells."

Men staggered out of the darkness and became the Emperor's men.

"To Blachernae!" shouted Henry, and his men took up the cry all the way back up the Mese, waking the city as they marched and perhaps striking a little fear into the enemy outside the walls.

Henry commandeered a chariot from somewhere, and I rode beside Isaakios, catching him up on everything that had happened since my last visit. By the time we reached the Blachernae wall, the rest of the Varangians were established throughout the palace and grounds. Their cheers resounded through the courtyard as we drove up.

Philoxenites came to greet us.

[248]

"Sire, I am your Treasurer, if you will have me," he said, bowing.

Isaakios motioned him to come up to the chariot.

"I understand that you were instrumental in bringing me back," he said quietly. "An Emperor thanks you."

"No need, sire."

"Now, a treasurer with no gold is like a shepherd with no sheep. I want you to seize all the possessions of my brother's family and raise funds any way you can, so long as it's fast."

"It is done, sire," said the eunuch, gliding away.

We entered the palace and ascended to the throne room. I guided the Emperor to the throne, one of the few things Alexios was unable to take with him. Isaakios sat down and placed his arms on the armrest. He looked old and shriveled compared to the previous occupant.

"There used to be some cushions here," he grumbled. "Someone fetch me some cushions. And a decent robe. If I'm to face the Crusader envoys, I damn well better look like an emperor. Which reminds me, I used to have a wife around somewhere. Does anyone know where she's gotten to?"

"Sire, she lives close by," said a courtier.

"Good," said Isaakios. "Wake her up, slit the throat of anyone you find in bed with her, and bring her here. And start dressing this place up as well. I don't care where you scavenge the drapes from. We may be impoverished at the moment, but I want everything that the envoys see to be the richest they have ever seen in their lives. Who will they send?"

"A delegation of French and Venetians," said Henry.

"We'll need the Imperial Interpreter," muttered Isaakios.

The courtiers looked at each other in consternation. One of them cleared his throat.

"What?" barked the Emperor.

"The Imperial Interpreter fled with the Emp—the usurper," he said.

"Wonderful," sighed the Emperor. "Well, find me ... Feste, you speak Venetian dialect, don't you?"

"Yes, sire," I said, my heart sinking.

"And langue d'oc?"

"Of course, sire."

"Good. You are now the Imperial Interpreter. Someone take him, clean him up, and dress him appropriately."

And before I could protest, I was led into another room, stripped of my motley, scrubbed of my makeup, and thrown into a blue tunic with a light purple robe.

"So that's what you look like," chuckled Henry as I was thrust back into the throne room. "I can see why you prefer the disguise."

The room itself had improved substantially in the short time that I was out. The Emperor was resting comfortably on silk cushions, his robes and buskins the peak of fashion. The walls had been draped with gold banners, and a second, smaller throne had been placed by his. As I took my place by his side, his wife was brought in.

"Is that you, Margaret?" said Isaakios, sniffing the air. "I remember that perfume. You wore it the last time you visited me. When was that, five years ago?"

She stood mute, clenching her fists.

"How does she look, Feste?" he asked.

"She is quite beautiful, sire," I said.

"I like to think that you are as beautiful as the day we wed, my dear," said Isaakios. "But of course, you were only nine then. I daresay you've become a real woman by now. Well, we'll resume conjugal relations tomorrow. In the meantime, you had better get yourself dressed up. We're having company."

Envoys were sent at dawn to the Crusader encampment. While we awaited their reply, the preparations for parley continued. The road from the Blachernae Gate to the palace was decked with banners and every remaining flower in the city. All the nobles who had remained were charged with appearing in their most sumptuous robes. They were placed along both sides of the street and ordered to stay on penalty of meeting the nastier end of a Varangian axe.

Soon, we heard cheering from without and the blare of trumpets. The doors were flung open, and a guard announced the envoys from the Crusaders.

There were two from the army and two from the Venetians. Geoffroy de Villehardouin, Marshal of Champagne, was the leader. He was of some fifty years, with gray hair, a stern mien, and a calculating look. His armor was so fine that I doubted it had ever come close enough to an enemy to receive even a token scratch. He looked about the room as if measuring it for his own furniture and glanced at the bejeweled ladies with an eye of appraisal, but only for the jewels. With him was Mathieu de Montmorency, ostensibly Villehardouin's superior but more a soldier than a diplomat. He was a pallid man—we learned later that he was deathly ill, despite his valiant command in battle, and would not live another year. The two Venetian representatives were a Tiepolo and some nephew of the Doge, both of whom spent more time spying on their allies than they did watching us.

Villehardouin stepped forward and knelt before the throne.

"Your Imperial Majesty," he said in stentorian tones that reached the farthest corners of the room. "On behalf of the most holy Crusade, I praise God that our assistance has restored you to your rightful throne."

"We thank you," said Isaakios gravely after I translated.

"We bring words of joy and thanksgiving from your noble son, whose tears first moved us to divert our forces from their original purpose."

"Then our own prayers have been answered," replied the Emperor. "And we seek no further hindrance to your holy quest. We wish you Godspeed and success in your endeavors."

Villehardouin smiled.

"We will leave," he said, "once the terms of our covenant with your royal son have been met."

"What covenant is that?" asked the Emperor.

"To submit this empire and its church to Rome; to pay the army two hundred thousand silver marks for its service on your behalf; to donate, as a charitable gesture, a year's provisions to the Crusade; and to contribute ten thousand men and arms, along with ships to transport them, to join our venture to Beyond-the-Sea."

There was a long pause after I finished translating this to the Emperor. Then he leaned forward on his throne and beckoned to the Frenchman. Villehardouin stepped closer.

"You must be joking," muttered the Emperor. I translated, keeping my voice at the same low level.

"Perhaps we should adjourn to a more private setting," suggested Villehardouin.

This was met with instant agreement. The Emperor, the Empress, his newly-appointed advisers plus Philoxenites, the envoys, and I retreated into an adjoining chamber with a large oaken table, normally used for small banquets. Philoxenites closed the door and sat next to Alexios Doukas, who was resplendent in his Chamberlain's garb.

"Now, let us talk about the real terms," said Isaakios. "What do you really want?"

"Milord, your son agreed to this covenant," said Villehardouin, unrolling a scroll which he placed before the Emperor. "By oath and sealed charters, witnessed by your royal son-in-law, King Philip of Swabia."

"My son was in no position to agree to anything," said the Emperor evenly. "He does not sit on the throne."

"Not yet," returned Montmorency, with a hint of menace in his voice.

"Nor can the terms be met as things presently stand," said the Emperor. "My brother fled, it is true. But he took most of the Imperial Treasury with him. Had you intercepted him in his cowardly flight, you would have had ample means of meeting all of your needs. A pity that you let him escape so easily."

There was a quick huddle among the envoys, with whispers of chagrin floating back to our end of the table. I translated what I could pick up, murmuring in the Emperor's ear.

"Our army is still at your gates," said Villehardouin finally.

Isaakios shrugged. "But your cause has vanished," he said. "You vanquished the usurper. If you fight now, it is only for gain, not for honor."

"And we outnumber you," said Doukas in a harsh voice that startled everyone.

"You outnumbered us yesterday," said Montmorency acerbically. "Yet we prevailed. You may have as large an army as you like. It matters not when they flee. And who will lead them? That blind, doddering man?"

"Perhaps I should challenge the Doge personally," said Isaakios. "A battle of blind, doddering champions. We could sell tickets and use the proceeds to fund your departure."

The Frenchmen did not know what to make of this statement, but Dandolo's nephew actually chuckled.

"Look, we're both in a hard place," said Villehardouin, dropping his showy diplomatic manner. "We've been at this for over a year, with precious little to show for it. My fellows must be satisfied. We have your son and heir. Agree to the covenant now, make him co-emperor, as is his due, and meet the terms once things settle down. We've seen the display you've put on. There's plenty of gold left in this city. You're the Emperor—have your treasurer raise the funds from the people, and we'll be square."

"Where's my treasurer?" muttered the Emperor.

"Here, sire," whispered Philoxenites.

"Do we have enough gold to hold them off for a while?"

"We can make an installment or two," said Philoxenites. "But the full amount would take months to meet. Even years."

"Then we shall agree, but stall them as long as we can," said Isaakios. He turned to the envoys. "My friends, our gratitude is boundless, even if our resources are not. We shall accept your terms, on condition that you give us time to persuade our people. The submission of their church will not be taken lightly. We ask that you remove your encampment to Estanor again, and as a token of our good faith, we will send you immediate provision, which should improve the morale of your men greatly."

"Agreed," said Villehardouin, so quickly that I knew he would have settled for much less.

"Fetch the Imperial Seal," ordered Isaakios grandly. An adviser whispered something to him. "Well, find something that will work," he muttered. "What a shambles this is."

After a brief delay, something was brought in that looked official. The Emperor's hand was guided to the appropriate space on the covenant. A quill was dipped in the philter containing the ink mixed with the blood of Our Savior, a relic reserved for only the greatest of occasions, and the Emperor proceeded to sign away the Empire.

The seals were affixed. We entered the Imperial Throne Room, and a herald proclaimed the terms to the shocked assemblage.

The gates to the city were thrown open. In the afternoon, Alexios was led in to publicly embrace his father while the crowd cheered uncertainly. The Emperor proclaimed that the boy would be coronated on the first of August, twelve days hence.

"On the Feast of St. Peter in Chains," Isaakios said to me as he waved to the crowd. "Too appropriate, don't you think, Feste?"

"If I was a fool, I would comment, sire," I said, shifting uncomfortably in my borrowed bureaucratic habiliments. "But I am only an interpreter."

"Well, I'd rather you were a fool," he said. "I'll be needing some entertainment. In fact, we should have some celebratory games at the Hippodrome. Do this affair right. Go, get your motley back on, my friend. We can get another interpreter, but a good fool is hard to find."

I bowed, grateful and relieved, and left to rejoin my wife.

And so peace was restored to Byzantium.

NINETEEN

Lift thy head, unhappy lady, from the ground; thy neck upraise; this is Troy no more, no longer am I queen in Ilium.

—EURIPIDES, *THE TROJAN WOMEN*

I chatted with Niketas for a while after Feste left. We strolled out to a balcony, watching Laskaris giving orders in the courtyard. I wasn't certain that the orders were being carried out, but the servants and soldiers scurried about in a semblance of obedience.

I spotted my husband returning with Henry but drew no attention to the fact. Shortly thereafter, Varangians began drifting through the courtyard, quietly passing the word. At a quick signal, Laskaris and his men found themselves inside a ring of axes. They were disarmed and led away.

"Fascinating," exclaimed Niketas. "This may be the most bloodless coup this city has ever seen."

"They haven't reckoned with Euphrosyne," I replied. "I think I will go find out what is happening there."

"Tell me everything you see," he begged me.

Euphy looked as though she had not slept in days. Her hair was a rat's nest, her crown askew, and her makeup applied so haphazardly that it made her face look lopsided. She was screaming at every servant and lady-in-waiting unfortunate enough to cross her path while waving an old sword that she had found somewhere.

"We shall attack them at dawn!" she cried. "Fetch me armor. When the men have fled, it shall be the women who shall repel the invaders. There will be no surrender, no suicides. The Trojan women were cowards and traitors to our sex. Fetch me armor!"

Anna, her middle daughter, rushed into the room.

"They've arrested my husband!" she wailed.

The Empress turned to stare at her.

"Who dared lay a hand on Laskaris?" she asked.

"The Varangians!" cried Anna. "They're saying Father's not the Emperor anymore."

Euphrosyne drew herself up to her full height.

"I am the Emperor!" she shouted. "Fetch me the Varangian captains. I shall execute them myself."

No one seemed particularly anxious to carry out this order.

There was a tramping echoing down the hallway, coming closer and closer.

"Shut the door and bar it," commanded the Empress. "We shall hold them off from here."

Her servants hesitated.

"Do it!" she screamed.

Two women heaved the doors closed and dropped an iron bar across it.

"There's no other way in," she declared. "Bring me my bow."

She strung it herself and notched an arrow in readiness. The door shook, then a regular pounding began. As the thick planking began to shiver, I inched closer to Euphy. She drew the arrow back steadily.

The door shattered. Just as the first Varangian poked his head through, I knocked Euphy's arm up. The arrow sailed high over the doorway and stuck halfway up the wall.

She turned to me in fury. "How dare you!" she thundered, raising her hand. She swung, but this time I was ready for her. I ducked the blow and gave her a nice, solid head-butt to the stomach. She staggered back, momentarily winded, and collapsed onto her throne.

The Varangians swarmed in and seized her and Anna. Evdokia came into the room and froze. A Varangian took a step toward her, but the one in charge stopped him with a glance. They placed the two captives in manacles and started hauling them away.

"You can't do this!" screamed Euphy. "Someone help me!"

"Wait," said Evdokia. The Varangians stopped and looked at her. She stepped forward and ripped the crown from Euphrosyne's head.

"Goodbye, Mother," she said, and the Varangians started walking again.

"How could you abandon me, ungrateful child?" cried Euphy.

"Mother, how could you say such a thing?" smiled Evdokia. "You know that I'll come visit you. I was always good at visiting prisoners. How is Wednesday?"

She laughed as her mother and sister were led shrieking out of the room. The servants and ladies-in-waiting took the opportunity to flee.

Which left just the two of us. She hadn't noticed me. It wasn't until she looked into the glass while posing with the crown on her head that she saw my reflection behind her. She whirled around in surprise.

"Well," said Evdokia. "How do I look?"

"You're not the Empress yet," I said.

"I know," she replied. "But I am closer than I was. By the way, I won't be needing you anymore. Good day, Aglaia."

I walked out of the Empress's chambers for what would be the last time. Somewhere in the distance I could still hear Euphy sobbing. Then a door slammed shut, and the noise stopped.

I'm out of a job, I thought.

Niketas was waiting outside the throne room. He brightened when he saw me.

"Come," he said, taking my arm. "I'll escort you to my home."

"What about Feste?" I asked.

[258]

"He's busy," he said, chuckling. "He asked me to take care of you. I'll tell you all about it on the way."

Niketas lived in a good-sized palace northeast of the Hagia Sophia, in a district called Sphorakion. The entrance was through a low portico that was architecturally unimpressive but eminently defensible from within. His servants unbarred the front gate and welcomed their master with a palpable sense of relief. He, like us, had been up and about since the previous dawn.

I was given a room that was far above our current status, with a bed so soft that my eyes closed the minute I lay upon it. When I woke, it was afternoon, and I was starving. I staggered down to the kitchen, where I was taken in hand by the cook, a jolly woman in her fifties who immediately divined my pregnancy and loaded my plate over and over, chatting amiably about the eleven times she had given birth, along with reams of advice on how to rear children, tame husbands, order about incompetent servants, and generally run the world.

I had my fill of both food and advice, thanked the provider, and waddled back up the Mese to Blachernae. There were hordes of people blocking the way. I learned from a soldier that they were getting ready to cheer the entrance to the city of the boy Alexios. I wonder how many of the cheerers had hurled stones at his ship only a few days before.

I thought I could get a better view from the monastery on top of the Fifth Hill and started up the familiar road to the top. I decided to drop by the house of Bastiani's lady. I was curious to see how she had fared.

I arrived at her gate. It was open, which surprised me. I peeked through, and saw with horror that the house no longer stood. Instead, there was a pile of charred timbers and stones, a thin wisp of smoke rising from it.

I heard the sound of a shovel breaking ground and turned to see the gardener working, despite the ruin behind him. Then, on closer look, I saw that he was shoveling dirt onto a grave beside the garden. I walked up, making sure that he could see me well before I got to him. He stopped shoveling and waited for me.

"She's gone," he said, tears running down his cheeks.

"How?" I said.

He could read lips, apparently, for he responded.

"I sleep in that shed in the corner," he said. "I didn't hear the fire. I didn't smell the smoke in time. When I did, the flames were already reaching the sky. The house collapsed like it was made of twigs. It happened so fast. By the time I got help, she was dead."

He resumed filling the grave.

"She once told me that she thought she would not live past this year," he continued. "She wanted no priest, no ceremony. Just to be buried by her garden. It was the last thing she kept of all her finery."

"What was her name?" I mouthed.

He looked at me. "I called her Lady," he said.

I looked around. All of the other houses on this street were untouched by the fires that had raged across the base of the hill. And this fire had happened at night, after the others had been doused.

I picked up a clod of earth and crumbled it over the grave.

"Good-bye, Lady," I said softly. "I hope, wherever you are, that you find him."

We met briefly with the troubadours once things had settled down a bit. It was at this meeting that we learned that Tantalo had died in the battle at Galata.

"So, I will be assuming the leadership of the Guildmembers," asserted Raimbaut haughtily.

Feste shook his head. "I am the Chief Fool in Constantinople," he said quietly. "Nothing has changed that. As far as I am concerned, the three of you are cowards and traitors to the Fools' Guild, and I will see to it that you are expelled."

"But—" spluttered the troubadour.

"But nothing!" shouted Feste, standing abruptly. "Did you cover yourself in enough glory to impress Montferrat, Raimbaut? Have you drenched your sword in enough blood to win his eternal subsidy? There is peace here, no thanks to you. Peace because we worked for it. You've done nothing to call yourself our leader."

"It won't last, Feste," said Gaucelm.

"Then when it's threatened, we'll think of something else. If we need you and think we can trust you, then maybe we'll get in touch. Until then, stay the hell out of our city!"

He stormed out of their tent, Plossus and I trotting after him. I noticed a knight staring after me. He removed his helmet.

"Sebastian!" I exclaimed.

Feste and Plossus stopped and turned to watch. My twin looked back and forth at the three of us. I took a few steps toward him. He shook his head, replaced his helmet, and walked away.

It was an uncharacteristically gloomy trio of fools who gathered in the Hippodrome a few days later. We had come to rehearse for the games to be given in honor of the coronation. Apart from that, there had been little call for our services as entertainers. Plossus had picked up some extra pocket money by giving guided tours to small groups of awestruck Crusaders.

"I swear you could tell the French the most outlandish tales, and they will believe them," he said. "I tell them that the figures in a frieze will move when no one is looking, and they will stare at it, waiting. I tell them that the scenes on a column foretell the fate of the city when all they really show are stories from the Bible, and they will gasp, 'I' faith? 'Tis so?' If they ever get the money they claim they're owed, we shall be able to do quite well."

"But until that happy day, let's do what we are supposed to do," said Feste as we passed through the stables and waved to the boys exercising the horses.

We had performed at the Hippodrome before several times, of course, but it was somehow eerie to be doing our routines when there was no one present to observe us except for the statues. The statues were everywhere, ringing the top level of the stadium and fighting each other for space on the euripos, the lengthy oblong divider in the center of the course. On each end were a pair of enormous columns, and in the center was the fabled Serpent Column that once stood before the Oracle of Delphi, the three carved snakes intertwined and supporting a massive bowl.

We sat on the edge of the euripos, opposite the Kathisma, the two-story royal box from where our new co-patrons would be watching. It was hard to summon up any enthusiasm for rehearsing. We were all still weary, even emotionally spent, from our exertions during the last battle. I found myself regretting not having made more efforts to help Bastiani's lady. Feste, in addition to everything else, had been morose since learning of Tantalo's death.

"But you said yourself that they had betrayed the Guild," argued Plossus, continuing a debate that had raged between them since morning.

"I said it, and I meant it," said Feste. "But Tantalo is someone that I've known for years. I can forgive him for being weak in these circumstances."

"Only because he's dead," retorted the younger fool. "If he lived, you would want to kick him out of the Guild along with the other three."

"Maybe," said Feste. "But he was the best of them."

He leaned back against a bronze lion, his eyes closed.

Plossus leapt to the dirt track.

"This is no mood for a revel," he growled. "How are you going to entertain the multitudes when you can't even crack a smile?"

"Enough, boy," muttered Feste, his eyes still closed.

"What is bothering you?" Plossus persisted. "This should be our triumph as well. We brought about an end to the war before it got completely out of hand. I'm sorry about Tantalo for your sake, but I don't see why you need to mope about for so long."

"Who killed Bastiani?" asked Feste abruptly. "Who killed his lady? It irks me that we haven't found out the answer."

"I don't know, and I don't think it matters anymore," replied Plossus. "Bastiani was probably killed by Viadro or Ranieri."

"They said that they didn't kill him," said Feste.

"Have you considered the possibility that someone capable of murder is also capable of lying about it?" said Plossus.

"Yes, of course," said Feste. "But I don't think that they were. And they both died before his lady was burnt."

"Which could have been an accident or coincidence," said Plossus. "In any case, it never was the Guild's problem to begin with, and now that the world has changed, even our Lord Treasurer has lost interest in pursuing it."

"That's true enough," I said.

My husband looked at me. "Do you think that his lady was the victim of an accident?" he asked.

"No," I said. "But I have no idea how to find her killer, and I am no longer certain that it's worth the effort."

Feste stood and stretched, then dove over Plossus's head, flipping through the air and landing on his feet behind him.

"There," he said to him. "Better?"

Plossus grinned.

"You know, O chieftain, there is a method that you have not considered," he said. "And it stands here before you."

"What is that, my lad?" asked Feste.

Plossus capered over to the euripos and held his arms up before the Serpent Column.

"Behold," he cried. "The Oracle of the Ancients, whose powers of divination surpassed those of mortal men such as we. I suggest that we invoke them, rouse the spirits from their centuries of dormancy." He sank to his knees. "Hail, Oracle! We beseech thee, answer our most fervent prayers. Grant us some augury to relieve our master's mind."

"This is heresy," I scolded him. "I want no part of it."

"Besides, you're doing it all wrong," said Feste, smiling for the first time in days. "There was supposed to be some kind of oil or incense burning in the bowl, and a crowd of vestal virgins undulating in a state of frenzy."

"Like this?" said Plossus, wiggling before him.

"Not bad," observed Feste critically. "But do you qualify as a vestal virgin?"

"That's personal," said Plossus. "But I can reveal to you that—"

He stopped. Feste was staring over his head, his eyes thoughtful.

"I've seen this before someplace," he said.

"Where?" asked Plossus.

"Quiet," I whispered. "I've seen that expression before."

We watched as he walked around the euripos, looking at the column from every angle. Then he stopped again, a slow smile spreading across his face.

"You've figured something out, haven't you?" I said.

"I think that I have," he said. "And I think that you were right all along."

"Well, good," I said, pleased. "It's about time that you came around to my view of things. I'm delighted to hear it. Thank you."

"You're welcome."

"Now, if you please, dear husband, explain to me exactly what I was right about."

"Figure out the how, and you figure out the who," he said. "Are the two of you free for a little expedition?"

"Right now?" said Plossus.

"Right now."

"But what about our rehearsal?"

Feste sighed. "We'll do the Two Suitors, the Shepherdess and the Sheep, you do a few minutes on stilts, then we'll finish with three-man juggling, clubs, axes, and torches. Good enough?"

"Could I be the First Sheep this time?" asked Plossus.

"Yes, you can be the First Sheep," said Feste wearily. "Let's go."

"Where are we going?" I asked.

"Back to Bastiani's."

TWENTY

Ravelli: Yeah, it'sa my own solution . . .
Captain Spaulding: Come on, let's go down and get the reward. We
solved it, you solved it. The credit is all yours.

—*ANIMAL CRACKERS*, GEORGE S. KAUFMAN
AND MORRIE RYSKIND

I walked toward the quarter at such a brisk pace that Plossus had to pluck at my motley to slow me down.

"What's wrong, lad?" I snapped. "Can't keep up with the old man?"

"Primus, you'll draw attention to all of us, barging through the city like this," he said. "Secundus, I seem to remember that one of our party is pregnant, although it escapes me at the moment which one it is. I don't have a tertius."

I slowed down until my wife caught up with us.

"Considering we've done damn little to catch this person, it's rather odd to rush now, don't you think?" she said.

"I want to get there when he's not there," I replied.

"Now, there's a strategy," commented Plossus. "Your average murderer-catcher would want to catch the murderer when he is there. But you have always been one for the subtle approach."

We came to the house of Vitale around noon. The landlord was not about, fortunately. I glanced up at the front of the house and saw no sign of stirring.

"Good," I said. "Come with me. Keep your weapons handy."

They glanced at each other. Aglaia grinned and Plossus shrugged, then they followed me inside.

Bastiani lived and died on the top floor, but I stopped on the middle one and listened for a moment, making sure that no one was about. Then I approached the middle room of the three in back and knocked softly on the door. There was no response, so I quietly opened it.

The room was used by Vitale for storage, with linens stacked neatly on shelves to the right, lumber, old furniture, and some tools on the left. I lit a lamp and held it up, looking around until I saw what I was looking for.

"Very good," I said. "Come with me."

I led them across the hall to the opposite room where John Aprenos and Tullio stayed. The huntsman and the carpenter were not at home, but the remnants of their professions were still scattered about the room. I took the three spears from their mounts on the wall and handed them to Plossus, then I took his shield and gave it to my wife.

"Are we hunting something?" asked my wife.

"And what are you going to carry?" asked Plossus.

I picked up a small metal tool by the head of Tullio's pallet. "Back to the other room, if you please," I said.

They followed me, puzzled looks on their faces.

"The problem has always been how was Bastiani killed, if no one gave him poison at his meal and if his lady did not administer it before she left," I said. "And what type of poison would have been strong enough to kill him but leave him enough strength to first bar his door and shove the blanket against the crack at the bottom to seal off outside noise? Right now, we're underneath his room. Aglaia, where would you say the head of Bastiani's bed would be, given the identical proportions of the two rooms?"

"About here," she said, pointing to a spot by the left wall.

I took the three spears from Plossus and rested their points on the floor. "Look," I said, holding the lamp near the floor. There were three small holes on the spot she had indicated.

"Someone has done this before," said Plossus.

"I think I'm beginning to understand what you're doing," said Aglaia.

I placed the spear points in the holes, then rested the shafts against each other, tying them together in the middle with a piece of string. The ends stopped just below the ceiling. I held the lamp up and pointed to what I had observed before. There was a lattice of tiny holes cut through the boards that made up this room's ceiling and Bastiani's floor. The wood here was blackened compared to the rest of the ceiling.

"What worms bored those holes, I wonder?" said Plossus.

"Worms with tools. This augers well, I should think," I said, holding up the tool I had taken from Tullio's bedside. It was a small one, with a fine, thin blade the size of the holes in the ceiling.

"And this?" Aglaia asked, holding up the shield.

I took it and slid it carefully over the tops of the spears. It nestled snug between them and the ceiling, covering the scorched spot completely.

"There's your tripod," I said. "Let's see what burnt offering they made."

I took the shield down and inverted it, then rubbed its interior with the tip of my finger. It came away black. I sniffed it, then passed the shield back to the others, who repeated the process.

"Charcoal," I said. "They placed burning charcoal in the shield and kept it pressed against the ceiling. The fumes had nowhere to go but up. They knew about Bastiani's peculiar habit of keeping the doors sealed tight. That habit sealed his fate as well."

"That's what killed him?" exclaimed Plossus. "Fumes from burning charcoal?"

"I got the idea when you drew my attention to the Serpent Column. Bastiani died in a stuffy, airless room, and when his neighbors broke the door down, Vitale had a coughing fit and nearly fainted. I have heard tell of foolhardy blacksmith apprentices dying in such a manner by working with burning charcoal indoors. I would bet that that was what killed the merchant and gave him that odd pink complexion as well."

"Then you're saying that Tullio killed him," stated Aglaia. "Or Tullio and Aprenos. But why?"

"We'll have to ask them," I said. "And unless I miss my guess, that's the huntsman coming now."

It was Aprenos's mutterings floating up the stairs as he stumbled home from another midday bout with a barrel of ale. We watched the doorway as he entered his room. There was a pause, then a burst of expletives as he realized his gear was gone. He started to rush out of the building, then saw us in the opposite room.

"And just what the hell are you doing here?" he demanded belligerently. Then he stopped, the blood draining from his face as he saw the tripod standing by the wall and the auger in my hand.

"We'd like to talk to you," I said.

He nodded, then bolted down the stairs.

"Plossus, fetch!" I said.

He nodded, but instead of pursuing Aprenos down the stairs, he ran to the opposite room, stood by the window for a moment, then jumped through it.

There was a cry and a thud, then the sound of a man being dragged up a flight of steps. Plossus appeared, his arms under the huntsman's and his hands locked around Aprenos's chest. He brought him into the room and unceremoniously deposited him on the floor.

"I wanted him conscious," I said.

"Well, be more specific next time," replied Plossus as he rolled Aprenos onto his stomach, tied his hands behind his back, then sat him up in the corner of the room and slapped him a few times until his eyes finally opened.

"What do you want?" he asked when he saw us bending over him.

"I am willing to make a deal with you," I said. "Tell us who hired you to kill Bastiani."

"Who says I did?" he said defiantly.

"I do," I said. "And your reaction to seeing the tripod set up confirmed it. Tell us who hired you."

"And in exchange?" he said.

"We let you go," I said.

"Tempting, but no go," said Tullio, standing in the doorway. "Hello, Feste. Are you buying us that drink that you promised?"

He had a hatchet in each hand.

"Same deal goes for you," I said as the three of us turned to face him.

He held a hatchet up.

"There's a certain code involved," he explained. "A course of conduct that is expected of one, especially when one was paid in advance."

"I suggest you put those hatchets down if you want to live," I said, stepping away from the others. "There are three of us. I have a dagger and a knife, my wife has a pair of daggers, and Plossus—quite frankly, I'm not sure what Plossus uses in a fight."

"Oh, I'll think of something," said Plossus easily.

He looked back and forth at the three of us.

"You are more than fools, I see," he said.

"Just as you are more than a carpenter," I said. "A convenient profession for arranging accidents. And you have a talent for arson as well."

He bowed slightly, keeping his eyes on our hands.

"Can you guarantee our safety?" he said, suddenly.

"Not only your safety, but I know a man who might find good use for your skills," I said.

He looked at his companion, then lowered his hand.

"All right, then," he said, resigned. He turned away from the door, then whirled abruptly and hurled the hatchet at me.

So, I caught it.

"Really," I said. "My wife throws axes at me harder than that."

But he was already dead, slumping down into the doorway, a pair of daggers in his breast.

"Mine hit him first," said Plossus.

"Maybe," said Aglaia dubiously.

I turned back to Aprenos, who was shaking with terror.

"The deal still stands," I said.

"Go hang yourselves!" he said, spitting at us.

I looked at him sadly. "I suppose this code of yours requires avenging your friend's death."

He didn't reply. I shifted the hatchet to my right hand.

"I'm sorry," I said. "But I can't spend the rest of my life looking over my shoulder."

"Just make it quick," he muttered, closing his eyes.

I did.

Plossus untied his hands. We left Aglaia's dagger in the carpenter's body and dragged him over to the huntsman, then placed their hands on each other's weapon.

"What do you think?" I said as we looked down at the little tableau we had arranged.

"It might convince someone that they killed each other," said Aglaia.

"I don't think anyone will look too closely," said Plossus. "Hey, maybe Philoxenites will want you to investigate it."

"Let's get out of here," I said, and we slipped quietly out of the building and left the Venetian quarter unremarked.

"And that's an end," said Plossus as we walked back to Choniates's house.

"No, it isn't," said Aglaia. "We don't know who hired them."

"I can't prove anything," I said, "but I can make a pretty good guess."

"Let's hear it," said Plossus.

"Bastiani and his lady were lovers," I said. "The lady was married, but we never learned the identity of her husband. She wasn't killed until the night that Alexios fled and Isaakios was restored. I think that the timing was significant."

"How so?" asked my wife.

"Her husband could have had them both killed, but chose to have her lover killed first. He left her alive for some reason, but needed her dead later. The last time I saw her, she had just been visiting Chalke Prison. Tullio and Aprenos had also been there, supposedly visiting a friend. I'm guessing that she had gone to the prison to visit her husband, perhaps to plead for his forgiveness. Whether she obtained it or not, we'll never know. But when Isaakios was released, and had his supporters released as well, the husband needed her dead if he was going to take his next step."

"His next step being what?" asked Plossus.

"To marry a woman of position and influence," I said.

"Evdokia," said Aglaia. "Bastiani's lady was the wife of Alexios Doukas. But why would he leave her alive before that?"

"He was hedging his bets," I said. "While he was in prison, he could have two women working independently toward obtaining his release. But once he actually had it, he no longer needed both of them. And marriage with the Emperor's niece, the only member of the usurper's family to visit Chalke and show some sympathy, would cement his influence at Blachernae. Before, he was married to an impoverished woman who was cheating on him while he was imprisoned. Now, he's the Chamberlain and a member of the royal family. Quite a step up."

"And it won't be his last," said Aglaia. "Evdokia wants to be Empress. I have a feeling Doukas has no strong objections to the idea."

"I think I had better warn Philoxenites," I said.

With all of the preparations for the coronation taking place, it was hard for me to get an appointment with the Imperial Treasurer. He had been busy selecting particular enemies of the new regime to hit with onerous taxes and forfeitures. I figured he had settled a few personal scores along the way. When I finally gained entrance to his office, he was chortling with glee over the discovery of a small horde of gold buried in the garden of one of Euphrosyne's cousins.

"The idiot never gardened in his life until the siege hit," he laughed. "Suddenly, he's spouting gibberish about marrows and beans, pretending it had been a lifelong hobby. We only had to dig down a foot before we struck the casket."

"Well done," I said.

"So, Feste, what news?"

"I found out who killed Bastiani," I said.

He sat behind his desk and frowned.

"Do you know? I had forgotten all about that," he said. "Well. Good. Who was it?"

"Had you heard about a pair of killers-for-hire known as the Huntsman and the Carpenter?"

"Rumors only," he said. "Some say the Carpenter arranged the collapse of the floor in Blachernae Palace. He just missed the Emperor and got Palaiologos instead. Are you saying that they killed him?"

"Yes."

"And where are they now?"

"Dead."

He sat back, toying with a ring on his finger, looking at me closely.

"I heard about a pair of fellows who killed each other in the Venetian quarter yesterday," he said. "That was them?"

I shrugged. "I guess they had a falling out."

"A pity," he said, smiling. "With Will and Phil gone, I could have used them. Oh, well. And I suppose that with them gone, you'll never find out who hired them."

"As a matter of fact," I began, then I stopped.

The ring that he was playing with was one I had never seen him wear before. It was an emerald set in an enameled cross on a band of gold. He saw me staring at it, and held it up so that it sparkled in the light.

"Pretty, isn't it?" he said. "A gift from a new patron."

"One with bushy brows," I said.

"Yes," he said. "So generous, even in mourning. He lost his wife recently. Tragic. Funny how one small burning ember can be carried on the wind until it singles out just one house for disaster. But listen to me, trying to tell a jester what's funny."

I looked at him for a moment. He returned my gaze evenly.

"There's a murderer standing by the Byzantine throne," I said.

"There's one sitting on it," he said. "Several more around it, a few married into the family, and others waiting in the wings. If the emperor is strong and smart, he survives and the Empire thrives. If not, then someone who is strong and smart becomes the emperor. That's how it has always been."

"Sometimes, the successor is only ambitious and lucky," I said.

"The next best thing," he said. "Isaakios is old and weak, Alexios is young and weak. I do not intend to lose this empire."

"You've already lost it," I said.

He sighed. "I think that it is time for you to leave," he said.

I stood. He held up a hand.

"You misconstrue me," he said. "I meant leave Constantinople. Take your wife with you. I understand that you are expecting a child. My felicitations. You should raise it in a place of safety, don't you think?"

"And Plossus?" I said.

"He may stay," he said. "He's just a lad. Talented, but no Feste. And besides, he makes me laugh. Go, Fool. I know that you have a performance at the games on the first. By the second, I expect to find no trace of you in this city. And I will be looking."

At the games, Isaakios and his son sat on a pair of matched golden thrones. The men who sat in the Kathisma with them spoke many languages. Few of them spoke Greek. Doukas sat where he could observe everything and everyone. He was relaxed and calm, as only a man who knew how to wait patiently could be.

One part of me wanted to pick up the nearest weapon and hurl it at the point where his bushy brows met. But he was beyond my reach, and would remain so.

We buried our feelings and turned into a trio of performing fools. Most of it was dumbshow, given the variety of tongues in our audience. But we did the Two Suitors in Greek, so that the blind man on the throne could enjoy at least one bit of our act.

When it was over, Philoxenites came up to us and handed me a sack of silver. He said nothing in farewell, nor did we want him to.

We went back to Niketas's palace. The three troubadours were waiting for us.

"You sent for us, milord?" asked Raimbaut, bowing.

"Yes," I said. "Aglaia and I have been banished."

"We know," he said. "A pity. Still, that leaves four of us. I shall be glad to assume the mantle of responsibility."

"Very good," I said. "Of course, under Guild rules, I have the right to name my successor. I name Plossus."

"What?" he shouted.

"Ridiculous," said Giraut. "He's just a lad. We have been in the Guild longer than he's been alive."

[275]

"Plossus is Chief Fool of Constantinople," I said. "You will report to him and follow his directions. If I learn that he's come to an untimely end, I will drop whatever it is that I am doing and come back here. I will then hunt the three of you down and kill you. I will not be in fool's garb, I will not engage in any chivalric challenge, I will simply use every sneaky, underhanded method I know, and I know many, to bring about your deaths. Am I understood?"

They looked at each other, then at Plossus.

"Plossus, it is," said Gaucelm.

"Gentlemen," said Plossus. "I have a few ideas that I would like to discuss with you. Meet me tomorrow morning at the Forum of Arkadios."

Aglaia and I packed the few things that we had purchased since the fire. At dawn, we rose. Niketas escorted us to the stables. Plossus had taken it upon himself to rise earlier and get our horses ready for our departure.

Niketas embraced each of us in turn.

"Stay alive, my friends," he said. "We need you to make this world laugh again."

"Take care of yourself, Nik," I said. "We must sit and gossip again someday."

Plossus was doing everything he could to hold back tears.

"I really hadn't planned on running this place this early in my career," he said. "I was hoping you'd last a few more months before I had to step up and take over."

"You'll be fine, lad," I said. "Watch your back. Go to Father Esaias if you need to hide out. And don't drink any of Philoxenites's wine."

He hugged me, then turned to my wife.

"There's no one like you," he said. "I wish that there was."

She stood on tiptoe and kissed him gently.

[276]

"Farewell, Plossus," she said.

He helped her onto her mare. I swung myself onto Zeus, and we rode a short distance until we came to the public gate that led through the double walls.

The Via Egnatia started here, the old Roman road built when the Empire was a great one. We headed west. About two miles from the city, Aglaia called for a brief halt, dismounted, and pulled a shovel from her gear.

"Wait here," she said, and headed into the nearby woods.

I sat there, thinking how a pregnant wife adds to the length of a journey. A few minutes later, she came back. To my surprise, she was carrying a small, wooden casket. She came over to me and opened it. There was a sack inside, with enough gold to keep a pair of fools going for years.

"My earnings from Euphrosyne," she said. "When she was generous, she was generous to a fault."

"My word," I said, impressed.

She put it inside her saddlebags, then mounted her steed and looked back at the walled city for the last time.

"I liked it here," she said.

"It was interesting, challenging, and dangerous," I said. "What's not to like?"

She smiled at me. "Interesting, challenging, and dangerous," she said. "You're going to love being a parent."

CODA

[Y]ou'll tender me a fool.
—William Shake-
speare, *HAMLET*,
ACT I, SCENE III

We reached Rhaidestos in a few days. Alfonso was waiting for us, strumming his lute in a backstreet tavern. He greeted us with relief, which shortly turned to outrage when he learned of how his fellow troubadours had turned against the Guild. He immediately left to shore up Plossus.

Three weeks later, we reached Thessaloniki, whereupon my wife declared that she was not going to ride another foot in her condition, and that I was a brute if I thought that she would, especially considering that the next part of the journey was through mountains with winter approaching and bandits and wolves gathering, and if I thought that she should endanger our baby just because . . .

I had actually conceded the sojourn at her initial statement. I thought about pointing out that it was only the end of August, and that we could have made it over the mountains before winter, but never let it be said that I would spare my wife a good harangue when she got her wind up.

We stayed with Fat Basil, who was glad for the company. He and I did a lot of two-man work, with Claudia (for I must use our Guild names again at this point—Aglaia and Feste were left behind in Constantinople) accompanying us on various instruments from a comfortable cushion on the side. She also would sing and throw in any ribald remark that crossed her mind. All in all, our months in Thessaloniki provided some of the more pleasurable performances of our joint careers.

To the east, events took their dreary and disastrous course. Isaakios, having regained the throne, settled into his old, debauched ways again and died before the year was out. He may have been helped along by his son, or his wife, or just about anyone close to him. It doesn't matter much at this point.

Alexios the Fourth was as fit to rule as a goose, and with less morals. He kept Alexios Doukas close by and quickly ran what was left of the government into the ground. Doukas quietly gained sufficient support among the aristocracy and the bureaucrats to make his move and deposed the boy in the middle of the night, with Philoxenites suborning the Varangians yet again. After a couple of attempts to poison the youth failed, Doukas took matters and a bowstring into his own hands and became Alexios the Fifth.

Mourtzouphlos, the people called him, a word meaning bushy-browed. He stood against the Crusaders and called the covenants made by Isaakios and his son void and against God's divine will. The Greeks stood by him, grateful for any display of resistance.

There were two more fires. The first was when the locals rose against the Venetian quarter. In their rage, they extended their anger against the Pisans, the Amalfitans, and the Genoese, who fled across the Golden Horn into the Crusader camp. Thus, the Greeks accomplished what no one thought possible: The unification of the Italians.

With the addition of so many thousands of arms to the Crusader cause, the ultimate outcome was not in doubt. The Venetians, having learned from experience, refined their battle techniques. After some initial attempts at negotiation, they tied pairs of the giant merchantmen together and sent them once again across the Golden Horn to lash their flying bridges to the towers of the seawall. Mourtzouphlos proved to be a poor general and followed the example of his father-in-law by fleeing the city. For the first time since the walls were erected around Constantinople, an enemy had conquered from without.

For the best account of the carnage and destruction that took place within the city after, I must refer you to the history compiled by Niketas Choniates. Only he truly does it justice. It isn't surprising that he became a historian. What is history but gossip written down? I ran across a copy of his tome years later when my wife and I were at the court of Frederick II. Nik survived, barely, and even a bit heroically, but lost his palace to one of the fires and most of his possessions to the Crusaders.

Mourtzouphlos and Evdokia decided to flee to her father and throw themselves on his mercy. Alexios welcomed his new son-in-law and rival and treated him like family. By which I mean to say, of course, that he had him blinded. Mourtzouphlos wandered for a while and, as fate would have it, ended up back in Constantinople. The Crusaders took him to the top of the Pillar of Constantine, spun him around several times, then laughed as he staggered around, and laughed even harder as he went over the edge.

Alexios the Third, having another daughter to trade, gave Evdokia to some king somewhere, another cruel marriage. He carried on as Emperor of a dwindling empire as long as he could, but the money ran out, his troops deserted, and he was captured by the Crusaders. They did not execute him. They sent him into permanent captivity with Euphrosyne, a fate he probably considered worse than death.

We lost track of Rico. The Guild may know of his fate, but not I. That's what happens sometimes in our profession. You work with someone in one part of the world, then you take separate paths to who knows where and never hear from each other again. I enjoyed my time with the little fellow. We often wondered if he ever got anywhere with the flutist. She we would encounter again, under quite different circumstances, but that's another tale.

The Crusaders never made it to the Holy Land, spending their energy squabbling over the remains of Byzantium. The Doge died soon after the conquest. They say his intestines erupted from his body, but that was probably just wishful thinking. Montferrat died in a battle with the Bulgarians trying to keep control over some spit of land somewhere. They say Raimbaut died with him, although it's not certain. Nobody bothered to write any songs about it.

And Plossus continues to this day as chief fool in Constantinople and is generally accounted in Guildlore one of the greatest fools in history. My tutelage, of course. We think he got Philoxenites finally. I hope that's true.

When I look back at the Guild's efforts to stop the Fourth Crusade, I see from the perspective of Time and old age that it was impossible. But that is not to say that we failed. A handful of men and women in motley staved off the initial launch and kept the sack of Constantinople at bay for three years. You may say, Well, the rape, slaughter, and desecration happened anyway, so what was it worth? I reply simply: three additional years of life for thousands of people. And if that seems like just postponing the inevitable, let me ask you this: given the choice between dying today and dying three years from now, which would you prefer?

I thought so.

What survived were Nik's history and Raimbaut's songs, which are still being sung even today. Not a bad legacy when you think about it. We are lucky if anything survives us, whether it's a stone, a song, or a history.

Or a child.

Most stories in life begin with a birth and end with a death. But this is a fool's tale. Since it began with a death, I shall end it with a birth.

On the morning of the Twelfth Day of Christmas, Fat Basil and I galloped around Thessaloniki, searching for a sober midwife. We finally located a dour but competent woman and carried her back to Fat Basil's house. Then my brother fool kept me pinned outside in the cold while I listened to the screams of my wife, helpless to do anything about them.

Shortly after the sun set, there was one final yelp, and then a higher, weaker cry joined them. The midwife came out and smiled for the first time, and I hugged this woman who I had never met before like she was my own sister.

Inside, my wife was pale without the assistance of whiteface, but as happy as I have seen her. She beckoned to me, as if I needed any prompting to come closer. In her arms, a small, red-faced little girl bawled lustily.

"Meet your daughter," said Claudia, and she sat up and handed her to me. I took her in my arms with a feeling of disbelief mingled with joy.

They say that newborn infants do not smile, that they do not know how. I will swear by the First Fool, Our Savior, that when she opened her eyes and gazed upon me for the first time, seeing a fool in makeup cooing at her, she smiled, and my heart melted.

"Milady, I find I must break an oath I once made to you," I said.

"What oath is that, Fool?" asked my wife, smiling at me.

"I swore when we married that I would never love any woman but you," I said. "But I find I must make room in my heart for this little one."

"I expected no less," said my wife.

"What shall we name her?" I asked, sitting next to her in bed and handing our daughter to her.

"I've already named her," said Claudia. "Portia. I hope you don't mind."

"Portia," I said, rolling it around in my mouth.

"Yes," said Claudia. "She will be a woman men should listen to or ignore at their peril."

"I like it," I said. "Portia it is. A daughter of fools, born on Twelfth Night."

In late March, the snows melted sufficiently for my wife to agree to travel once again. We purchased a mule to add to our two horses, bade our host farewell, and once again rode the Via Egnatia. We planned to take it west to Durazzo, then north to visit Claudia's children in Orsino, and thence across the Adriatic and back to the Guildhall.

We passed Lake Ochrid around Easter. Claudia had mastered the art of nursing on horseback, a delicate matter for both parties. She was fussing over the baby when suddenly she reined her mare to a halt. I immediately had my sword out, but she shook her head and pointed to the road ahead of us.

Someone had drawn a crude circle in the center of the road, the compass points marked by piles of stones and strange markings that seemed to be Latin incantations.

"I think it's meant to be a magic circle of some kind," I said.

"Yes," she agreed.

We looked down at it for a while.

"Could be that it's supposed to be some sort of trap or other," she observed.

"Yes," I agreed.

We looked at it some more.

"Of course, I don't believe in magic," she said firmly.

"Neither do I," I said equally firmly.

We looked at it one last time.

"But there's no harm in being careful," I said, guiding Zeus carefully around it.

"None," she agreed, following me.

I could have sworn that someone muttered, "Damn!" from behind a nearby tree, but we moved on.

HISTORICAL NOTE

History is more or less bunk.
——HENRY FORD

It is hoped that with the addition of these chronicles of Theophilos the Fool more light has been shed upon the origins of the Fourth Crusade. A debate has been raging for decades among literally dozens of scholars worldwide over whether the Crusade had been subverted from the start by the Venetians toward the elimination of their trading rival (the Byzantinist view), or whether this change in course came about later, during the winter after the conquest of Zara, at the instigation of the Germans who used the boy Alexios as their tool (the Venetianist view). The French historian Achille Luchaire wrote in 1907 that the issue was not settled, nor was it likely ever to be, while another medievalist scholar writes of a conference in the 1980s where the two camps divided so bitterly that they nearly came to blows.

I, for one, would gladly have paid to see this last. In my fantasy, the Venetianists and the Byzantinists are at opposite ends of a large field. Each side is given a disassembled mangonel, operating instructions in the appropriate thirteenth-century manuscript, and a pile of stones. The last historian standing gets to write the definitive work.

My own timid forays into the field have convinced me that what historians prefer above everything else is to denounce other historians, usually through the use of spectacularly catty footnotes ("What Professor So-and-so fails to take into account..." "Unaccountably, Ms. Such-and-such has relied upon a simple misinterpretation..." "Herr Something merely parrots the long disproved observation that..." and so on). However, a reasonable book on the subject may be found in *The Fourth Crusade: The Conquest of Constantinople*, second edition, by Donald E. Queller and Thomas F. Madden. While unabashedly apologists for the Venetianist view, they at least discuss opposing ideas before demolishing them in the aforementioned footnotes, and their bibliography is extensive.

I would, however, take issue with their conclusion that the diversion came later. The two, citing the argument of John Pryor, suggest that the vast amount of time spent by the Venetians constructing horse transports with ramps for easy beach access could only mean that they meant to attack a target with an easily accessible beach, such as Egypt. Let me point out that the Venetians also built the giant transports with the extended bowsprits, which remained the only machines of war used successfully against the walls of Constantinople from their inception until the Turkish cannons finally blew them apart nine centuries later. Further, the design of the *Eagle*, with its massive metal plates coming to an edge at the bow, was perfectly suited to breaking the great chain guarding the Golden Horn. These huge vessels had to have been designed and built for these purposes from the start. Given the great familiarity of the Venetians in the quarter with the layout of the sea-walls by the Golden Horn, all of this smacks of something resembling a plan—one that had been set in place from long before the fleet even left Venice. And the horse transports worked just fine when they landed and attacked Galata.

One small mystery is cleared up by the translation of Theophilos's report of the first siege, and that is how a Venetian banner came to be displayed from a Byzantine tower at the seawall. This was mentioned in passing by Geoffroy de Villehardouin, who "affirms that more than forty people solemnly assured him that they had seen the banner of Saint Mark flying from the top of one of the towers, but not one of them knew who had planted it there." Even with flying bridges, taking a forty-foot wall from the water is no simple feat. It is not surprising that the Crusaders had help from the Venetians within the city.

What is impressive about this particular battle is how many contemporaneous accounts have survived it. I have mentioned the Chronicle of Geoffroy de Villehardouin. The translation by M. R. B. Shaw is available from Viking Press. Villehardouin gives much of the higher negotiations as well as the military take on the whole event, all while tilting the moral balance to the Crusaders in general, the French in particular, and Geoffrey de Villehardouin most of all.

A rare and fascinating grunt's eye view of the war may be found in the memoir of Robert de Clari, which was translated by Edgar Holmes McNeal and published by the University of Toronto Press. This ordinary soldier was in the thick of several battles, including the final taking of the seawall in the second siege of 1204. He also gives the reader the tour of the city, albeit with enough misinformation to suggest that Plossus may have been his mischievous guide. De Clari passes along gossip, fact, myth, and hearsay in equal measure but provides a slightly more cynical counterpoint to the self-serving justifications of Villehardouin.

Finally, from the Greek point of view comes our old friend Niketas Choniates, and I once again refer the reader to the marvelous translation by Harry J. Magoulias, *O City of Byzantium, Annals of Niketas Choniates*, from Wayne State University Press. Choniates was as good a historian as ever lived through a cataclysmic event, and his lament for the city unites reporting with poetic grace to produce a work of powerful beauty rivaling that of the Old Testament prophets.

The events set in motion by the Fourth Crusade are still being played out. Had the Crusaders not defeated Byzantium, there might still have been a strong enough empire to withstand the Turks later on. The thrust of the latter into Europe and the creation of the Ottoman Empire led to the long-term tribal faultlines whose tremors culminated in World War I. The pockets of Muslim-Catholic-Orthodox division deposited by the dissolution of the Ottoman Empire are still erupting in civil war and ethnic "cleansing" in the Balkans to this day.

On May 4, 2001, Pope John Paul II visited Orthodox Archbishop Christodoulos of Athens. In a powerful symbolic gesture, the Pope prayed to God to forgive the Catholics for their history of sins committed against Orthodox Christians, specifically singling out the Fourth Crusade. "How can we fail to see here the *mysterium iniquitatis* at work in the human heart?" he said. "To God alone belongs judgment and, therefore, we entrust the heavy burden of the past to His endless mercy, imploring Him to heal the wounds that still cause suffering to the spirit of the Greek people. Together we must work for this healing if the Europe now emerging is to be true to its identity, which is inseparable from the Christian humanism shared by East and West."

Perhaps we need another Fools' Guild to help us bring peace back to this troubled world.

Sections of the city walls still stand. If you chance to travel to Istanbul, go look upon them and think of this passage from Choniates: "As we left the City behind, others returned, thanks to God, and loudly bewailed their misfortunes, but I threw myself, just as I was, on the ground and reproached the walls both because they alone were insensible, neither shedding tears nor lying in ruins upon the earth, and because they still stood upright. If those things for whose protection you were erected no longer exist, being utterly destroyed by fire and war, for what purpose do you still stand? And what will you protect hereafter . . . ?"